D0407239

FIRECRACKER

FIRECRACKER

⌒

SEAN STEWART

Weidenfeld & Nicolson
LONDON

First published in Great Britain in 2005
by Weidenfeld & Nicolson

First Published as *Perfect Circle* in the United States
in 2004 by Small Beer Press, MA

© Sean Stewart 2004

A CIP catalogue record for this book
is available from the British Library

ISBN 0 297 84826 7

Printed in Great Britain byButler & Tanner Ltd,
Frome and London

Weidenfeld & Nicolson
An imprint of the Orion Publishing Group
Orion House, 5 Upper St Martin's Lane,
London WC2H 9EA

www.orionbooks.co.uk

For my family

FIRECRACKER

CHAPTER ONE

I woke up sweaty and shaking. Tense. I had been dreaming about ghost roads again. This one was leaving an apartment complex swimming pool, and there was a little girl walking down it. She was looking back over her shoulder at me, eyes solemn behind a cheap kid's snorkeling mask, and wearing pool flippers; slow dreamy duck-steps, a trail of wet inhuman footprints disappearing into the dim black-and-white houses, the humming silence.

I looked at the clock display on my VCR, but the glowing blue numbers just flashed

– 00:00 –

– 00:00 –

– 00:00 –

Time unstuck and drifting. That lost feeling, like when you're a kid with a fever and the night breaks around you forever.

I lay on my dingy mattress in my tiny living-room, body humming with the premonition of something terrible about to happen. That copper taste in my mouth. Eyes wide in the darkness. Waiting.

The phone rang and I grabbed for it. 'Hello?'

'DK?'

'Who the hell is this?' Nobody had called me DK in ten years, not since my cousin AJ died. DK had been her nickname for me.

'It's your cousin, Tom. Tom Hanlon. My dad married your Aunt Dot's half-sister.'

I dredged up a vague memory of a strident woman in puffball hair lecturing my Uncle Waylon on the evils of drink while he sipped Coors Lite from a paper cup. 'Okay. I think I got it.'

'Now we're talking,' Tom Hanlon said. 'Do you remember me at all?'

'Not at all.'

'We talked at that one family reunion. I asked you what ghosts were like.'

'What did I say?'

'"Dead."'

That sounded like me. There are other things to say about ghosts, of course. They're all different, like demons, not all the same, like zombies. Some can touch you and some can't, some are sad and some are mad as hell. The main thing is, they all want *something*, and they want it way worse than you want anything. If you've got the sense God gave a cockroach, you stay the hell away from dead people.

Just to be polite I said, 'Tom, are you aware that it's the fucking middle of the night?'

'There's a dead girl in my garage.'

'Call the cops.'

'No, not dead like that. I mean, more dead.'

Oh. 'Shit, man. Can't help you. I don't do that any more. Good ni—'

'I'll give you a thousand bucks,' he said. 'Think about it.'

I thought about it.

'A thousand dollars, just to get rid of one ghost. That's a lot of money.'

One thousand dollars. Six thousand packages of Ichi-Ban noodle soup. Lunch at my current lifestyle for about . . . fourteen

2

years. Ten good trips to Six Flags for me and Megan, Dr Peppers included and all the Frito Pie we could eat.

'I notice you aren't hanging up,' Hanlon said with a tired laugh. 'You know what they say, every man has his price –'

I hung up.

Six hours later I was out on my every-second-Sunday visit with my twelve-year-old daughter, Megan. Megan is short and fast and scrappy, not only the captain of her soccer team, but the only girl in the entire Greater Houston AYSO to get a red card this year. 'Great eyes, ref!' she had said after a terrible no-call, clapping sarcastically and paying no attention to the blood dribbling from her split lip.

That's my daughter.

If she got a certain streak of cussedness from me, Meg inherited from her mother her blond hair, her athleticism, and – thank God – a complete inability to see the dead. I never told Megan about me and ghosts. No kid wants to think her daddy is a freak.

I don't drive, so Megan and I take the bus when we go out, which she is beginning to think is lame. Today we'd spent an hour bumming around the Cactus Records on Shepherd listening to the free tracks. My current shitty job was at Petco, and on my budget, free was good. This had been a reliable outing even six months ago, but this time Meg was so obviously unimpressed that I decided to spring for a root beer float at the 59 Diner to salvage the afternoon, only to hear Meg say that she was trying not to drink extra calories.

Jesus.

'You're too young to give up beer,' I said.

She rolled her eyes.

The bus ride back to her house in Woodland was long and awkward. Woodland is a professional suburb on the north side of Houston, all carefully manicured pine trees and midscale housing developments. Even the Taco Bells are clean and neat.

3

There was a dead woman on the bus, Chinese or Vietnamese, clutching a plastic shopping bag, with the usual grim expression. All in black and white, of course. Caught myself wondering why, of all the places in her life, she chose to come back here. Not a really useful line of thought. The dead have their reasons, and by and large the living are better off not knowing them.

'Earth to Will?'

I flinched. 'Hey, sorry. Day-dreaming.' Usually I'm better at ignoring the dead, especially when Megan is around. I don't want her to . . . as I said, that part of my life isn't something she needs to know about.

'Day-dreaming?' She was giving me a Knowing Look spookily like her mother's.

'Hey, this is like every second Sunday, here. Pay attention to me.'

'So, how are Trish and Fonda these days?' I asked, hoping I had remembered the names of Megan's posse.

Meg reached to ring the bell for our stop. 'I don't even know or care about Trish. Fonda and Azul are at Six Flags today.' Tickets to Six Flags are $39.99/day for each person over forty-eight inches tall, and that doesn't include bus fare, balloons, or Dr Peppers. Not easy to do on Petco money. 'They asked me to come, but . . .'

But your mother made you come out with me.

In twelve years I have never missed a Christmas pageant, a Brownie merit badge ceremony, or a school concert. I planted pumpkins at Megan's daycare, I picked up books at library sales and donated them to her school, I sold raffle tickets to send her to science camp. Josie, my ex, once said, 'Will, you've been a great . . .' She floundered. '. . . the best estranged father I can imagine.'

Best Ex-Dad in the Lone Star State. I'm thinking of putting it on a T-shirt.

Megan and I stepped into the steamy Houston air at the bus stop in front of Jamison Middle School. Heat waves shimmered off the metal slides in the playground. 'How come your name isn't on my birth certificate?' Megan asked.

'What?'

'Mom had it out last night. She was looking for my shot records. Your name isn't on my birth certificate. Dad's is.'

Dad meaning Don, the jarhead fucking ex-Marine Josie married a year after leaving me. 'My name's not on the certificate?'

'That's what I was trying to communicate.'

I said, 'By the time you were born, your mother and I weren't together any more. I guess she decided it would be easier to have Don's name there.'

'Don't they do a blood test or something?'

'No, I think they just take the mother's word.' Or maybe the nurses didn't even ask Josie. Maybe Don went and filled out the paperwork himself. 'She never told you I wasn't your dad.' Silence. 'She never said Don was your biological father.'

'No. She always said you were.' Meg not sounding convinced here.

As we turned up the walk to Meg's house, Josie waved at us from the living-room window. 'See you, kiddo,' I said. When I leaned forward to kiss the top of her head, I saw she was wearing a bra.

My daughter stood a moment on the front steps, her hand resting on the doorknob. 'Will, why don't you even have a car?'

Then Josie pulled the door open, and Megan disappeared inside.

I ride the bus a lot, which is not a very Houston thing to do, but I have my reasons. Every second Sunday for twelve years me and Megan had been going out together; half my memories of her are about riding buses. Megan nine months old and screaming with laughter as I zoomed her around like a fighter plane, until an old hag at the bus stop said, 'I never did see anybody treat a child so reckless!' Megan gurgling with laughter the whole time, pounding on my arms with her fat fists to make me

5

do it again. Bottles of formula sticking out of the pockets of my leather jacket.

Megan, still chubby at three, kicking her feet until one of her canvas sneakers – she called them her slip-offs – went sailing into the head of a Vietnamese grannie across the aisle.

Megan skinny and eight, absorbed in a classroom copy of *Charlotte's Web*. Me watching the way her bangs fell in front of her eyes. When she came to a hard word she would squint, and the tip of her tongue would stick out.

Now she was wearing a bra, and I didn't even have a car. She was looking nowhere but forward, at thirteen and sixteen and twenty-one. All those little Megans were invisible now. Ghosts, and only I could see them.

My name is Will Kennedy. I'm smart, but not as smart as my cousin Andy, who took up computers in Boy Scouts and now works in Austin's Silicon Gulch. I've been in trouble with the law, but not like my uncle Jerome, who is currently in jail for assault after catching his wife in bed with his parole officer. I'm considered a bit peculiar in the family, but not as peculiar as my Aunt Dot, who – though still a Baptist – believes that in a past life she was the queen of the planet Saturn. (Aunt Dot got into past-life regressions as a weight-loss therapy, and since discovering that she died of famine in eighth-century Ethiopia, she's lost forty-eight pounds. And kept it off.)

Aunt Dot once told me it was thinking about me that got her interested in the idea of reincarnation. Personally, I have a hard time believing we all live many lives. The dead folks of my acquaintance have a hard enough time getting over just one.

When I was six years old, my Uncle Billy was killed in the K-resin facility of the Philips Petroleum complex. Vaporized, actually, except for the steel soles of his work boots, which he left behind on the factory floor like wet silver footprints. Statistically, this was not surprising. If you're a boy growing up

6

in Deer Park, or Pasadena, or any of the other little suburbs east of Houston, the odds are pretty fair that Refinery Row will get you sooner or later. Before he died, Billy had been a deacon at the Deer Park Church of Christ, where we used to go before Mom got too heavy to fit in her Sunday dresses. Once a month he spelled Missy Pierce in the Sunday School rotation. As I recall, he took the Journeys of Paul very seriously, and could not abide a spitball.

The explosion came on the first Friday of first grade for me, during Show and Tell. We ran to the classroom windows and watched a black cloud seep into the hazy Texas sky like blood staining a gauze bandage. I didn't know then that Uncle Billy had dissolved into that dark air; I didn't hear about that until almost five o'clock, when the school decided it was safe to let us hurry into waiting cars, breathing through our hands, to be whisked home. My mom still likes to tell how the company and county officials came on TV to tell everyone that the fumes billowing from the plant weren't *dangerous*, but we citizens should stay inside for the rest of that ninety-nine-degree August day. With all the windows shut. And the air-conditioning off.

Like a lot of kids in Deer Park, I woke up in the middle of that night with a nose bleed. There were bloodstains on my pillow the next night too, and the night after that. 'Solvent vapor,' said my twelve-year-old cousin AJ wisely. Her daddy was a Brown & Root pipe fitter. AJ (short for Julie-Anne) had an abiding interest in industrial pollution, on account of she'd been born with the second and third toes on both her feet stuck together.

The next time I saw Uncle Billy was three weeks later, at the family reunion. This was back when the reunion was still on the Labor Day weekend, in a campground down on the banks of the Little Blanco River. What I remember best about those reunions is the food. The picnic tables were heavy with lemon pound cake and potato salad, brisket and fat quarters of watermelon. That year Uncle Raider's pretty Mexican wife, Juanita, had brought

7

tortilla soup and chile rellenos and cinnamon cookies and jalapeño spread and chicken tacquitos, which my dad said was trying too hard, and my mom said you couldn't blame her. I said their oldest boy, Carlos, told me his grandma Braunfeltzer (Raider's mother, this would be) didn't like Juanita on account of she was Catholic. Mom and Dad looked at one another for a spell and then Mom told me to hurry up and fix my plate.

I went for the hot dogs (made special with Hill Country German sausage and slathers of ketchup and chow-chow) and a little bit of slaw, the kind with raisins, and also a fat splotch of banana pudding with Nilla wafers in it. I had just grabbed a handful of Fritos when I bumped into Uncle Billy. He was so cold my sunburned shoulder puckered up with goose bumps, and he was black and white, as if he had come out of an old movie. I had seen plenty of ghosts before, and I knew right away that him being black and white meant he was dead.

Having left his boots on the refinery floor, Uncle Billy stood woefully barefoot, staring at Aunt Dot's famous Ambrosia salad, which was always a favorite on account of she used fresh pineapple instead of Del Monte fruit cocktail, and real cream instead of Cool Whip. Uncle Billy turned to look at me, and I felt guilty, because he was never going to experience the sticky tug of banana pudding against a spoon, or taste the fizzy burn of a cold Coke. I was so guilty, and so glad. So glad it was him dead and not me.

By the time Uncle Billy met his maker at Philips Petroleum, I had learned not to talk about dead people. Even my mom's mouth pulled down and her eyes got worried every time I mentioned ghosts. Everybody knew I saw them, of course – this was small-town East Texas, after all – but I kept my mouth shut with everyone except my cousin AJ.

AJ wasn't like the rest of Deer Park. She wore John Lennon glasses and burned incense in her room and told people she was a witch. When the cousins were over at Uncle Walt and

Aunt Patty's house, the grown-ups would hunker down in the heavily upholstered front room to 'set for a spell,' which meant talking slowly but loudly over the baseball game on the TV. Us kids, meanwhile, would rush outside, ignoring our mothers' warnings about being out in the heat of the day. This was the '70s, and if sunscreen *had* already been invented, word of it had not come to Texas. It was the business of any self-respecting white kid to burn to the point of peeling over every square inch of exposed skin twice a summer. The best place to peel was at your ear-tops, where sometimes, if you were very careful, you could slough a whole curled layer in one piece, translucent and slightly bendy, like the abandoned shell of a cicada, which we called katydids back then.

AJ was expected to mind the rest of us. Sometimes she would grab the magnifying glass out of the garage and let us try to burn pinholes through a Cornflakes box on the patio, but most often our general holler and hubbub would be too shattering on Aunt Patty's nerves, and she would order AJ to take us back to the rumpus room at the back of the house where they kept a TV so old it didn't know any programs but *Gunsmoke* and *Popeye* cartoons. We'd fight awhile about what we were going to play next, until finally AJ would drawl, 'Hush you up, vermin!' and turn off the lights and bring in one of her tapers of incense. We would happily hush and pull the curtains closed while she told us truly terrifying stories about the bloodthirsty ghosts left over from Jean Lafitte's pirate crew; or about this friend whose sister had picked up a Cajun hitchhiker who turned out to be a homicidal maniac just bust out from a Louisiana prison for the criminally insane.

Once AJ even brought out the skull of a monster baby that had been given to her by an old blind prophetess in Lake Charles. Trying not to seem impressed, my cousin Doreen said it looked like a cat skull to her, but AJ said that was how they knew it was a demon baby, because it had been born with fangs and eyes where the pupil slits ran catwise, up and down, which is why as soon as the parents got home from the hospital they killed it themselves by emptying half a can of Raid into the baby's bottle. Then we all felt sorry for the kid, even if it was a cat-headed demon baby, and everyone got quiet and very respectful because we all knew this story was particularly true and poignant for AJ, on account of her toes.

When I was twelve, AJ was the object of my very first crush. Of course, she was a senior in high school and I was only a seventh grader, but I found I could use my stories about dead people to make myself interesting. I told her about Mr. Johnson, the old black janitor at my school who was still wearily scrubbing down the bathrooms even though he'd hung himself from a beam in the boiler room with a bright orange extension cord when I was in second grade. AJ seemed kind of disappointed by how ordinary most ghosts seemed to be, but when I tried to make my stories more exciting, like hers, she could always tell right away that I was lying. She'd look at me over the tops of her little round sunglasses and put on the heavy Black Girl accent she used to aggravate her daddy. 'You axin' me to b'lieve dat, DK?' DK short for Dead Kennedy, which was her nickname for me. So I learned to stick to the facts.

Then AJ left high school, moved out of Uncle Walt's house and disappeared into the world of grown-ups, which it seemed to me then was another kind of dying.

I had other crushes, and dates, but after that first love I didn't talk about the dead until my junior year in high school, when I started going out with Josie Wells. Josie was the only girl in the history of Deer Park High to make the cheerleading team and then drop out without getting pregnant. She was blond, with six rings in her left ear and two useless doper parents. We got married a month after senior prom and moved to Houston proper. First, because I was damn good and ready to live someplace where nobody would start humming 'Ghost Riders in the Sky' when I walked by, and second because it's never the wrong time to get the hell out of Deer Park.

Two years later Josie left me. She was pregnant at the time.

For the next ten months, I crashed in many shitty places: friends' apartments, shared houses, parked cars, and, twice, the playground at Hermann Park. You know your life has taken a wrong turn when you're trying to get your beauty sleep in a tire swing.

I finally got my shit together enough to move into the Parkwood Apartments complex, which lies between the Astrodome and the Texas Medical Center. Parkwood is six square blocks of poorly maintained brick fourplexes built in the 1950s, all owned by the Baylor College of Medicine. Baylor doesn't specialize in real estate. As a result, both the maintenance and the rent are five years behind the times. On my budget, an excellent trade-off. Most of my neighbors were grad students from exotic places like China or Pakistan or Idaho, many with little kids. There was also a mix of old people on fixed incomes, and a sprinkling of the sort-of-working poor, like me. By the time Tom Hanlon called me about the dead girl in his garage, I had lived there for almost eleven years, getting fired and laid about the same number of times.

Every Monday night, my buddy Lee had me over for Foreign Film Indoctrination at his place, which is the other upstairs apartment in our fourplex. Lee had introduced me to Hong Kong action flicks, Jackie Chan and Jet Li, as well as Indian disaster movies. He was also partial to Soviet-era Armenian musicals. You don't know how good you've got it, he liked to say, until you watch the Armenian proletariat burst into joyous song on the floor of a tractor-parts factory.

We were scheduled to watch a flick the day after my not-so-great outing with Megan, but I managed to lose my job at Petco, which took the zest out of me. A definite sign of aging, there. In my early twenties, the days I got canned were three or four of the finest in a calendar year. I'd get bored with my current job and start experimenting, searching for management's exact snapping point. At the Galleria Men's Wearhouse, for instance, mascara alone isn't enough for them to risk a wrong-ful dismissal suit, but even one pretty lame coat of lipstick puts them into a comfort zone, firing-wise.

Anyway, it was back to job searching. (I've done welfare, but I don't like it. It's embarrassing to show up and stand in line with, you know, single-parent amputees. Besides which, welfare doesn't pay enough if you have to buy chocolate-covered almonds at a dollar a box to send your daughter to science camp.)

I headed across the foul hallway to tell Lee I was going to bail on Monday Movie Madness. Parkwood Apartments does-n't bother air-conditioning public areas, so the foyer, staircase, landings and hallways in my building stay at a more or less con-stant ninety-three degrees from May until October, and stink like old gym socks from the mildew in the carpet. I slapped a couple of heat-drugged mosquitoes into small splotches on Lee's door by way of knocking.

Lee appeared holding two bottles of Pacifico with the tops already off. He's about my age, with the kind of scruffy good looks that make grown women want to tuck in his shirt. He gets fired less than me, and laid a whole lot more. Tonight he was wearing a peach-patterned bowling shirt and jean shorts. '*Bushmen!*' he said, handing me a brewski. 'Tsui Hark moves the Chinese Hopping Vampire genre to the Kalahari desert. A classic.'

'Can't do it.' I took the beer.

He glanced sharply at me. 'Uh, oh. You've got the chit, don't you?' Lee and I have this deal where only one of us is allowed to feel shitty at a time. If one guy has the feeling-shitty chit, the other one is honor-bound to suck it up. 'Did you get fired again?'

'Screw you. It might have been my love life.'

'You don't have a love life. So . . . you gonna skip the movie, just stay home and lay low?' he said, holding the door open.

'Yeah,' I said, coming inside. I sat down at his kitchen table.

'I got leftovers. How did you get gassed this time?'

'Ate cat food.'

'Meaning, you ate cat food so you're not hungry for leftovers,' Lee asked, 'or ate cat food in regards to Got Fired?'

'Numero dos. See, the first thing is, when I got in this morning, I found the weekend crew had screwed up the dog food displays.' Lee's dog, the Frankenterrier, padded in to scope me out. 'This story isn't really about dog food,' I told him. 'The dog food is just the teaser.' Frank's ears drooped, and he settled down under the table to snooze.

Lee took a long pull on his beer. 'You're making me hungry.' He strolled into his kitchen. 'Want something? Vicky did a chicken molé before she went to work.'

'Of all your current girlfriends, she's my favorite.' I'm a Pierce-Top-With-Fork man, myself, when it comes to cooking.

'How long until we get to the part where you fuck up?' Lee fussed at the stove, dumping a drumstick onto a plate of rice and ladling molé sauce over it. 'I bet that's the funny part.'

I drained my Pacifico down to the halfway point, still trying to wash away the lingering taste of cat food. 'Long story short: I'm already tired and cranky when Mrs. Belton rolls in. The Belton is this vicious scamming old hag who drops by three times a week to pass off color-xeroxed cat-toy coupons and complain about the service. So today she shows up claiming the NutroMax we sold her was spoiled. This is dry food in a vacuum-sealed bag. So I politely reached into the bag for some—'

'And ate it.' Lee grinned. 'Shit, that's just standing behind the product. They should have given you a raise.'

'You'd think.' But I had gritted my teeth (still spackled with cat food) and told Dickless Phil, my manager, that his general point – you can't spray customers in the face with lamb-flavored cat-food crumbs – was well taken, and that I would be careful not to do it again, even to vicious scamming old hags. He canned my ass anyway.

Lee and I considered my situation over Mexican food. I

dropped out after eleventh grade. I knew even then it was a stupid thing to do, but there's a big gap between knowing something and *getting* it. 'The trouble is, I haven't got anything to fucking *sell*,' I said, somewhere through my third Pacifico. 'When I was nineteen, I used to despise the whole idea of growing up into, you know, nine to five in the suburbs. The shows I watched on TV just wanted to sell me beer. Now it's ads for life insurance and financial planning. And the bitch of it is, *I want them.*'

'Next it will be heart medication,' Lee said. 'Home improvement supplies.'

'Viagra,' I said gloomily.

'When would you ever need it?'

'Fuck off.' I grinned into my beer. 'Lee, she was wearing a bra today.'

'Like that wasn't going to happen?'

'I just worry she's trying to grow up too fast. She's flatter than a West Texas highway.'

'You're stressing, dude.' Lee shrugged expansively. 'There's no drama here. They chafe.'

'What?'

'Nipples. The year before the breasts actually develop, the nipples get real sensitive. The bra's just there to keep her shirt from driving her nuts.' He looked at me. 'How do you not know this stuff? Didn't you have sisters?'

'Little ones. I guess I wasn't paying attention. So you think it's not about wanting to . . .'

'Dude, they chafe.'

'Okay,' I said, obscurely relieved. I shook my head. 'Lee, the older I am, the harder it is to get even shitty jobs. Fuck, I hate worrying about money.' I was pissed and even scared about losing a job that ten years ago I wouldn't have been caught dead taking. How humiliating. 'Jesus, Lee, I don't have my G.E.D. I can't drive big trucks. I can't even type.'

'There's the Army,' Lee suggested.

'Or Refinery Row.'

'Same thing,' he said. We drank to that.

We finished eating and left the dishes in Lee's sink. I stretched out on the couch while Lee started the VCR and then settled into a fat armchair as the FBI warning played across the blue TV screen. The Frankenterrier assumed his movie-watching position, slumped across Lee's feet. 'You know what they say about that which does not kill us,' Lee said philosophically, tipping back another mouthful of Pacifico.

'¿Qué?'

'It can still hurt like hell.'

'Amen,' I said.

That night I couldn't get to sleep. Long after midnight my crappy A/C unit was still beating like a tired heart, losing its long war with the sweltering Houston heat. I lay on the mattress in my 'studio' apartment, sweating and itching, while my mind stupidly circled: I couldn't even take my kid to Six Flags – how did I think I was going to help her through college? Why wasn't my name on her birth certificate? When the *hell* had she started wearing a bra? Around and around, as useless as that old A/C unit, a record with a scratch in it.

Funny to think Megan had probably never seen a vinyl record.

When she was seven she made me a 'CD slipcase' in an after-school beadwork class. It seemed un-dadlike to explain that little metal beads and wires weren't the best thing to carry a compact disc in, so I picked one album to sacrifice and carried it around in there all weekend, scratching the shit out of it. Joy Division, I think. When you've got a kid, the whole suicide thing loses its glamor.

I rolled off my mattress and dug the Classifieds out of a three-day-old copy of the *Houston Chronicle,* looking for high five-figure jobs for guys with a keen interest in alternative music and no high-school degree. The pickings were slim.

At two in the morning I gave up and went outside. Houston is basically a concrete saucepan full of swamp water. The sun heats it up to a slow boil in May and keeps it simmering through to the end of October. Even at two o'clock in the morning it was still sweltering, sweaty and restless. A tree roach as long as my thumb went hurrying along the sidewalk, big enough to throw a shadow by the yellow gleam of the streetlight. I walked up Cambridge to Holcombe and took the path along Braes Bayou. 'Bayou' is our romantic Southern word for 'big concrete drainage culvert.' The bayous are theoretically there to protect us in case of heavy rain, but they don't stop flooding; they just give you an extra hour to get to high ground.

I walked west along Braes Bayou until the path dipped under the Fannin overpass. From down in the gully, I couldn't see the cars as they passed overhead – just catch the sweep of their lights going by, and the hiss of tires.

Before me, the path disappeared into the darkness under the bridge. The silhouette of a man was standing there like a gatekeeper in the gloom. I slowed up. A lot of homeless people hang out under these bridges. This guy was wearing a construction worker's battered hard hat and no shoes or socks. I wondered if I should give him a buck, or if that would just make me a good target for a mugging. I slowed up more. Now I was close enough to hear him muttering, some kind of Bible verse.

I had just decided to turn back when he raised his face and I saw that he was dead. His bare feet and pale cheeks and hard hat were all in black and white, and he had the lightless eyes the dead so often have. Those underground eyes. 'His *feet* like unto fine brass, as if they burned in a furnace,' the dead man said. 'And his *voice* as the sound of many waters.'

'Jesus,' I whispered. '*Uncle Billy?*'

He was still wearing his Brown & Root jumpsuit. His naked feet stuck out from his pant legs, white as cut mushrooms. I always remembered him as grumpy and middle-aged, but now I realized

16

he had died at only thirty-two or thirty-three. My age. I got a powerful feeling that he had been waiting for me: waiting years for me to come down to the concrete bayou and be washed in that black water.

One cold distant streetlight showed in the strip of night sky overhead. The banks of the bayou seemed very tall. Down here the darkness was pooled, heavy and deep. Dirty water gurgled and whispered, echoing under the bridge. The smell of decay was thick as mud in my mouth. My heart beat. My chest shook with the thudding of it. Billy's eyes slid across my face, blind as stones. 'Be thou *faithful* unto death,' he said, 'and I *will* give thee a crown of life.'

I jumped off the asphalt path and bolted up the embankment, digging my fingers into the muddy slope. Bits of cardboard and old beer cans rattled and pinged as I scrabbled up the hillside. Sliding and slipping, I grabbed at the tall grass, tearing out clumps of it, pulling myself up until I scrambled out of the dim ravine. 'I have somewhat against thee,' Uncle Billy called, from down in the gloom. 'Because thou hast left thy first love.'

Up at street level, the night seemed normal, flat and wide. Lights on in the office buildings of the Texas Medical Center. Traffic humming through the intersections. I ran and I didn't look back, ran like a bastard down Fannin and then along Old Spanish Trail, my feet thudding and the sound of my own ragged breathing loud in my ears. I didn't stop running until I banged up the back stairs of my apartment building and found myself safe in my own kitchen again.

The last time I saw Uncle Billy, it was 1977. I was watching *Batman* every day after school. My grandpa Jay Paul was still alive, lingering on in the nursing home that would later be shut down after three orderlies were investigated for elder abuse. Back then, David Bowie was in Berlin, making great records like *Low* and *Lodger*, but in Deer Park even a rebel like AJ only

17

knew 'Space Oddity.' In 1977, Josie was already starting to look after her useless doper family. It would be years before we met.

The present is a rope stretched over the past. The secret to walking it is, you never look down. Not for anyone, not even family. The secret is to pretend you can't hear the voices of the people who have fallen down there in the dark.

There was a red light blinking on my answering machine. The message was from Tom Hanlon, telling me his offer was still on the table. A thousand bucks to come see about the dead girl in his garage.

I stared at the machine for a long time, thinking about Megan, and bus fare, and rent, and the fact that I didn't have a job any more. This is how girls get to be hookers, I thought. You get into a jam where you've only got one thing left to sell.

I called him back.

CHAPTER TWO

'It started with the crying,' Hanlon said. 'A couple of weeks ago I came in dead beat, must have been past midnight. It was raining. Anyway, I was in bed, just falling asleep. All of a sudden I find myself real scared, and I'm listening for this girl crying, so quiet I would have thought I imagined it, only my body knows I didn't. She's crying out there in my garage. I'm all tensed up and my skin is crawling. The next night it's the same. I tried getting drunk before I went to bed, but that made it worse. Now, I hear her all the time. She knows I can hear her.'

'You ever see her?'

'No.'

Oh, great. When it's all sounds and voices, nine times out of ten you're talking schizophrenia. Schizophrenia is every bit as real and scary as ghosts, in its own way, but nothing I can do jack shit about. 'You know who she is?'

'No clue.'

'Do you hear her more often some times than others?' I asked. 'Only at night, for instance?'

'M-maybe a little more often when it rains. DK? Do you have any ideas?'

'Call me Will. Nobody calls me DK any more.'

'She's driving me crazy, DK. I can't eat, I can't sleep, I'm missing appointments, I'm blowing sales. I truly need your help. I'm good for the money. If you can think of anything I can do to make her go away, I'll write you a check tomorrow.'

Shit. 'I just don't think—'

'Jesus, Will. This is family. Family *and* a thousand dollars.'

I looked out my living-room window, wishing I didn't need his money. My reflection looked back at me, tired and pale. 'What the hell. Pick me up tomorrow and I'll take a look.'

Silence. 'Pick you up? Can't you just . . . ?'

'Write you a prescription? If you're paying me to check it out, I'm going to check it out.' Long silence from Hanlon. 'Hey, Tom, piss or get off the pot. Your choice, man.'

'The thing is, I'm really busy right now,' Hanlon stammered. 'I don't have . . . I don't think I can work that in.'

'Then buenos fucking noches.' I slammed the phone down on my thousand dollars. If there's anything worse than being a whore, it's being a rejected whore. 'God *damn*.'

Probably it was for the best. Probably cousin Tom was beginning the long awful slide into schizophrenia, and nothing short of heavy-duty medication would get rid of his ghost. In the long run, we would both be better off this way. Except . . . a *thousand dollars!* 'Fuck!' I shouted, and I kicked my wall hard enough to leave a bootprint on it.

Then I stomped over to my stereo and played 'Wild Child' thirty-eight times in a row.

I was listening to Bauhaus when Hanlon called back two days later. He hadn't slept in forty-two hours, he was calling from his car, and if I had time, could I come to his house that night?

About eight o'clock on a wet July night, Hanlon rolled to a stop in front of my apartment in a Nissan Stanza that had seen better days. I reached into the back of my hallway closet, trying to decide if I should put on my old leather jacket, the one with the fish-hooks sewn onto the undersides of the lapels. I hadn't worn it since the day I'd taken Megan to a movie and nearly had a heart attack when she made a grab for the shiny fish-hooks with her fat toddler fingers.

But tonight, going to the house of a possibly crazy dude, I kind of wanted it on. The experts at the Ultimate Fighting Challenge tell us that sooner or later ninety percent of fights go to ground. I can confirm from my wild youth that the first couple of times some son of a bitch grabbed me and found his hands full of Eagle #8 brass hooks, our tussle was a head butt and a broken nose from being over. Of course that was semi-decent neighborhoods in the good old days, when the other guy was packing maybe a butterfly knife or a roll of quarters in his fist, instead of a Mac-10 with blazer ammo.

On the other hand, it was a muggy ninety-two degrees out and the whole city smelled like a crawdad boil. I put the jacket back in the closet with the feeling I was probably making a mistake.

The rest of my gear was suitably bland: a Men's Wearhouse shirt and black jeans over my ancient but classy pair of black Doc Martens. I don't wear jewelry any more. My wedding ring lives in an aspirin bottle in the medicine cabinet. I always mean to throw it away, but I never do. I wore a stud or a hoop in my left ear for years, but Megan grabbed it when she was little, so I took it out and the hole grew in and the whole idea of a guy in clip-ons seemed to miss the point. Now that Meg was older I could have gotten the ear re-pierced, but these days I'd need to hang a cowbell from my nipple to keep up. It's hard to make that commitment when you're over thirty and sober.

My mohawk I had shaved off when it began to recede.

I headed out of my apartment, not bothering to lock my door. The rotting gym-sock aroma of the hallway was duking it out with the scent of Vicky's cooking – homemade tamales tonight, to judge by the smell, and pico de gallo.

I clattered downstairs and stepped out into a warm drizzle.

As I walked out to the curb, a discarded condom drifted by on the current of run-off and disappeared into a gaping storm drain.

Hanlon leaned across the front seat and rolled down the passenger-side window. 'You don't have any tools,' he said. 'Bells and candles and Bibles.'

'Is your ghost Catholic?'

'I don't know.'

'Me neither.'

Tom Hanlon was balding and tired. He was wearing a London Fog raincoat that was probably expensive when he bought it, some time before the Berlin Wall came down. Now it was smudged with coffee stains and newsprint. Two of the bottom buttons were missing. His car felt pitifully lived in: Doritos bags and misfolded maps in the back seat, 7-Eleven coffee cups stacked three deep in the cup holder. The dashboard was littered with receipts from Whataburger and Dairy Queen. My powerful brain worked out that Hanlon was a salesman. My dad spent a year thinking he could get rich moving cheap air-ionizers. I know the signs.

Hanlon peered up at me. 'Remember me now, DK?'

'Not at all.'

'You haven't changed much,' he said.

I stood beside the passenger door, rain trickling down my scalp. I wasn't crazy about getting in a car with a haunted driver who hadn't slept in two days.

Hanlon tapped his raincoat pocket. 'I have the money right here. All cash. Crisp three-dollar bills.'

'OK, that was funny,' I said. And besides, I needed the money. I got in the car. My cousin stuck out a hand and we shook. He had the Bieler nose, like Aunt Dot; and of course the spooked eyes the haunted always have.

We crept down to the end of my block and turned right on Old Spanish Trail. The rain left needle-tracks on the windshield and the wipers cleared them off. A car rolled by with a swish, leaving treadmarks on the wet road that dissolved as I watched.

At the Fannin Street intersection, an old Korean woman carrying a sack of groceries froze suddenly in Hanlon's headlights. I grabbed for my door handle and yelled as the Stanza plunged through her. My skin prickled in a burst of cold air.

Hanlon jumped. 'What the *hell*?'

'Sorry.' I forced myself to let go of the door handle. 'Thought I saw something.'

'A ghost?'

'Yeah.'

We passed the Astrodome, heading for the 610 Loop. 'You working a shtick on me, DK?'

'Didn't know she wasn't real,' I said. 'Thought you were about to hit someone.'

'You can't tell?'

'Not in the dark.' I didn't feel like explaining the black and white thing, but it makes it harder to tell the living from the dead at night.

'Isn't that dangerous?' Hanlon said. 'How do you drive?'

'I don't. I smashed up my dad's car twice, braking for dead people. Let my license lapse. Mostly I take the bus.'

Hanlon stared at me. 'You don't *drive*?'

I have ways to shock even the most jaded Houston native.

My cousin took the ramp onto 610, accelerated onto the freeway and sifted over one lane, letting traffic drift into place around us. He drove like a man who drove a lot. His shoulders were high and tight and he kept shaking his head. The wipers made their tired heartbeat sound, squeak-chonk, squeak-chonk. We headed east, pouring down the freeway, me staring through the side window as the lights streamed by, apartment blocks and billboards.

'Hey, Will. How long since you've been back to Deer Park?'

'Not long enough.' I thought of Uncle Billy, his blind eyes sliding off of mine. *I have somewhat against thee, because thou hast left thy first love.*

Be thou faithful unto death, and I will give thee a crown of life.

It's harder to tell the living from the dead at night, and harder to tell the ghost roads from the real ones. There weren't many ghost roads in Deer Park when I was a kid – not like they have them in Galveston, say, or over in the Fourth Ward – but I saw at least one every time I rode the bus to school. They don't stay put, though. One day there might be a long gray alley stretching out behind the 7-Eleven. Everything in it would be in black and white, real sharp and clear so you could read the grain of the cement, or pick out the shadowy pits in the telephone poles and see the rusting staples where old flyers used to be. But the next time I went in for a Slurpee, the alley would be just normal again, with crows on the telephone wires and red-and-white Coke cans tangled in the hedges.

I never walked down a ghost road myself, not even when Josie left me. There are some places we just aren't meant to go.

Hanlon said, 'A ghost can't actually hurt you, can it? She can't actually . . . you know. Touch me.'

'Most ghosts don't. But they can still scare you to death. You ever hear about those people who think they're Jesus? They believe it so hard that nail-holes open up in their hands.' AJ had told me about that. 'I knew this guy once who was haunted by a dead girl,' I said. 'She kept trying to slash him with a switchblade. At first he couldn't feel anything, but after a couple of weeks, these cuts started opening up on his skin.'

Hanlon stared. 'My God. What did you do?'

'Got him a box of Winnie-the-Pooh Band-Aids.'

'Like hell.'

'They weren't bad cuts. Once he realized he could take the worst she had to dish out, and fix it with a Piglet Band-Aid, he got less and less afraid, and she did less and less damage.'

Hanlon gave a little choked laugh. 'I guess that's why they pay you the big bucks.'

Amber taillights fled along the highway in front of us. I asked one of the questions I always ask the haunted. 'What did you want to be when you grew up, Tom?'

'Spy.' Hanlon grinned self-consciously. 'I wanted to be a secret agent. American James Bond. This was when I was maybe eleven or twelve. Spring-loaded Walther PPK. Microcamera. Stealing secrets from the Russians to save America. Very hush-hush. Nothing in the papers, no appearances on TV. Handshake from the President. Fast car.'

Big dreams, small life. Loner. Haunted. Well that's just great, I thought. He's a fucking Cobain.

Generally speaking, I divide people – living and dead – into five groups:

1) Buddhas
2) Tell-Tale Hearts
3) Cobains
4) (Jack the) Rippers
5) Zombies

I use the rating scale two ways. First, to identify what kind of ghost I have to reckon with. If someone is being haunted by a guilty conscience, that's a Tell-Tale Heart. A mom who let her kid drown in a swimming pool, for example. If you can get her through the worst of the guilt, the ghost will stop coming.

I also use the scale on living people, judging how likely they are to return after death. Buddhas never come back: they have their shit together and they keep their accounts in order. The Buddha said, 'Desire is the root of all suffering'. So if you don't want to suffer, all you have to do is stop wanting anything. That's the part that gives me trouble.

Cobains are a funny bunch. They brood to the point of obsession. They mix guilt and bitterness. They nearly always feel betrayed, by lovers or parents or life, and especially by themselves. They tend to be introverts with a need to act out: clowns, lady poets, vengeful suicides. Spy – that was perfect. A perfect Cobain.

Hanlon cleared his throat. 'I shouldn't be telling you this, but I actually did some work for the CIA when I was selling in

Belgium and Germany. I was a mule. That's covert ops jargon. You know, a courier. Mule. Get it?'

I said I got it.

Hanlon smiled, remembering. 'Got recruited in Brussels, at Rick's. Rick's is a complete replica of Bogart's joint in *Casablanca*. 344 Avenue Louise, Commune of Ixelles. Very upscale address. It's a hang-out joint for American ex-pats. The guy who worked the territory before me got a hamburger named after him. His case officer picked me up. Always looking for patriotic single men, he said. They paid good money, too, before they cancelled the Cold War.'

Hanlon swung around a slow-moving Volvo station wagon. 'If I just didn't give a damn, the noises wouldn't matter,' he said. 'What's a ghost? Nothing. All I got to do is stay away from the garage. And I'm scared as hell to go in there, it makes me want to throw up I get so scared. So what the hell do I do every night? I go into the garage. Why do I do that?' He squeezed his eyes shut. 'I lie in bed listening, and now if I *don't* hear the little bitch, I get up and I creep into the laundry room and I stand at the garage door for hours. Listening.' An eighteen-wheeler started to pass us on the left. Reflected in the rearview mirror, its headlamps spread harsh white light slowly over Hanlon's face, exposing it. His pupils shrank in eyes bloodshot and pouchy from sleeplessness. 'I hit her,' he said.

'What?'

'I was driving. It was dark. She just walked into the road before I could do anything about it. Maybe she was committing suicide, I don't know.'

'You killed her. With your car.' Classic: a ghost pulled back by a guilty conscience. I didn't bother saying, *You lied about not knowing her!* Haunted people lie a lot.

'This was in Germany,' Hanlon said. 'I didn't know what to do. I dragged the body into the bushes on the side of the road. She didn't have any ID, there was no point calling in the accident. They don't like foreigners, you know. The Germans don't.

None of the Euros do. They all feel this kind of contempt for Americans. Those Germans, they've forgotten about getting their asses kicked in '45.' Hanlon's hands were shaking on the wheel. 'It was her fault,' he said. 'I didn't think she'd find me, not back here in America. But she did. She did.' His voice was hoarse. 'What the hell does she want?'

'You,' I said.

Hanlon's house was on one of those dreary suburban streets where all the children have grown up and moved away. He turned into an anonymous driveway and parked in front of what I assumed was the haunted garage. 'Maybe this isn't such a good idea.' He turned off his engine but left his headlights on, spraying white light through the drizzle, two big white spots on the garage door. He sat in the car with his hands tight on the wheel. 'Sell me, Will. Make your pitch. It's your fee.'

'It's your ghost.'

Hanlon laughed and rubbed his eyes. 'Yeah. Yeah. I love a product like that. Sells itself. Something the customer needs.' Rain creaked and ticked on the roof of the car. 'When I was over in Europe, I worked for this company that sold signals. Flashers, strobes, sirens: all that stuff you see on cop cars, fire trucks. Great product. Every town's got to have 'em, and it's always public money.' Hanlon set his parking brake and turned off the lights. 'Do you ever see these ghosts? I mean, maybe even when the haunted person can't?'

'Sometimes.'

'Son of a bitch.' My cousin pulled his key out of the ignition and the red brake indicator winked out. We sat together in the dark. I could feel the bulk of his body in the next seat. Think about the thousand bucks, I told myself. Hanlon's coat rustled. In the darkness he said, 'What it comes down to is, I need the product.'

*

27

He opened his front door and I followed him into an old person's living-room. A flower-pattern couch, a large color TV, a china cabinet filled with the kind of knick-knacks my Mamaw Dusty used to love – egg-cups and ceramic owls and coffee spoons with the crests of the different states on top. 'This your mom's house, Tom?'

'Eugenia's. My daddy remarried. They both passed away last year, is why I came back. House being paid for and all.'

Eugenia had done like my Great-Aunt Rebecca and laid down little walkways of clear plastic to keep her champagne-colored carpeting from getting dirty and flattened out. In one corner of the room sat a black piano with its feet in oversized plastic coasters. Sheet music for a hymn was open above the keyboard: 'There is a Fountain Filled With Blood.' I had a sudden dim memory of singing that in church: *There IS a fountain FILLED with blood* – breathe – *drawn from Emmanuel's veins. And sinners plunged beneath that flood* – breathe – *Lose all their guilty stains.* The throb of the electric organ and the boom of Uncle Billy's voice behind me. *Lose all their guilty stains, lose all their guilty stains.* And after, the decorous rustle of people sitting back down, and then the stealthy advance of the communion tray, heading toward me with its little shot-glasses full of grape juice.

And SIN-ners plunged beneath that flood
Lose all their GUIL-ty stains.

On a hat stand by the front door was a furred cap. Hanlon picked it up and turned it slowly in his hands. He was still wearing his London Fog coat. 'See this? Genuine Soviet Army.' He held the hat up so I could see the small red hammer-and-sickle pin stuck to the side. I had a flashback of myself at nineteen, grinning at Josie over a pitcher of beer, thumping a bar table with my fist and thunderously quoting Stalin. *You cannot make a revolution with silk gloves!*

A sharp scream came from the garage, ending in a muffled grunt. My guts cramped up. Shit, shit, shit. So much for schizophrenia.

Hanlon twitched. 'Did you hear that? I thought I heard something.'

'Yeah,' I said. 'Maybe a little something.' Obviously I was hearing the ghost a lot more clearly than he was. That's why they pay Comrade Will the big bucks. 'These sounds always come from the garage?'

'Mostly. Mostly from the garage. Near the car.'

Hanlon put back his genuine Soviet Army cap and headed to the kitchen. He pulled a box of grapefruit juice from the fridge and drank from its spout. His hand was shaking. My cousin had killed this girl and wasn't man enough to stick around and face the music. I didn't feel as much contempt for him as you might think. One thing I've learned from watching the dead is that you can never be sure what you'll do when the very worst happens. But after I had looked in the garage I would tell Hanlon he had to confess, or at least call in a tip about the accident. It's for your own good, I would tell him. But mostly I was thinking of that girl's parents, waiting at home while pictures of their kid got old and yellow in photo albums they couldn't bear to open.

'You can wait here while I poke around the garage,' I said.

'No.' Hanlon looked over the refrigerator door and tried to smile. 'Count me in, buddy.' He put away the box of juice and dug a small key out of the silverware drawer by the sink. I followed him through the kitchen into a little laundry room, with a washer and dryer and some shelves overhead. Beyond them was the door to the garage. There were new locks on it: a deadbolt Hanlon turned back, a chain lock he unlatched, a padlock he opened with the key from the kitchen drawer, and a combination lock.

'Are these here to keep the ghost from coming in,' I asked, 'or you from going out?'

'Both.' He dialed the combination lock and opened the door to the garage. The darkness smelled of damp concrete and sawdust and mold. Hanlon flipped a light switch and a bare bulb came on over three unpainted stairs leading down to a concrete floor.

I clattered down the steps. There was a lawnmower in the near corner of the garage, and a wheelbarrow with a few of last year's leaves still blackening at the bottom. A hacksaw and a drill hung on a pegboard against the back wall. Below them was a worktable – screwdrivers and hammers and tackle boxes whose slide trays were jumbled with nuts and nails and screws. In the shadows under the worktable, I saw a gallon can of gasoline next to a plastic bucket full of rags. There was also a utility sink hooked up to the near wall. The tap was leaking, a slow steady drip that had left a trail of rust like a bloodstain on the white basin.

Huddled under the sink was the battered body of a young woman. She was nineteen or twenty, soaking wet, wearing a dripping vest over a wet T-shirt. She was naked from the waist down. Her hips and legs were covered in bruises; they had spread like smoke-stains across her clammy flesh. Her face was mottled and bloated, as if she had been beaten first and then drowned. Her mouth was clumsily gagged with a man's silk tie. Two more ties bound her wrists and ankles. The ties were gray. She was all gray, I realized. All in black and white. This was Hanlon's ghost.

Only this girl hadn't been hit by a car. This girl had been tied up and beaten to death.

Stairs creaked behind me. My cousin's right hand was hidden in the pocket of his coat. He wet his lips. 'See anything?' he said.

And right then I realized that sometimes a guy is haunted for a really good reason.

CHAPTER THREE

I rocked back and forth, trying to force the shakes out of my legs. Hanlon had murdered this girl, and not just in a traffic accident. She had come back to haunt him, and when he couldn't take it any more, he had called me.

But then I told him I'd have to come to his house, and he was screwed. Haunted, his life was shit, but he didn't want to risk me finding out who the dead girl was and what had happened to her. So between the first time he called me and the second, he had made up the story about hitting her with his car. If I never actually saw her, that would explain why she was in his garage. It would even be sort of true, emotionally: he was admitting he had killed her. If I could make her go away without seeing her, great. But if not . . .

Hanlon was still wearing his raincoat. He had his hand in the pocket. He sure as shit had a gun. We can carry concealed, here in the Lone Star State. This is the kind of thing you think about when you grow up wanting to work for the CIA.

Oh, shit.

I sucked in a long unsteady breath. So I had to pretend not to see the ghost, that was all. 'Okay, yeah, I can . . . sense, I can sense the presence of a young woman.' My voice sounded terrible, strung too tight. Relax, comrade. You're Dead Kennedy, remember? This is just one more ghost out of hundreds. 'Let me take a look around.'

The dead girl under the sink was soaking wet. Drip, drip. Hanlon heard her when it rained. Water was her ghost road. Maybe Hanlon drowned her. Maybe he beat her to death and threw her body into a river or lake. Probably he really had killed her over in Europe. Offed her in Amsterdam, or Bonn, and then dumped her in the Rhine or the Danube. That would explain why he wasn't still cruising the autobahn, pushing flashers to German cops and Dutch fire brigades. That's why he had come back to live out of his mom's house and his old Nissan Stanza.

And SIN-ners plunged beneath that flood
Lose all their guilty stains!

The dead girl under the sink strained against her gag. There were little bubbles of spit at the corners of her mouth. Her eyes were dark, like Uncle Billy's. She couldn't see Hanlon, but she could feel him there.

Creak, creak, said the wooden steps. Hanlon must be shifting his weight back and forth, back and forth. Listening for the dead girl. Sleepless, exhausted, terrified. Do you ever see these ghosts? I mean, maybe even when your client can't?

I walked over to the far side of the garage, away from the sink, pretending to look around. Was Hanlon a serial killer, or was this girl strictly a one-off? On TV, serial killers are crazy and they feel no guilt. That didn't sound right. This guy was no cool, calculating killing machine. He had a Tell-Tale Heart, didn't he? He must be capable of some remorse.

Still, he was a murderer. If he thought I had seen her, would he shoot me to keep me from turning him in? Would he risk killing me here? Maybe nobody would hear the shot, or call the police. Thirty-two-year-old loner disappears after losing job – probably nobody would even notice I was gone until I failed to pick up Megan the Sunday after next.

Quick nightmare image of Megan roped and gagged underneath that dripping sink.

'Hey, Will?' Hanlon said. 'You got this thing figured, kemosabe?'

'Mostly.' I frowned, real professional. 'There's a couple of things . . . tell you what. Why don't you drop me at home, I'll do a little research, then we can come back tomorrow and fix you up.'

Hanlon shook his head. 'You've got to do for me, Will. Now. I can't take another night of this.'

'Hey, do you want the job done right?'

'I want the job done now!' Hanlon yelled. He pulled a gun out of his right pocket. The barrel stared at me, a cold black eye. Hanlon blinked at the gun in his shaking hand, like How the hell did this happen?

'Whoa there,' I said softly. 'Easy, big fella.'

'I just can't stand it, DK.' He was weirdly apologetic. 'One more night, I'm like to blow my brains out.'

My legs were shaking uncontrollably.

'"I'll get back to you tomorrow."' Hanlon shook his head. 'I heard that a time or two. I don't even do follow-up on that one any more. I'm real sorry, DK.'

'Chill, dude. Tonight is no problem. You can count on me,' you sack of shit. Angry. Okay, maybe the planet wouldn't miss me if I got whacked by Secret Agent Man, but I didn't have to make it easy. I have always prided myself on being one sore fucking loser. And I did have one piece of leverage: Hanlon needed my product.

I walked over to the shop area. 'Ah,' I said seriously. 'Hm.' Maybe I could palm a screwdriver and stick him in the kidney? Nope – not through that London Fog coat, Comrade Will. I looked along the bench for something I could throw at Hanlon, or hit him with. Circular saw on the worktable, not plugged in. Power drill, hammer, wood chisel. I didn't have to kill the fucker, I just had to knock him out, or distract him enough to run like hell, with enough of a head start that he couldn't shoot me before I got to the door.

The dead girl huddled under the sink, grunting and work-ing at her gag with swollen fingers. The silk tie cutting into her wrists made it hard for her to use her hands. Hanlon could obviously hear something. He backed up to the top of the wooden steps, feeling behind him for the doorknob, gun wavering in his hand. His eyes settled on the sink. Water drip, drip, dripped down into darkness. The salesman licked his lips. 'Qué pasa, DK?'

'Thinking.' I forced myself to consider each item in the workshop. T-square. Crescent wrench. Gas can.

Gas can. *His feet like unto fine brass, as if they burned in a furnace.*

Thank you, Uncle Billy.

A can of gasoline. I found myself grinning, my body lit like I was nineteen again and up two Black Mollies, with the good hard whine of speed in my veins. 'All righty. This is looking bet-ter than I feared.' *There is a FOUNT-ain FILLED with blood . . .* 'It's a pretty straight-ahead case here.'

'You said you needed to do research.'

'I like to be sure. Two hundred proof. But looks like you need a straight shot of bourbon here and now.' I was babbling. Shit. 'Your ghost is pretty much, you know – off the rack. But the same name-brand quality you'd expect in one *twice* this expensive.'

'What the *hell* are you talking about?'

Great question. I moseyed back from the shop area and forced myself to meet Hanlon's eyes. 'Look, this chick, she is after you. I mean, your car is the last thing she ever saw. The dead are like that. They get fixated.' Ten feet in front of me, the gagged girl grunted and struggled.

Two tears rose and spilled from Hanlon's haunted eyes. 'She was so beautiful.'

Yuck. 'Do you have any candles in the house?'

'Emergencies, in the kitchen cabinet. Mom bought them after Hurricane Alicia, in case the power went out. Why do you need them? She was Catholic?'

34

I stared stupidly at Hanlon.

'The ghost,' he said. 'She was Catholic, then? That's why the candles?'

'Oh. Right. Catholic.' Shit, it would be just my luck if she had been a Buddhist or something and Hanlon would know my whole spiel was bullshit. 'Or raised Christian, definitely.'

My cousin nodded. His face was wet with tears, his eyes half-blind with guilt and exhaustion.

Okay, Will, push the pace, push the pace. 'I could use a few candles, maybe five if you've got them, and some matches. Perfect. And a Bible.'

'I don't think there's a Bible.'

'For fuck's sake, Tom, Eugenia must have a Bible stashed around here someplace.' Shit. Shut *up*, Will. 'That's not the important part, though. The candles are my ammo here. My silver bullets.'

'Wait a sec.' Hanlon backed into the laundry room, closing the door behind him. I could hear him turning the deadbolt and rehooking the chain lock. I took a long slow breath as Hanlon rummaged in his kitchen. I crept to the workbench, knelt next to the gas can, and twisted the rusty old cap. It squeaked like a stabbed rat. The footsteps in the kitchen went still. I held my breath until I heard cabinet doors creaking open.

A sharp grunt made me turn back to the drain. The dead girl was reaching up from under the sink with her bound hands, groping around the basin. The flesh around her bonds was dark and swollen. In black and white you could see the burst veins on her bruised arms. All her guilty stains. The hands gripped the basin's edge. Drip. Drip. The girl's face emerged from the shadows underneath the sink, staring blindly around the garage. Searching.

Locks rattled and Hanlon opened the door from the laundry room. 'I only found one,' he said, holding up a stubby emergency candle in his left hand.

I tried to smile but my mouth was dry and my lips wouldn't

move. The dead girl inched forward, slow as a crab, until she was crouching with her back to the sink, as if she couldn't bear to leave the basin and the pipes below. She went back to working at the gag in her mouth.

I said, 'Stand over by the sink, cowboy.'

'No. Why?'

'That's where the ghost is, Tommy.'

Reluctantly Hanlon walked down the three creaking steps. The girl stopped working on her gag and reached out as Hanlon edged closer. Her straining fingers trembled two inches from his coat. She rocked forward and then fell back, grabbing clumsily for the basin. 'Did you hear something?' Hanlon's voice was hoarse and cracking. 'I thought I heard something.'

'I heard it. Get over on the other side of the sink. That's it. Muy bien.' When I threw the gasoline on him and he caught fire, I needed a clear line to the laundry-room door. My heart was pounding like a runaway train.

Hanlon rocked nervously, head bobbing, holding the stubby candle in his gloved left hand. 'You gotta do for me here, Will.'

'You bet your ass I will. Did you fetch me those matches?'

'Got 'em.'

I made a show of inspecting the garage, squinting and sniffing. 'All right. Light the candle.'

'Why me? Aren't you supposed to do the exorcism?'

'Who is getting his ass haunted here? Trust me, Tom. Light her up.'

Watching me every second, Hanlon put the revolver back in his pocket and pulled out a lighter with his right hand. Stalin would have rushed him while he wasn't holding the gun, but I was too chickenshit. 'I hope you know what you're doing,' Hanlon said. He flicked his lighter and held it to the candle. A bud of light swelled around the wick, and opened into a thin leaf of white flame. Slowly the salesman straightened and put his lighter away. His right hand settled back into the pocket of his coat. So much for that chance.

The dead girl managed to pull off her gag at last. She threw it into the corner of the garage, where it hit with a faint swish. Her chest heaved. She dragged her bound hands across the front of her mouth, leaving a wet smear of blood around her lips, black against her white skin.

Shit, shit, shit. I turned and walked back to the workbench. 'Now, I need something to mark with . . . a paintbrush? Piece of chalk, maybe?' I bent down so my body blocked Hanlon's line of sight. I grabbed the handle of the gasoline can. Another buzz of adrenaline drilled through me, making my hands shake. I'm fixing to draw a pentagram, I tried to say, but I was strung too tight to get the words out.

'Hey, mister,' the dead girl croaked through battered lips. 'Aren't you American?'

I straightened up, turned, and lunged for the center of the room, swinging the gas can. Hanlon stared at me as a glittering ribbon of gasoline stretched out through the musty air. It splashed into the sink and through the dead girl. It splashed onto Hanlon's London Fog coat and his business slacks and the hand stuck in his pocket. It splashed onto the candle flame and put it out.

I stared stupidly at the stubby wax candle in the salesman's hand.

There hadn't been enough gasoline vapor in the air. The gas had been too cold and liquid when it hit the candle; instead of exploding, it had doused the flame like a cup of cold water. The can dropped from my numb hands and clattered to the concrete floor.

Hanlon blinked. 'Is this part of the—?' He stopped. 'You saw her.' He pulled the revolver out of his coat pocket and pointed it at my chest. 'You tried to kill me.'

'Tom. Take it easy, man.' My eyes were nailed to the barrel of his gun. 'So I saw her. So what? What am I going to do? Tell the police I saw a ghost in your garage? You think they give a fuck?'

Gasoline ran out of the can I had dropped, a dark pool of it creeping toward a drain under the sink. I should have been diving for a hammer off the workbench, or ducking under the table, or some damn thing. Instead my legs were shaking and shaking.

(Megan at four, crawling into my lap on the bus, frowning and serious. Are you going to died, Daddy? That was before she had stopped calling me Daddy. Shh, honey. Not for a long time. Megan lunging forward for a fierce hug, mashing my nose with her forehead. Daddy, I don't want you to died.)

I squeezed my eyes shut. No fucking time for that.

'I would have given you a thousand dollars, Will.' Hanlon's hand was shaking. The gun barrel wobbled around, pointing at my neck, my balls, my lungs. 'I ought to shoot you. You could describe her. The cops would start looking. They would find out.'

Adrenaline was screaming through my blood. I felt myself grinning like I used to back in my bar-brawling days, just before the punches started to fly. I held up two fingers, very slowly. 'Hey, I won't tell, Tom. Injun swear. I don't give a shit about her, she's your ghost.' Obviously he wasn't the cold-blooded serial-killer type, or he would have capped me already. 'You think you're the first sorry motherfucker I've met with a ghost following him around?' The gasoline was starting to evaporate. The smell of it rising around the salesman was strong enough to make my eyes water. 'You think I'd still be alive if I went around ratting out every brother with a body in the trunk of his car?'

The dead girl jerked on Hanlon's coat. 'Hey, mister,' she said. 'I need a ride.'

Hanlon jumped away from her touch. 'Shit!' His eyes flicked back to me. 'That's a hell of a product, Will.' He was breathing very fast and there was sweat beaded all over his forehead. 'Get her away from me. Get her away from me, Will, or so help me I'll shoot you where you stand.'

'And make another ghost to follow you around? I don't

38

fucking think so, Tom. Looks to me like you're in enough trouble already.' *Shut up!* I told myself. For Christ's sake, Will, why can't you stop ragging this guy? But my whole body was shaking with adrenaline and I couldn't stop grinning. I have *plans*, you asshole. I'm going to *Six Flags*.

The dead girl leaned away from the sink, groping blindly for Hanlon's coat with her bound hands. 'Hey, mister,' she said. Her voice was low and ugly. 'Do you know your way around?'

'Shit!' Hanlon's gun hand was trembling wildly. 'I loved her.' The girl strained forward. Her forearms were a mass of bruises. She had probably tried to cover her face while Hanlon beat her to death. The salesman's eyes filled with tears again. 'I loved her.'

'Oh, yeah,' I said. 'I can see that.'

Hanlon licked his lips. 'Fuck you.'

I jumped for the door. Hanlon's bullet slammed me in the chest. I spun and smashed face down on the laundry-room steps. The gunshot crashed deafeningly around the garage. Something exploded and suddenly there was fire everywhere. The flash from Hanlon's gun had set off the fumes from the evaporating gasoline. Burning air roared and popped behind me.

Gasping, I turned my head and looked back into an inferno. Hanlon was a mass of flames. He staggered backward and stumbled into the far wall of the garage. His arms beat wildly against the air. Evil yellow light flickered everywhere. Black stains flowered on the concrete.

His feet like unto fine brass, as if they burned in a furnace.

Fire thundered down on Hanlon like a waterfall. He fell over and his body jerked. His arms flapped like the wings of a burning wasp, crackling, little fanning motions getting weaker and finally weaker. His screams dried up. His body began to pull in, withering and contracting. I heard bones snapping. The garage was hot. My chest hurt. I coughed and it hurt more.

I squinted at the sink, trying to catch a glimpse of the dead girl. She wasn't there. Hey, mister, I thought, looking back at Hanlon's smoking body. I got rid of your ghost. Where's my thousand bucks?

Oh God.

Oh God.

It was getting harder and harder to breathe. The garage was hot. I tried to get my shit back together. Okay. Okay. So I had been shot. It wasn't too bad, really. My chest had a funny, ringing, buzzing hum in it, but there wasn't real agonizing pain. No gouts of blood. I looked back. Doing better than some, hey, Tom? Hanlon's body snapped and popped. Sometimes the fucking bear gets you, mister. Long live the revolution.

Ropes and strings of black smoke were spreading through the garage. It smelled like burning plastic, and I coughed, a little hack. That hurt. I crawled into the laundry room and closed the garage door behind me. The chain lock jingled. I gulped a big lungful of air and yelped as pain shot through my back. I was beginning to pant, fast shallow breaths separated by that little hacking cough. My right shoulder felt heavy and useless.

A gust of feeling swept over me, Hanlon's gun trained on my chest and the memory of Megan in my lap. What if I had died there? *My, like, biological father, he got shot to death in some pervert's garage.* No, not fair. Megan would come to my funeral. She would cry. No father left but fucking Don the ex-Marine. Kennedy lets his kid down again.

A thick, terrible pressure spread from my shoulder to the veins on the right side of my neck and then across my face. It came like a hit of dope, leaving me warm and calm where it had passed. I thought, Better call the cops. I seemed to recollect Hanlon having a phone on the kitchen wall. I grabbed the top of his dryer with my left arm and hauled myself upright, then waited for the stars to fade from in front of my eyes. I felt warmer and calmer by the second. That can't be a very good fucking sign, I thought. Calmly.

Yellow light gleamed and danced under the laundry-room door.

It took forever to walk into the kitchen. Time stretched, dreamlike. Each footstep would begin, my heel would lift, my toes would scuff on the linoleum, my weight would shift unsteadily forward . . . and already the beginning of the step would have tumbled back into the past, like a dream scared off by an alarm clock. Each moment like waking up again, clueless and blinking.

I was standing by the refrigerator. There was a plain gray phone on the wall next to me over a set of matched canisters, Flour-Sugar-Rice-Cookies. The phone was over Cookies. My right shoulder wasn't working worth a damn. I grabbed for the phone and dropped it.

A long time later I woke at the smack of the receiver hitting the linoleum floor.

Pant. Pant. Pant. Cough. Every time I breathed I felt a slicing pain from the right side of my chest to my backbone, as if I were getting run through a meat shaver. Pant, slice. Pant, slice, cough. I bent over for the phone and the damn slicer nearly cut me in half.

Because thou hast left thy first love.

What the hell had Uncle Billy meant by that? I hadn't had a steady girlfriend since Megan was born. The occasional screw, but nothing serious. It was Josie that left me, anyway. I keep my accounts settled. I will never be one of those sorry bastards who comes back after he dies. I would do anything, I would burn to death a hundred times rather than come back.

I wasn't going to die today. I would call 911. The cops would rescue me. I would live happily ever after. Happy ending.

Josie left me over happy endings. Said I didn't believe in them. Said I wouldn't try. Josie never needed more reasons to be sad. Her dad did beer, pot, worker's comp, smack, and prison. Her mom stuck to weed and welfare. By the time she was eight, Josie was holding that family together with Scotch

41

tape and unnatural competence, cooking tuna casserole made with no-name cream of mushroom soup and hiding the grocery money.

I always thought she liked me because I was smart and saw a world bigger than Deer Park. Maybe that was true, but looking back it's easy to see how much I owed her dad. She had been born into this world to love a loser, after all.

She quit cheerleading because she got bored. Everybody assumed she was pregnant but too stuck up to admit it. When she never got fat, they figured I'd sent her to Houston to get an abortion.

Pant. Pant. Pant. Cough. I slid down to the floor with my back against the refrigerator. It took a long time. I reached for the phone with my left hand and listened as the dial tone got louder, approaching my ear.

I punched a nine.

Josie's eyes were faded blue, like old jeans. She had six rings in her left ear, and wonderful ash-blond hair she kept in a ponytail. When we made love, I used to tease the scrunchie out, a gentle tug that would lay the back of her neck bare, and I would kiss it. Her hair like corn silk, slipping across my cheek. Then one day she showed up at our apartment cropped back like that chick in the Eurythmics, Annie Lennox. When I went to kiss her neck, there was only stubble. It was all gone and she hadn't asked me.

She put some food in a backpack and told me to get in the car. I was twenty and between jobs. We headed down I-45 for the Gulf of Mexico, looking across hazy East Texas scrub at the distant refineries of Dickinson and Texas City. We made it to Galveston in just under an hour, rolled over the long causeway and kept on driving to the western tip of the island, where nobody comes. There had been a storm the day before. The sand was littered with little blobs of black oil, and when we walked along the beach we had to step over a thousand dead jellyfish.

I punched a one on Hanlon's phone.

We tried to make a fire out of hackberry scrub and drift-wood but it was all too wet. We ate the food Josie had packed, peanut-butter sandwiches and a bottle of red wine. We got drunk and I loved her helplessly. The sun guttered out. The sea grew dark, then the trees. The clouds went out like cigarettes, gold at the tips, then red, then smoke and ashes. I caught glimpses of Josie in the twilight: a line of leg, a dim cheek, hands appearing and disappearing as she drank. I made a joke and she laughed. I taught her a hymn, 'Will the Circle be Unbroken.' I had the solo on that one in the church choir, back when I was a boy. We sang it together, very badly. *By and by, Lord, bye and bye.*

Josie drank another thermos cap of wine. 'Will,' she said, 'I want a divorce.'

I punched another one on Hanlon's phone. Pant. Pant. Cough. Pant.

She said she didn't want to spend the rest of her life rescu-ing me. She said I made everything seem hopeless. 'You look at me sometimes and I know you're seeing me dead, or dying. Paralyzed after a car crash or something.'

'Cancer,' I said. 'Considering your family.' Her granddaddy had died with a tumor in his colon the size of a grapefruit.

'Christ, Will.' She cupped her face in her hands. I couldn't believe I was never going to kiss her again. 'Is that what you're going to teach your kids?' Josie screwed the lid back on the thermos. 'Not mine,' she said. Then she packed up our picnic and we hiked back to the car in the dark.

Later, I figured out that must have been the week she found out she was pregnant. Will Kennedy, raising my child? she must have thought. Better no daddy at all. Another reason I never missed a soccer game or a school concert. Wanted to show fuck-ing Josie she was wrong.

When we got back to Houston, Josie said I could sleep on the couch but I said maybe not. I spent the night out walking, marching through the Rice campus and up into the Montrose by the Rothko Chapel. I saw a lot of ghost roads that night, three or four of them. Long quiet gray streets. I remember, there was a pick-up truck rolling slowly down one and I thought about catching up to it, hopping into the bed like I was seventeen again, the summer I did farmwork for my Uncle Chase down by Brownsville, breathing pesticide all day and fainting from heatstroke while the lazy wetbacks around me laughed and dabbed my head with water. Tireless sons of bitches. I told them they better stop working so hard or they'd never fool La Migra into believing they were Americans.

I didn't sleep for seventy-two hours after Josie dropped the bomb. Just walked and walked. Disaster is better than Dexedrine that way. In my exhaustion I remember thinking, Love turns you into a refrigerator. You think you're a person, you can laugh and talk and move around, but it's not true. At any moment your lover can pull you open and rummage around inside, pull out your heart and walk away. And you can't stop it. You can't hold the door closed. All you can do is sit there while she takes your heart and walks away.

I couldn't eat, I couldn't sleep, and I couldn't stop walking. Lost ten pounds in three days. You too can get these fabulous results with our easy new Miracle Heartbreak Diet! Josie tried to make me see a doctor, but we didn't have insurance and anyway I didn't deserve it. What did I feel? Relief. A big empty balloon of relief in my chest that just kept drifting up and up. What kind of loser can't even work up a good cry over his marriage falling to shit? Well, me, apparently. I didn't collapse at all. I felt sharp as a fishhook. Hard and light.

Never told Josie that.

A year later she married this guy named Don. Just finished his tour in the Marine Corps. I came to the wedding and behaved myself. Watched Josie's mom dandle Megan through the service. I even brought a present. China, I think. Me and Josie only ever had cheap crappy plates when we were together. In the receiving line Josie said, 'I hope we can still be friends.'

I have somewhat against thee, because thou hast left thy first love.

A woman's smooth voice woke me up. '911. Do you need police, fire, or ambulance?'

'Uh-oh,' I said. 'Hard question.' I coughed. I felt like I was trying to breathe through a hot towel. I was panting like a dog but I still couldn't get enough air.

'Sir, are you hurt? Do you need an ambulance?'

'Yes, ma'am.' Pant, pant, cough. Little choked-off coughs, but they hurt like hell. Between the coughs, time was stretching and stretching. 'Shock,' I said. 'I think I'm in shock.'

'Where are you located, sir?'

'Don't know.' It was hard to spare the air for talking

I went away and came back again.

'Sir, I have you located at 610 Juanita Lane. I'm going to transfer you to the ambulance now.'

'Transfer? No, you can't —'

Then I was on hold.

I drifted back to the night Josie told me she wanted a divorce. Darkness spreading along the beach like black water. Gulls rising over the ocean until the vanished sun caught them, wings suddenly white and dazzling against a sky gone cold.

Lights winking on a trawler running far out to sea.

'Medical emergency. Are you the injured party?'

I talked to the voice. It said an ambulance was on the way. I dropped the phone. I didn't hear it hit, but when I woke up later I could see the receiver still quivering on the floor. Back in the garage, the fire was talking to itself.

From my gut to my skull, the whole right side of my body felt strange and swollen. The pressure behind my face was horrible. Pant, pant, pant. Cough. A coil of smoke drifted into the kitchen from the hallway. Then a muffled boom came from the garage. Can of spray-paint exploding, or WD-40, or paint thinner. It sure would be ironic if Hanlon's house burned down, with me inside it, before the ambulance could arrive. Sometimes the big Russian bear gets you.

I told myself I ought to get to the front door. That way the EMTs could find me. I rolled over so I was lying on the kitchen floor, my head a few inches off the linoleum, my weight on my elbows. Best to stay down, with all that smoke. I was coughing continuously now, choked-off gasps between every pant for air. I pulled myself on my elbows across the length of the kitchen, then turned left into the living-room. It was very hot. I gulped for air and the pain in my back dropped me to the floor. The carpet felt rough and hot against my face. I snuffled, gasping up carpet fibers and coughing hard. My mouth was so dry. I dragged myself forward, making for the flowered chintz sofa. I hoped I would cross one of the little plastic runners, so I could follow it to the front door. I wondered if I still had my Petco health insurance, and if it covered bullet wounds. Probably only if you were gunned down on Petco property.

Somehow I had wandered off course. My useless right shoulder smacked into a coffee-table leg and I dropped mouth first into the carpet again. I could just make out the bottom of Hanlon's front door. I heard another crash from the garage, followed by a cascade of falling steel tools. I meant to scramble forward, but then darkness blew me out like a match.

The next time I woke up I was flat on my back in an ambulance, naked, and my first thought was: Who took my pants?

It was bright inside the ambulance. There were hot blankets on me, from my feet all the way up to a huge mound of slimy gauze on the right side of my chest. That's covering a bullet hole, I thought. Son of a bitch. I went away and came back. The hot blankets felt good. A cute black EMT in navy coveralls was holding a clear plastic mask over my nose and mouth. The mask gurgled and hissed like a fire. The EMT's fingernails were painted gold with swirly designs. 'Oxygen,' she said, smiling. 'It's the real thing, baby.'

The ambulance sped through the city, sirens screaming. The flashers would be going too, fine American colors, red and white and blue and red and white, spinning and strobing. I gathered my breath, which was a mistake. Hell of a product, I thought. Then I passed out again.

We were at the hospital. The EMTs had stuck an IV in my arm. I could see the drip bag swinging overhead as they heaved me onto a gurney and started hauling ass. The whole operation was hellaciously bumpy and noisy, metal wheels chattering up the concrete ramp from the ambulance bay, automatic doors swishing open, another jerk and then we were on linoleum and the ride smoothed out. It's very weird to be moving fast while lying on your back. I rattled through Emergency until they parallel-parked me against a corridor wall. I stared up at the ceiling, which was made of squares of wafer-board with lots of tiny circular holes in it, with every fifteen feet a stainless-steel sprinkler head. At least I wouldn't burn to death.

The EMTs talked with a doctor somewhere out of sight. I tried to eavesdrop, but all I could make out was something about carbon monoxide that I didn't understand. They wheeled me into another room and put me on a bed. A pale nurse with freckles and sensible brown hair took my pulse and blood pressure. Then she drew off a syringe of blood. I watched the needle fill. I felt shivery, not so warm and not so calm. Don't put me in a room, I tried to say but couldn't. I can't afford a room. Just stack me on the floor.

Periodically an impatient voice crackled from speakers over-head, but I couldn't understand it. Maybe it was Spanish.

I coughed. That hurt. It also hurt when I tried to move my shoulder. Wheels rattled on passing gurneys. We should have corridor races, I thought. Zoom down these halls on our backs like bobsledders. I went away and came back. The nurse with the sensible hair was standing over me with a clipboard. 'Is there someone we should call, hon?'

My first love was home with her husband. My daughter who no longer called me Daddy would be asleep under a poster of the U.S. women's soccer team.

'Mr. Kennedy?' The nurse knew my name. Must have looked in my wallet. Those pants sure were getting around. 'Is there someone we should call?'

I pretended I couldn't hear her and pretty soon I went away again.

When I came back, a lady doctor was holding up an x-ray and tapping it with one hard finger. 'You have been shot through the chest and your lung has collapsed. The bullet has entered just below your clavicle, broken your fifth rib on its way out, and made a small hole in your scapula. It will heal.' She was a small woman from India with streaks of gray in her short black hair. She spoke decisively and rolled her Rs. When she said the word 'rib' it sounded like a ziploc bag being closed in a hurry. 'The collapsed lung is the reason for this cough.'

I coughed.

The doctor looked at me sternly. 'Some blood has collected in your chest cavity. We will be inserting a chest tube to drain it.'

'My chest,' I said, panting. 'My neck. They feel—'

The doctor gave me a brief professional frown. 'There is no lung to keep your organs in position,' she said brusquely. 'Things slosh around.' She scribbled something on a clipboard. 'Everything here is highly routine.'

The freckled nurse came back later pushing a small wheeled stewardess-type cart loaded with medical supplies. I didn't have a good feeling about it. She started to lift my dead right arm, but I thought that would hurt. We fought over it and she won. She slathered my side with brown stuff that smelled like iodine. The PA system crackled angrily in Kurdish. The doctor returned and held up a syringe. 'Anesthetic,' she said. 'This will sting.'

It did.

CHAPTER FOUR

That night my body was dull and heavy with drugs. For hours before I woke I was lying on my back with my eyes open, looking up through cool blue layers of Demerol at the wafer-board ceiling far overhead. The smells of rubbing alcohol and latex rippled into me.

I took a slow breath. Pain eddied out from my chest. There was an IV in my right forearm. With every heartbeat the plastic needle trembled in my skin.

My eyes closed.

My heart beat.

Hospital sounds, muted and murky, came to me as if underwater: many footsteps, phones ringing, distant announcements on the intercom. Creaking gurneys rolled by with conversations attached, talking suddenly louder as they passed my door and then fading down the corridor.

'I baptize you with water for repentance, but he who is coming will baptize you with the Holy Spirit and with fire.' The rustle of a Bible page turning.

Who's there? I tried to say.

So cold.

It's like this to be dead. Cold dirt stuffed into your mouth and ears. Life just a rumor – the whisper of people talking as they walk around in the bright air. Packed in the earth, muffled thump of feet overhead and inside my room, a faint gurgling hiss, as if someone far away was sucking the last of a Slurpee through a straw. I let my head loll to the side and opened my eyes again. A nurse was standing in a pool of light by the other bed. Her white uniform was shining, shining. She looked down at an old man who stared at her, frightened and blinking. A whispering mustache of plastic tubing disappeared up his nose.

I wanted very badly for the nurse to go away because if she stayed I thought the old man would die. I didn't want anyone else to die. No more ghosts.

Tom Hanlon an angel with bright wings smoking in the yellow light. The gleam and flickering.

I drifted through the long night, eyes open, eyes closed. Busy nurse shoes squeaked across the linoleum. White uniforms doctored my IV bag or bent over the old man or walked briskly into my dreams. I heard the rustle of pages, and once I saw my mother's face looming over me. After some hours it floated up like a balloon, dwindling into the ceiling until it slipped into a hole in the wafer-board. Many dreams later I saw her again, sitting quietly in the chair beside my bed, her face still and grieving.

The intercom hissed and crackled. A hungry sound, like fire burning in the next room.

I am eleven, tagging after my cousin AJ, who is seventeen and beyond cool. She reads poetry. She's saved up money from her after-school job at the fabric store and bought a Walkman, on which she plays The Clash and Roxy Music instead of George Jones and Dolly Parton.

AJ is not my baby-sitter so much as my parole officer. She takes me out on weekends when the grown-ups have other things to do. Today we're going to the hospital to visit one of her classmates. 'Jamie says they just went into the closet and necked for a while.' AJ and me don't believe that for a minute.

'Barb says Sandra said he raped her, kind of. Not all the way.'

AJ always treats me like I'm old enough to handle it.

Outside it's greasy August heat, the air like hot motor oil, but when the hospital doors swing open a wave of chilly A/C spills out, smelling of formaldehyde. We get directions from the information desk and head up to the psych ward, me in an *Empire Strikes Back* T-shirt, AJ sporting tinted John Lennon glasses and hauling around the big denim purse where she keeps her Walkman and tapes and feminine products and probably some drugs although at this age I've never actually seen any.

'Ten days after the party, this girl, Sandra, tried to kill herself,' AJ tells me. 'Her mom found her half-passed out in a bathtub full of red water. She broke open a Bic razor and tried to cut her wrists.'

I hate hospitals. People die in them.

'She had a huge crush on Jamie. After all, he *was* on the football team,' AJ says witheringly.

When we get to Sandra's room her mom is there, bustling around to cover the silence.

Sandra is a Zombie. She is very thin. Her hair is long and greasy, her pale face is dotted with pimples. Whether it's the drugs or just sadness, she's white and stiff. If you poked her with your finger, her skin would stay pressed in, like cooling wax. She moves in a slow, jerky shuffle. She's a broken thing, and you can't imagine she could ever be fixed. The plastic hospital bracelet looks empty around her wrist.

So glad AJ should drop by, Sandra's mom gushes. It does Sandra such good to have company! Spots of color high in the mother's cheeks.

Sandra doesn't talk. She has gone to a place where words don't help.

We stay for fifteen minutes, and I am so glad when AJ says we've got to be getting on. As we get into the elevator, AJ's lips are thinned out that way they get when somebody's going to catch some shit. I'm hoping it isn't me. The elevator is a little one, with shiny steel walls. I'm trapped in there, with blurry AJs reflected all around me. They consider blurry me's disapprovingly. 'I wanted you to see that, DK.'

'Why?'

'Someday it will be you going into a closet with some girl.'

One of the AJ's splits in half as the elevator doors open. She strides out through the hospital lobby, and I scurry after her. I understand I should feel guilty for being a boy, and I do: but I don't want to give up the good stuff, like being able to make gross jokes and take my shirt off in summer. I'm pretty sure AJ can sense this unworthy thought. I'm careful not to make eye contact, except I look up and find her reflection staring at me from out of the glass of the hospital door. 'So don't be a jerk,' she says.

The next time I woke up, daylight was streaming into my hospital room. My mother was gone. I felt less drifty. There was an IV in my wrist and my chest hurt, but it didn't bother me as much as it should have. Still drugged to the gills, presumably.

A humongous black nurse ambled into the room. The name *Darla* was stitched into her white nylon blouse above a pocket big enough to stash a dachshund. 'Good morning, Mr. Kennedy.' She scooped up my wrist and took my pulse. Her fingers were like dinner rolls still warm from the oven. 'How you feelin'?'

I coughed. Little firecrackers of pain went off inside my ribs. 'My chest hurts.' The slack muscles in my face pulled into a smile. Darla glanced at my IV bag and then jotted a note on her clipboard. 'What's in my IV?' I asked. 'Just Demerol?'

Darla chucked me under the chin. 'Percodan. A spoonful of sugar makes the medicine go down.'

I laughed, which was a mistake. A flurry of little hot rips and tears of pain came from the various holes in my chest. 'I wouldn't move around too much,' Darla said placidly. 'Your mom was in for a while last night. Nice lady.' (A fragment slipped up from my underground dreams: my mother's still face, staring sadly down at me, as if I were lost at the bottom of a well.) 'I'll be back wit' your breakfast directly. Best you eat up. The police are waiting to talk to you.'

Oh. Great.

In my stupid teenage years I had a few run-ins with the Harris County Sheriff's Department. By the time I got out of high school, I had scaled back my life of crime to scoring the occasional dime or handful of poppers, but I did backslide during the year after Josie left me. There's a big Marine installation just down Old Spanish Trail from my apartment, and I started going to this one bar where the jarheads liked to hang when they crawled off base to nail the local girls. I can talk some pretty good trash when my need is great and my cause is just; it never took long for me to get an invitation to dance in the parking lot. Then there would be the brief obligatory bit of posing, while Mr. Professional Soldier pretended like he was going to box me scientifically. But sooner or later we would clinch, doughboy would grab my lapels and discover a handful of Eagle #8 Fishinghooks with the No-Rust Guarantee. He'd scream and I'd break his nose with a head-butt. Fight over.

It wasn't my most mature period, I'll admit, but justice was finally served. One night I started chatting with this black Marine from one of those little Louisiana towns where they live on crawdads and Wonder Bread. He caught my attention by loudly announcing that the Violent Femmes were all lesbians. I began a gentle correction, only to find myself ten minutes later draped over a Handicapped Parking sign with a mouthful of blood and a growing suspicion I had been set up. Not only did this guy lose all interest in alternative music once I joined the conversation, he had a left jab like a staple gun. Two teeth, one cracked rib, and a broken jaw later, he told me he was a Silver Glove welterweight. It took me six months sacking groceries at Kroger's to pay off my dental bills.

After this guy left me flat-faced in the parking lot – to loud applause, I should add – the bouncer squatted down to let me know the cops would be coming by to toss me in the can for creating a public disturbance. I should have run away, or at least crawled behind a dumpster to hide, but instead I was still dragging around the handicapped spaces groping for my missing teeth when the black & white pulled up. The cop was a friendly middle-aged guy named Earl. He took one look at me, called an ambulance, and then whiled away the wait by chatting about his current passion, which was gourmet salads. I couldn't afford to go to Emergency, but it's hard to argue when you're covered in blood and the friendly cop might have decided to run your ass into his precinct instead.

I think that was the first time I ever heard the word 'arugula.'

That was my best-ever encounter with the police, but ten years later, under the present circumstances – self-defense, an armed murderer who had already beaten a girl to death and dumped her body in a river or something – I guess I was expecting a certain amount of sympathy from the Men In Blue. As it turned out, the Harris County Sheriff's Dept. had dealt me a couple of your basically suspicious and unnurturing-type police officers. It soon became obvious that from their point of view, they had a guy with a bunch of JV misdemeanors and a spotty work record who had burned a tax-paying citizen's house to the ground with said citizen inside it. I told them Hanlon had confessed to killing this girl and then decided to get rid of me. They didn't sound thrilled with that explanation, but no way was I going to start telling them about the ghost.

I suggested they do a background check on Hanlon and see if there were any links with possible dead women in Europe, and then said maybe it was time to call my lawyer.

That afternoon I had another visit from my mom. She tried not to let me see how scared she was, but her eyes kept creeping to my IV and my bandaged chest. She chatted gamely, mostly about my sister Fonteyne's new baby, Violetta, but I was brutally tired, and silences kept spreading between us.

Mom bustled busily to cover them. Spots of color high in her cheeks.

My mother has worked as a receptionist in the same medical clinic for as long as I have been alive. There was a doctor there in the '80s who got addicted to morphine. He'd been making mistakes and missing appointments for two years before one of the nurses came in late to get a purse she had left behind and found him lying on his office floor with a needle stuck between the webbing of his toes. He had started using after a patient he diagnosed with routine back pain died of spinal cancer. Mom says a lot of doctors are addicts.

They hushed it up and put him in drug rehab. He actually kicked morphine. What he couldn't do was stop smoking. This mattered because he had a daughter with asthma. Once every couple of months this kid would wake bright blue and unable to breathe, and he would rush out of his bedroom in his bathrobe and shoot her up with a needle full of adrenaline and then take her to the hospital. But he never managed to quit smoking. Red light at the end of his cigarettes all the time, all the time. Smoke curling into every thread of the carpet, every crack in the ceiling.

Not all ghosts are dead, but every ghost is hungry. They are all hungry, and they can never, never, never get enough.

When we were kids, Mom carted home an endless supply of tongue depressors, happy-face stickers, and those crappy plastic toys they hand out after immunizations. But of all the things Mom brought home from the office, what I remember best are the back issues of the *MMWR: Mortality and Morbidity Weekly Report*. Every issue of the *MMWR* has three or four stories in it, and each story is like a little fable with a moral at the end. Every story starts differently –

'Three dentists in Omaha were sharing an egg-salad sandwich when . . .'

55

'Four hikers from San Diego had started through a difficult pass in the Sierra Mountains when . . .'

'A group of schoolchildren in Dayton, Ohio, were swimming in a local pond when . . .'

– But however differently stories in the *MMWR* start, they all end the same way.

I spent my whole childhood eating breakfast cereal while learning about mosquito-borne viral meningitis, or standing to pee while the *MMWR* on the back of the toilet detailed birth defects in Michigan children whose mothers were getting mercury in their tap water. It was a running joke in our family: 'Three kids were late for school in Deer Park when,' my Dad would say, pretend-scowling as he tried to hustle us out the door.

I don't know why Mom was so fascinated with the *MMWR*. I guess it's what there was before there was Oprah.

A young girl in Europe met a traveling salesman from Texas *when* –

So here's the thing about my cousin Tom.
I killed him.

I was just starting on my second hideous hospital breakfast when I heard the clip-snap of a pair of pumps walking up to my door. I looked up from my breakfast of grainy hot cereal (compare to: Cream of Wheat™), as a young woman slipped into my room. 'Suzette Colbert, *Houston Chronicle*,' she said. 'I want to do a story on your ghosts.'

'How the hell did you know about—'

'Used to be Suzy Friedlander,' she said. 'My cousin Travis used to be married to Marcia Jessup.'

'Aunt Patty's niece Marcia?'

'Yeah. We met once, at AJ's funeral.' Lying flat on my back I could only see her top half as she click-clacked toward my bed.

56

'Travis used to tell us stories about Marcia's spooky cousin, Dead Kennedy. I thought I recognized your name on yesterday's police briefing. My brother works in the Public Relations office. Nothing like family, is there?'

A revelation hit me in the head like a five-pound mallet. For as long as I could remember, I had been super careful not to talk about my ghosts, and yet everyone had always known anyway. Now, as I picked up my hospital-issue spork and poked at my side order of Browns In Microwave Shredded Potatoes, I realized it must have been my family that snitched me out. Specifically, all the deep dark secrets I told AJ when I was trying to make myself interesting had obviously been retold within hours to her friends and relations, like her cousin Marcia.

I couldn't believe I hadn't figured this out before.

Hell, probably my sisters had done the same thing, trying to look interesting for *their* middle-school crushes. I snorted with laughter, which hurt. What an idiot I had been not to see it before.

Suzy Colbert dug a little silver tape recorder out of her purse. 'Do you mind?'

'Usually I don't talk about this stuff,' I said. 'But since it's family . . .'

'I surely do appreciate it,' Suzy said, in a parody of a Texas cheerleader's voice. She hit Record. 'So tell me, Will – what is it like to see a ghost?'

I thought of my barefoot Uncle Billy waiting for me beside the dark water under the Fannin Street overpass, standing in front of the shopping carts and dirty bedrolls of the street people who had managed to fall out of life without even dying. 'You know homeless people? You know how most times you just try not to notice them? Like, they're there but you don't stare. You look away.' Suzy was nodding. 'It's like that. Only I'm not as good at looking away as everybody else.'

'You were investigating a ghost for Tom, right?'

'Yep.' I groped for my packet of boysenberry jam and struggled to open it. My shoulder hurt like hell and my hand wouldn't stop shaking. 'He got a little freaked out and pulled a gun on me.' Maybe the nursing staff had left a little too much Percodan in my drip, but this whole situation seemed weird and funny and very, very Texas. As Lee once remarked, there's a fine line between Houston and farce.

Suzy took the jelly packet, opened it, and spread boysenberry jam on my microwave-softened triangles of toast. 'That must have been scary.'

'No shit. I mean, You bet. Why, I haven't been that scared since the case of the Bayou Ripper, back in '99.'

'You do this kind of thing a lot, then?'

'I try not to, but sometimes the money's too good to turn down.'

Suzy blinked. 'What do you charge?'

'A thousand dollars a day.' I took a sip of reconstituted orange product with ten percent real juice. 'Plus expenses.' Got to remember to bill for expenses. See, all those childhood hours spent watching *The Rockford Files* hadn't gone to waste after all.

'Expenses?'

'You know. Candles. Computer research. Maybe a priest, if I need one.' There was definitely still some happy syrup in my IV. 'Those guys aren't cheap by the hour, you know.'

'Wow. This is great stuff,' Suzy said. 'I had no idea!'

My broken ribs made it easier to keep from laughing as I reluctantly revealed the secrets of William Kennedy, two-fisted ghostbuster for hire. AJ, you little snitch. You drama queen. This one's for you.

The next morning Darla brought me a copy of the *Houston Chronicle* with my breakfast tray. Suzy had put me on the front page of the Lifestyles section.

From the suburbs of Hell to Refinery Row, Houston-area paranormal investigator William 'Dead' Kennedy is no stranger to infernal landscapes.

There was a picture and everything, a photo of me in my hospital bed looking, as my Uncle Walt would say, like ten pounds of shit in a five-pound bag. I looked up at Darla in horror. 'Oh my God.'

She grinned.

I skimmed Suzy's story. It was all there, every wacky lie and truth mixed in, right down to my rating system – Buddhas, Tell-Tale Hearts, Cobains, Rippers, and Zombies. They had tapered the Percodan out of my medication, and somehow the idea that half of Houston was eating sausage and biscuits while reading the story of Dead Kennedy, Punk Exorcist, was a lot less funny than it had seemed yesterday. 'Aren't there supposed to be fact-checkers or something?'

'I think maybe that's in News. You're in Lifestyles. Your eyes is bugging out,' Darla remarked.

I could hear them spilling along the corridor, complaints and shushing, the squeak of sneakers, sounds of a scuffle as my sister Paris yelled 'Justin!' and dragged her two-year-old out of someone else's room. My four-month-old niece, Violetta, let out a long, astonished squeal; Dad murmured to her in babytalk.

'Okay, Meg,' Mom said, just out of sight, 'you go in first.'

My heart squeezed tight. Megan! *Megan* would know about me and the ghosts. Even if she didn't read the article herself, someone would tell her. She was going to find out. *That* was why I shouldn't have talked to Suzy Colbert. Oh my God. After eleven fucking years of trying to hide that shit from my daughter, I had blown it all in twenty minutes just to jerk the chain of some third cousin who worked at the *Chronicle*.

Fuck.

Megan came into the room. She was wearing make-up, brown eye shadow and pale pink lipstick. 'Hey,' she said.

'Hey, yourself.'

She held up my Discman. 'Grandma and me thought we should bring you this.'

I fumbled for the bed control. Motors whirred as the bed tilted me slowly upright.

I felt pitifully weak and not a little stupid. My right arm was basically useless, my broken rib stabbed me every time I laughed or coughed, and every muscle in my chest was hot and sore, as if I had been beaten with a baseball bat. 'You were in my apartment?'

Justin darted into the room with Paris in hot pursuit, and the rest of the family followed. 'God, what a pigsty!' Paris grabbed her son's arm and yanked him to a stop. 'Justin? Do you need to use the potty?'

'I'm a cat!' Justin said, jerking free and scrabbling behind my bed on all fours. 'Ruff! Ruff!'

Megan was wearing khaki pants with embroidered cuffs, and open-toed sandals. Her toenails were painted black, thank God. If they had been pink I would have lost all hope. 'I'm going to tell Mom I'm never cleaning my room again, if that's how grown-ups live,' Megan said. 'Now I know why you never take me there. Just kidding, Will.'

Megan's room was always immaculate. Probably Don carried out surprise inspections, with demerits if the bed corners weren't turned to Marine specs.

My dad paced into the room wearing a spit-up towel over one shoulder and gently jiggling my sister Fonteyne's baby, Violetta. Fonteyne claims the father was a male model. None of us have seen him, and I suspect that includes Fonteyne, whose track record would suggest she was drunk and had her eyes closed for the first few cell divisions of little Violetta's existence. 'Fonteyne couldn't make it this morning, but she said to send you her best wishes,' Dad said. 'She had one of her modeling classes.'

I might have rolled my eyes.

Mom sank heavily into the visitor's chair. 'We brought some things from your apartment. The Ramones and the Eels, and that *Sandinista* album you used to like so well.' She dug each item out of her purse and held it out at arm's length, peering through her bifocals to read the titles. 'Screaming Blue Messiahs. Jesus and Mary Chain. Stiff Little Fingers.'

'What? You didn't bring my Gun Club tapes?'

'We saw that article in the paper,' Paris said. 'You never told us you were making so much money! Hire a maid or something, why don't you? Justin!' she hollered. 'Get you out from under Uncle Will's bed this instant!'

Justin is a hider. Comes by it honestly, though, to judge by his dad, who hasn't been seen since the day Paris's pee turned pink on the home pregnancy test. My sisters don't have great taste in men.

'I don't think I've seen Suzy since her graduation,' Mom said. 'She hasn't been to a reunion in years. I think she used to run around with AJ and them.'

Justin grabbed the bottom of my IV stand from under the bed and gave it a furtive shake. The drip bag swayed overhead and the IV needle wiggled in my arm. 'Hey! Cut that out, Jus.'

Giggles from under the bed.

'When she saw you laid out, your mom came over all sentimental and volunteered to organize the next Smithers family reunion,' Dad said.

Uh oh. My father isn't wild about spending forty-eight hours a year sharing two campground porta-potties with upwards of a hundred Smithers, depending on how many are currently out on parole. For a kid, of course, the reunion is all sunburn and Fritos and poking snakes with sticks, but organizing it is like navigating the Fourth Army through North Africa.

'Family's what we have,' Mom said.

'Like Tom Hanlon,' Dad said. 'Gosh, if he'd just come to a few more reunions, he might have picked off quite a few Smithers before working down to Will here.'

'I told you, he wasn't really a Smithers,' Mom said, unruffled. 'Dot's daddy remarried after her momma died. She had one of those real aggressive lymphomas. The mother, that is. Just melted her down like a candle, six months from diagnosed to deceased.' Mom was still holding my hand, stroking it as if to make sure I was still there. 'I seem to recollect her people were from up by Abilene. Dot took it real hard when her dad remarried so quick. That's always the way, though. Men just can't stand to be alone. Women expect to be widows.'

Dad cocked one eyebrow. 'Don't get your hopes up, Mother.'

Mom spared him a quick smile. 'Dot was the one who had to go clean her momma's stuff out of the closets when Eugenia's mother moved in, and I think they had words. If I recall, Eugenia's husband – this would be Tom's dad – he died in an oilfield fire out by Andrews. Put his backhoe shovel through a natural gas trapping line and burned to death in the explos—'

Mom stopped suddenly, looking at me.

'Chip off the old block,' I said. Seeing Hanlon again, what I did to him. A clumsy angel, burning and burning.

'Ruff!' Justin started barking under my bed. 'I'm a cat! Ruff! Ruff!' Justin gave the IV another push.

My mother squeezed my hand. 'You look tired, Will.' I said I was fine, but she was already rising from the bedside chair. 'We'd best be getting on. Megan, why don't you just take a second and talk to your father? We'll wait out in the hall.'

They left me alone with my kid. I remembered looking at the dead girl in Hanlon's garage and imagining Megan there, tied up and beaten.

When I was a child, I remember thinking once that life is a firework, a burst of light in the sky. When you die, it's like the rocket is falling: glimmers and sparkles, memories, old stories, a few prayers maybe, and finally darkness. But for a ghost, for this girl Hanlon killed, death is a trap, a bad photograph trans-fixing you. All the color leaches out, the setting fades and the sky, everything goes dim and then stops, showing only one thing. The last, worst thing.

'So this guy who shot you,' Megan said. 'It was about a ghost?'

I flushed. Fucking Suzy Colbert, fucking AJ, twelve years of watching every word trashed in a day, twelve years of telling my family never to say one damn thing to my kid –

'Mom told me years ago,' Megan said.

Oh.

'I didn't say anything. I thought you'd be embarrassed.'

'Okay,' I said.

'Dad brings it up every time he doesn't want me to visit you.' Dad meaning Don the ex-Marine. 'He thinks you're a lunatic.'

'What about Josie?'

'She thinks it's real.'

'So who do you believe?'

Megan gave me a little sideways smile. 'Mom and me know you better.'

I nodded, very cool, but great ripping power chords were playing in my head. I gave Megan's hand a squeeze. 'I'm sorry about – I didn't want you to see me like this.'

'Someone's gotta keep an eye on you.' She kissed me before she left, a little peck on the cheek with those pink lips. Twelve years old.

I woke up late the next morning to the sound of my room door cracking open. I waited for the squeaking sound of busy nurse shoes, but –'Will?'

Josie's voice.

For some reason I didn't open my eyes. I lay in the bed as if I were still asleep. I don't know why. I was tired. And it was nice to think of her standing there and looking at me.

'You're not asleep,' Josie said dryly. 'I still know what you look like when you're pretending to sleep.'

She was wearing a denim shirt and faded blue jeans the same color as her eyes, with her hair in a ponytail. She looked every inch the soccer mom she was, except for the six rings in her left ear. 'I think you just like Don because with him you get to be the wild one,' I said. 'Mommy with an edge.'

'He envies you, you know.'

'Like hell.'

Josie settled into the visitor's chair. Her hips were wider than they used to be, and there were a couple of strands of gray in her ash-blond hair. 'Don's always been . . . He collects guns. He reads books of oriental philosophy. The year before he joined the Corps, he hitchhiked across Mexico.' Josie stopped. 'He never saw himself as the Assistant Mall Manager type. Now he provides for us. He doesn't complain. At least, not to me. But all this: wife and kid and soccer practice and a mortgage now – we have a mortgage for Christ's sake!' Josie looked tired.

'If Don envies me, he's even more of a dumb-ass than I thought.'

'You'd like Don, you know. If you ever got to know him.'

Motherfucking jarhead bastard. 'Okay,' I said.

'I pick good guys, Will.'

I thought about how once I could have unbuttoned her denim shirt. Josie's hand was on my bed. I reached out and covered it with mine. My skin was buzzing and alive.

'Don't,' she said. I could feel the bump of her wedding ring under my fingers. 'Will, don't.' She took her hand away. There was a diamond in the wedding ring Don gave her. I couldn't afford a diamond when we got married. My dad bought Josie's band for me. I never told her that. 'Don wouldn't like me being here,' she said.

I loved her. Hanlon's eyes filling with tears.

Josie shifted in the chair beside my hospital bed. When I looked back at her face, she was dead. Her lips had gone the color of wet concrete. Eyes like slate in her gray face, and the smell of cold dirt everywhere. A clammy flush spilled like ice water across my chest and up the side of my face. My chest was frozen and I couldn't breathe.

'Will?'

Jesus Christ. My meds must be fucking with me. I stared down at the IV needle in my arm, watching it shake with my pulse, two times, three.

I have somewhat against thee, because thou hast left thy first love.

'Will?'

Air rushed back into my lungs, making the IV in my arm dance. I coughed. It hurt like hell. Josie reached for the nurse's call button. Her fingernails were red. I looked up. 'Are you all right, Will? Let me get some help.' Her skin was pale but alive, her eyes the color of old blue jeans again, no longer blind.

'No, I'm okay.' I shook my head and pushed her hand away from the call button. Her fingers were warm. My whole body was still buzzing with the shock of seeing her dead. She bent over me, worried. I got drunk on the warm smell of her skin and hair. Herbal shampoo. 'I'm fine,' I said. I wanted to reach behind her neck and pull her face down to me and feel the warmth of her cheek against mine. 'J? Have you gone to a doctor lately?'

'What?'

'You check, right? For lumps and stuff?'

She went still. – *You look at me sometimes and I know you're seeing me dead, or dying.*

Not like this, I wanted to tell her. Not with your eyes gone out like candles and your skin the color of cement.

The cops came back that afternoon and told me I better watch my ass, which I took to mean they weren't going to put me in jail. A relief. I didn't want that added to the list of things to embarrass Megan with.

That night I asked the nurse to leave the light on in my room, but she said it was against regulations. I arranged myself around my IV cord so I could see the little strip of brightness under the door. I stared at it for hours, that faint wash of light bleeding through from the bright corridor beyond, and listened to the garbled voice of the hospital PA system, that crackled and popped and hissed all night. Burning and burning.

My cousin AJ was shot to death by her boyfriend when she was twenty-two. She burst out of their apartment at a dead run. A second later he followed, walking real slow. He held up a .38 caliber automatic, sighted over his arm, and shot her in the back. She dropped to the sidewalk like a bag of groceries. She tried to keep crawling, but something was wrong with her legs. He walked up to where she was thrashing on the sidewalk and shot her again. Then he went back into their apartment to wait for the police.

In the middle of the night I woke up, sweaty and gasping, with one thought circling around and around in my head.

I had never loved a woman enough to kill her.

CHAPTER FIVE

On Sunday morning I signed myself out of the hospital, putting $4,317.14 on my Visa at the cashier's desk. First installment of my $19,317.14 bill.

That's a lot of noodle soup.

My mother gave me a ride home, and I wasn't too proud to accept. I spent a few comical seconds trying to buckle my seatbelt with one bum arm, until finally Mom reached over and snugged me in as if I were a toddler.

When I made it back to my apartment, I put on a kettle and made some Gold Key, which is a cheap Mexican espresso. Without ever mentioning the word 'speed,' my dentist had told me at nineteen that if I kept grinding my teeth I would be lobbing dentures into a bedside jar of Efferdent by the time I was thirty-five. Gold Key was my favorite replacement for the buzz. If you drink five shots of that, and chase the last one with a couple of Valiums, which a lot of dealers sell loss-leader cheap, you can achieve a sort of mellow yet energized state, perfect for selling men's wear with a clean conscience. Also excellent for pizzeria work. For roofing in hot weather, not so good, but that's another story.

The phone rang as I was finishing my fourth cup. It was Megan. 'Mom said you'd be home.'

'Yep.'

'So . . . how are you doing?'

'Not counting bullet holes? Great. How about you?'

'Yeah, great. So you're okay?' Megan said.

'I think so.'

'You looked kind of lousy in the hospital.'

'I felt pretty lousy too.'

Awkward silence. Josie's kid, I realized. Looking after her shiftless dad, just like her mom used to do. 'Okay, look,' Megan said, 'I called Grandma, and she said she'll try and come see you today or tomorrow, just to check in.'

'She just brought me home.' I made my voice super cheerful. 'I'm doing great, honey. Thanks for calling, but you don't have to worry about me. I can take care of myself. That's not your job.'

'I know,' Megan said, sounding like she didn't believe it for a second.

We exchanged good-byes and hung up. The whole awkward conversation left me feeling weird and tired on the inside. I wondered if this was how Josie's dad used to feel when she was eleven years old, making him his dinners of Mac 'n Cheez when he staggered in drunk at eleven o'clock at night. Loved and humiliated. Tired. Wanting to do better.

I put 'Werewolves of London' on my CD player, cranked the volume and set it to Repeat, and lay on the couch with my headphones on, trying to fall asleep.

I am nineteen. Two weeks before our wedding, Josie and I are standing next to her daddy's grave. It's his funeral, which is another kind of family reunion. Bye and bye, Lord, bye and bye.

That fall he had gotten out of prison and found a new job, joined the local Promise Keepers and accepted Jesus into his life. But the reality is, when you are a drug addict and an ex-con with a tenth-grade education, just getting your shit together doesn't solve all your problems. And after a few long weeks of

68

turning the other cheek and cheerfully flipping burgers, it wasn't too surprising when a day came that he needed just one little hit. Yeah, it was wrong, sure it was, but Jesus knew temptation in the desert. Jesus understood about weakness. It wasn't like he was going to hit his useless wife or quit his job or anything. Just one little hit.

One thing a lot of junkies don't understand about going straight is that if you stay clean long enough, your body loses the tolerance you spent so many needles patiently building up. If you've been clean long enough, you can get pretty badly fucked up on nothing more than your usual dose. You can die.

Josie had stopped by his trailer with some groceries and found him sitting on the toilet, dead as a doorknob, with the needle still dangling in his arm.

We put him in the ground on a cold day in January. The live-oak trees in the cemetery were black with grackles. Chilly wind made the Spanish moss sway. The rest of the mourners were leaving. There were more than you'd expect. Family matters in Deer Park, no matter how much you fuck up. Not many fond stories at the graveside, just a kind of bleak endurance. Nobody surprised by the way things turned out, except for Josie's mom, who never would pass up a chance to carry on in public. She got all misty-eyed and talked about *if only* and *it was all because*, and how things had been fixing to get better, like they were always just about to . . . Shameless. As if she hadn't always, always known it would come to this. She took people aside one by one and whispered as to how she was looking for a few dollars to help with the cost of the funeral, and a place to stay until she could get back on her feet. Josie hated her.

Josie turned her back while her mother cried and complained of the cold and edged back to the car that would take her to the memorial reception my folks had paid for and the free food waiting there. Long after she was gone, Josie stayed staring at the grave in her jean jacket, face cold. She always was her daddy's girl. 'If you cop out on me like that,' she said at last, 'do me like that, I'll fucking kill you.'

I woke up in my apartment, thirty-two again. Hot. Confused. I reached to pull off my headphones and a stab of pain went through my ribs and shoulder. I tried again, more carefully. I rubbed my face and got groggily off the couch. The apartment smelled like Hanlon's garage – smoke and hot metal. Something was burning.

I lurched into the kitchen. The left front burner was on, glowing fiercely under my cheap kettle. Black char lines ran up its side, and evil little wisps of smoke curled from the spout. I grabbed the kettle and threw it into the sink, where it shrieked and cracked. I ran cold water over it, sending up a cloud of stinking steam. Then I turned off the burner. For a long time I stood there, my heart racing, watching the burner fade from bright orange to dull red, and finally to black.

'Fuck,' I said.

Who turned the burner on?

Okay. Me, obviously. I must have left it on when I made myself coffee.

Come on, Comrade Will. Get your shit together.

I thought about taking the smoke-detector batteries out of my kitchen drawer and putting them back in the smoke detector, but as always I was stopped by the knowledge that if I did, it would make this God-awful noise every time there was a little smoke in the air.

I headed back into the living-room, reached to pull the headphones out of my CD player, and swore as nails of pain punched through my chest and shoulder. I had strict orders from the physio at the hospital to 'encourage full range of motion' in my right arm as it healed. Well, screw that. I found an old bandanna and worked up a sling. Then I crammed the Pogues (Shane McGowan drunk and cursing at me) down into my CD player and settled in for some serious life appraisal.

I needed to make some money.

'Any man who isn't a socialist at twenty has no heart. Any man who's still a socialist at thirty has no brain.' Dad, of course. At twenty I assumed this was just typical bullshit to justify selling out. Older and wiser, I would put it this way: I was broke at twenty, and I was still broke at thirty-two. The difference was, now I couldn't make myself believe I liked it.

My dad had warned me about that, too, of course, but he wasn't a guy whose financial advice you took very seriously. 'You want a *career*,' he used to say, 'not just a *job*.' When Dad had jobs, they were strictly there to provide seed money for bigger things. But the 'careers' ended up more like 'schemes' somehow, and for all his ambition, Dad's resumé wasn't much better than mine. Mattress salesman, Wal-Mart clerk, a mail-order seed-catalogue company, a short stint as a Camera World clerk, followed by an even shorter turn as a freelance photographer. The best job, from my point of view, was the winter he drove the ice-cream truck. The worst was the seven horrible months of tenth grade during which he wore the little red change apron at the arcade next to my school. One fatherly hug in front of the *Star Wars* console ended my video-game career forever.

Other jobs . . . Parking-lot attendant, shuttle driver at the airport, night-school instructor. Real-estate agent. Import businesses that kept him fiendishly busy even though he was supposedly working from home: Mexican blankets and pottery, Indonesian batik, Hong Kong electronics, dehydrated food from a Swiss company looking to expand into the American market.

Working from home was tricky. He and Mamaw Dusty didn't see eye to eye, and of course he was always one moment's lapse of attention away from a kid-related disaster, as for instance the day two-year-old Fonteyne tore all his completed homework assignments for his Correspondence School Securities License into tiny little pieces and flushed them down the toilet with Dad pounding on the locked door.

An interesting fact most eleven-year-olds don't know is that you can go to prison for trading securities without a license.

Dad never talked about jail with us, but every year at the family reunion a couple of Smithers – Billy Joe who used to rob gas stations, particularly, and Floyd the roughneck, who used to get into fights every time he finished a six-month stretch on a Gulf oil rig – would strike up a friendly conversation with my dad about the Big House. They could tell he wasn't comfortable with his wife's kin, you know, and figured they ought to make him feel like one of the boys. It didn't much take, but they kept on trying.

I made myself another cup of Gold Key to steady my nerves. Okay.

The new, improved Will Kennedy, committed to moving forward in his life, swallowed his pride and called Petco. Dickless Phil said they'd already hired someone to replace me. No, he didn't expect there would be any part-time shifts coming up.

The hospital had sent me home with a stash of codeines, so I took one a couple of hours early. My chest still hurt like a bastard after two more minutes, so I foraged until I found a bottle of aspirin, and struggled to open it. When you've been shot through the shoulder, it's harder than you'd think to open a childproof cap. I finally beat the fucker into submission, but when I shook the bottle, all that fell into the palm of my hand was my wedding ring. I keep meaning to throw that damn thing away, but I never do. I stared at it for five or ten slow heartbeats, imagining what it would feel like to toss it out the window or drop it in the toilet.

Do me like that, I'll fucking kill you.

'Shit,' I said. I bottled the ring up again and stuck it back in the medicine cabinet. Once or twice a year I find that damn thing. It's a lousy experience every time.

I discovered some Tylenols lying loose in the drawer where I kept my shaving supplies, so I took four of them. My eyes in the mirror looked back at me, as tired as Hanlon's. That worn down. 'Dude, you need a fucking product,' I said.

Back in the living-room, I noticed the light on my answering machine blinking. I had missed twenty-two messages while I was in hospital. I touched Play. The first call was from some guy who wanted me to chat with his dead mother to settle an inheritance question. It had come in on Friday morning, right after Suzy Colbert's story had run in the *Chronicle*. The second message was an old lady asking me if I could talk to her dead dog. Two calls from Megan checking to see if I had made it home from the hospital okay. One call from Dickless Phil, explaining that because I had been fired for Gross Misconduct, I had voided my right to continuing health insurance. Messages from reporters, claiming to work for *Reader's Digest* and the *Houston Press*, the *Voice* and *Texas Monthly* and *Gnosis*.

A hate-o-gram from some guy who *really* talked to ghosts and knew I was lying about it. A call from the pastor at Aunt Patty's church, tactfully reminding me that he was there if I ever wanted to talk.

Then a message from the father of a missing seven-year-old. His voice was broken, and every time he started to say the kid's name, he would stammer and say 'my daughter' instead.

There were twelve messages from people who needed to talk to the dead. All of them wanted my help. A lot of them were willing to pay for it – a thousand dollars a day. Plus expenses.

Lee slid a plate full of Mexican food under my nose. 'Okay, so, what's the downside again?'

'It's crazy?'

'Besides that.'

'The clients shoot me.'

'Pussy.' Lee went rooting around his fridge for three bottles of Dos Equis.

I was feeling better. Lee and Vicky had made me a special welcome-home dinner, enchiladas verdes with mango pico de gallo. Vicky's enchiladas were incredible, all buttery chicken and cilantro and two kinds of peppers, roasted Hatch chiles and smoky dried chipotles, with just a touch of lime. She was a twenty-five-year-old waitress, what we'd call 'a pretty Mexican girl' in Deer Park, despite the fact that her family had been in Texas for five generations and she was a distant cousin of the mayor of San Antonio. She was standing by the stove, mixing sopapilla batter for dessert.

'I'm not an exorcist. I just see ghosts,' I said. 'I can't promise to get rid of them.' I waggled my sling at him. 'Could you get my beer open? I look like a complete gimp.'

Lee grinned through a mouthful of tortilla. 'I know.'

'Fuck you. Frank?' The terrier mutt that Lee was absolutely positively not allowed to keep in his apartment emerged from under the table. 'Chicken verde in it for you if you get me a bottle opener,' I said. Frank cocked his head and regarded me, ears pricked, alert but clueless. 'Go on, boy! Get an opener! Fetch!'

'Ruff!' Frank said.

'You think my dog takes orders from a guy who can't open his own beer?' Lee reached over and twisted the top off my Dos Equis. 'Good boy, Frank! Good dog!' He tossed a scrap of chicken in verde sauce into Frank's bowl. Frank liked Mexican.

'Dumb dog,' I said.

Vicky scooped gobs of Crisco into a big pot and set it to boil. Regular Mexican cuisine would add lard to milkshakes if it could get away with it, but Vicky was trying to use vegetable fat these days on account of she worried about Lee's cholesterol. 'That is all some crazy shit about you and ghosts,' she said. 'But you know, my abuela got El Mano Mas Poderoso to send a plague of fire ants at her neighbor's cat.'

'More things in heaven and earth,' Lee said.

It was damn fine to sit and breathe the aroma of enchiladas and beer instead of formaldehyde and starch. Nice to watch Vicky cook, for that matter, instead of seeing Josie turn black and white.

Lee dug a Buck folding knife out of his pocket to slice out a thin wedge of lime, which he poked down into his beer. The knife would be a present from his dad. Lee's great-grandfather had fought in the Spanish-American War, and his granddaddy had been in the Battle of the Bulge. His dad had done a tour in Vietnam and now lived a solitary but heavily armed existence in Alpine, where he worked servicing wells and painting desert landscapes in watercolor. He also owned a large selection of semi-automatic weapons, including a Barrett Light .50 that could put a round through a car body from a mile and a half. 'Whole damn Big Bend is crawling with these fucking survivalists,' he was given to saying. 'Nothing those people understand but superior firepower.'

Lee shook a dollop of sour cream next to his enchiladas. 'If you put an ad in the Classifieds saying you could talk to folks' dead relations, as seen in the *Houston Chronicle*, I bet you'd get a ton of business.'

'I bet I'd get peasants with pitchforks.'

'Possibly. But consider.' He thrust his drumstick at me for emphasis. 'A thousand dollars a day! Work one day a week, you're making fifty thou a year.'

'That is a lot of noodle soup.' The three of us looked at one another, chewing thoughtfully.

'I see an infomercial,' Lee said.

'Hold on, now. If Tom Hanlon was my first client,' I said, 'I would be eighteen thousand dollars in the red.'

Vicky paused to lick verde sauce off the side of her mouth. 'Plus a lung.'

'True.' Lee took a pensive pull on his Dos Equis. 'And yet there is that fifty grand.'

'Good point,' I said.

'William, the Good Lord done give you a gift. It is only right and pious that you accept it.'

'God wants me to take money from grieving widows and orphans?'

'You don't have to lie. Just tell them the exact honest truth about what you can and can't do. Cast some fucking bread upon the waters, man, and see what comes back to you.'

The Frankenterrier's sleepy head popped up and his ears pricked as Lee shoved back from the table and ambled across the hallway. I heard him opening my door. 'What the hell are you doing in my apartment?'

'Getting your mail,' Lee called. A moment later he was back, carrying the pile of envelopes I had left on my kitchen table. He dropped back into his chair and start to leaf through my mail. Frank put his head back down across Lee's sandaled feet and resumed his snooze.

'Phone bill,' Lee said, dropping my latest Southwest Bell notice on the floor. 'Gas bill. Hand-written letter – that looks promising. Another letter. Bill. Credit card offer. Bill. Dating service.' He glanced up at me. 'Better hang on to this one.'

'Fuck you.'

'I'd rather light a candle than curse my darkness, Will. But that's just me.' Lee shook a blue felt-tip-written letter out of its envelope. '*Dear Mr. Kennedy*,' he read, '*Surely you realize you will go to Hell for your—*'

'Skip,' I said.

Lee dropped the letter onto the floor, where it bipped Frank on his long-suffering head. The dog's ears twitched and then lay still. 'Next. *Dear Mr. Kennedy*,' Lee read. '*I am a forty-three-year-old professional woman with a good job and salary.*'

'You look damn fine in a business skirt, too, Lee.'

'*I have moved recently as the result of divorce, but I feel as if my new house is (for lack of a better word) haunted. It is also possible, of course, that the problem is psychological, brought on by recent stresses in my life. But before embarking on a long – and probably expensive – course of therapy, it seems worth my while to rule out the possibility of actual supernatural phenomena.*' Lee looked up from the letter. 'She doesn't sound crazy,' Vicky said from the kitchen.

'Money to spend, too.' I finished my Dos Equis, trying not to feel too hopeful. 'What else we got?'

'*Dear Mr. Kennedy. I have a problem with a dead man. Sometimes I have to hit my head very hard to stop from hearing him. I feel I have paid my debt to society, but he does not. Almost every night he . . .*' Lee trailed off and looked at the outside of the envelope.

'Huntsville Penitentiary return address?'

'As a matter of fact.'

'That would go in the junk pile.'

'You want to write him back?' Lee asked. 'I mean, you don't want him getting out after twelve-to-fifteen feeling disrespected.'

'Junk, dammit!'

'Since he knows your address and all.'

Jesus H.

Vicky came in with a jar of honey and a platter of hot sopapillas lightly dusted with icing sugar and cinnamon. By the time we finished them off, we had sorted all the mail. 'If you count the guys on the phone as well, I make it nine people who don't sound crazy and have a little money to spend,' Lee said, tapping the letter pile with one sticky finger. Vicky tried to get the honey off with a napkin. Lee just licked his fingers. 'You'd get a shitload more if you advertised. Dude, I think you should do it. Every time I want the chit, you're too gloomy to cheer me up. We need your life not to suck so much. Make some money. It's allowed.'

I washed down the last sopapilla with my third – it couldn't be more than my third – Dos Equis. 'I could be a Caped Crusader.'

'There you go! Grateful widows and orphans.' We drank more beer. 'Also, there's the money,' he added.

'Another good point.'

Vicky looked at the sling covering my bullet-ventilated chest. 'Besides,' she said, 'what's the worst thing that could happen?'

Which is how, two weeks after getting out of the hospital, I came to be on the phone to Don, my ex-wife's husband, asking him to teach me to blow shit up.

Long silence.

'You're going to do *The Exorcist* for money,' Don said slowly. 'But since you got shot last time, you figure you ought to carry some protection.'

'You got it.'

'And you're calling me because none of your alternative friends know dick-all about guns.'

'There is just no fooling you, Don.'

Another long silence. 'Okay,' Don said at last. 'I'll take you out to a gun range and teach you the basics if you answer me one question straight – no bullshit. Okay?'

'Fire away.'

'Was this Josie's idea?'

'Damn right.'

'Would you have asked me if she hadn't told you to?'

'You got one question,' I said. 'That was the deal.'

A beat, and then Don laughed. 'Screw you,' he said.

When I was five, my Uncle Walt – AJ's dad – gave me a puzzle to work. It was a Folger's coffee can full of bits of metal, springs and tubes and screws. He told me he'd give me a popsicle if I could figure out how to put them together. It took me more than an hour, but I finally got it. I ran into the kitchen shouting, 'I want my popsicle!' and waving the puzzle, which turned out to be Walt's .45 automatic from when he served in Vietnam. I can still remember Aunt Patty's yell.

I worked that .45 puzzle (over Aunt Patty's thin-lipped disapproval) dozens of times when I was a kid, but I never actually fired a gun. My own dad viewed gun-waving as one of those macho wastes of time that makes Texas look stupid to the rest of the country. Mom read an article in the *MMWR* that analyzed guns as if they were an epidemic, a deadly strain of plague. She'd no more have one in the house than lick the commode. Eventually she got wind of Walt's puzzle and made Aunt Patty put her foot down. After that I didn't touch a gun again for more than twenty years, until Lee's father, in a burst of Christmas sentiment, sent him his granddaddy's service pistol from World War Two. Lee was extremely jumpy about having a gun in his apartment, but he couldn't just throw it away, especially as his dad came to visit every six months. So I volunteered to break the gun down into pieces he could keep in a shoe box and put it back together when his father was coming to visit.

Long story short: I was secretly looking forward to the gun range experience. One of the big drawbacks with being left-wing is that you aren't supposed to want to blow shit up, which is purely unnatural in any full-blooded Texan male. My feeling is, if you're a James Taylor/Simon and Garfunkel liberal, you definitely aren't allowed to pick up a gun, but those of us in the Sex Pistols/Butthole Surfers crowd get a little more leeway for random acts of violence.

Three weeks after I got shot, I was waiting for Don to pick me up and take me to a gun range, when my phone rang. I grabbed the handset and brought it over to my living-room window so I could watch for Don's car. 'Hello?'

'Okay, Dad's on his way over,' Megan said. 'I figured I'd better give you a few tips.'

The line was crappy and I thought I could hear traffic. 'Are you calling from home?'

'I snuck out to the Stop N Go. Listen, first of all, no cussing. Dad thinks you're a potty-mouth.'

'Yes, ma'am.'

'Also, no jokes about drugs. He thinks you're just waiting for a chance to turn me on to pot. Which you'd better not be,' Megan added.

'No, ma'am.'

'Because I am not interested in that shit.'

'Hey! Potty-mouth yourself!'

'What are the rules?' Megan prompted.

'No cussing, no drugs.'

'And no acting crazy.'

'Gee, thanks.'

'I mean it, Will.' I heard the Stop N Go's door chime, and a rattle like someone walking by with a bag of chips. 'The kids at school know about the ghosts and everything, which is sort of a hassle but also kind of cool. But it's not *at all* cool with Dad, okay? So please, just . . .'

Don and Josie's Caravan rolled up to the curb in the street below. 'What?'

'Just *don't screw up*,' Megan said.

Don got out of the minivan and headed for the door of my building. 'I gotta go,' I said. My chest hurt. 'I'd do anything for you,' I said.

'Yeah, I know. You can take me to Six Flags when you're rich and famous.'

'It's a deal,' I said. She hung up.

Don knocked on my door. 'Rise and shine, Comrade Will.'

'Hey, Don. I'll be right there.' My chest still felt like shit, but I eased my arm out of its makeshift sling. I was going out with my ex-wife's husband, and there was no way I was going to look like a fucking gimp. 'Hey,' I said, opening the door. 'Let's rock and roll.'

Don was 6´3˝, with high-school football-player good looks. The Marines had been his ticket out of Quatro Huevos, Texas, population eight hundred seventy-three, most of them from family trees with not nearly enough forks. Don mustered out of the Corps after his second hitch and grew a blond mustache and beard. Think golden retriever. He was still wearing his Assistant Mall Manager costume: gray wool pants, white shirt, gray jacket. As he turned to head back downstairs, his jacket swung open to reveal the butt of a gun sticking out of a brown leather holster under his left arm.

We went down to the Caravan. Between us on the front seat was a Nike tote bag, presumably filled with a selection of constitutionally protected weapons of mass death.

(*A twelve-year-old girl in Houston and her friends were playing with her dad's guns when –*)

'You keep all this shit locked up,' I said.

'Ammo in a strongbox, the guns in the garage, unloaded, in a locked safe.'

'Nothing in the bedside table? In case of dangerous drug-crazed intruders?'

'Combat knife. You think I'd leave a firearm out, with Megan in the house?'

'Had to ask.'

Don looked at me. 'Okay,' he said. 'I'll give you that one.'

I clambered up into the WASP-mobile and struggled to put on my seatbelt with one hand. Unlike my mom, Don didn't lean over and help. 'We're headed over to your old stomping grounds. Pasadena,' he said. 'Man, that's a dump.' He headed up the entrance ramp to 680, barged into traffic and then slid over two lanes without bothering to signal.

It was just past six, and the late-afternoon sun came streaming in from the back window, low and golden, as if auditioning for a Mexican beer commercial. Sluggish waves of traffic oozed down the freeway, minivans and Plymouth Volares and Volkswagen bugs, round and glossy as M&Ms. A lemon-yellow Caddy with gold hubcaps swerved in front of us, driven by a hefty white woman with big orange hair. 'Bet she clubbed some hard-working black boy to death and stole that car,' Don said. He groped one-handed through a litter of tapes on the seat between us and jammed one into the player. *The Eagles, 1971-74.* Currently the best-selling album of all time, which goes beyond kissing your sister and into frenching your dog. 'Dessssssss-per-aaaado,' Don crooned.

'Jesus, Don. I'm begging.'

'*Why don't you come to your SEN-ses* – Hey, Will, what are

81

you going to do if the ghostbusting don't work out?'

'Get a real job, I guess. Maybe a record store. I could sell this stuff,' I said, stirring through his tapes. CCR, Eddie Rabbit, *The Beatles 1.*

God help me.

In 1974, J.D. and Margaret Sayers saw the old J.G. Long Movie Theater, a nice Art Deco building out on Highway 225, and thought the exact same thing you and I would have thought: By golly, that sure would make a fine indoor shooting range! 'I used to see movies here when I was a kid,' Don said, as we pulled into the parking lot. '*Robin Hood. The Lady and the Tramp.*' I got out of the Caravan and waited while Don hauled out the Nike bag.

There was a dead girl walking slowly back and forth under the old theater marquee. She was dressed 1940s style, tight long skirt and a big hat and a pair of white gloves. At first she stayed away from the front doors, as if they were crowded with long-dead moviegoers I couldn't see, but eventually her show must have started, because she drifted up to the glass and peered into the lobby. I wondered whether she had died here that night, picked off by a car in a freak accident. Or maybe the guy she was waiting for never showed, and she'd spent the rest of her life thinking she would have been happy if only she had married him, instead of staying at home to take care of her mom, who always felt a little poorly.

. . . Or maybe this evening had turned out just fine. Maybe her date did show up, twenty minutes late, breathless and apologizing, and the night she thought would be a disaster turned into something wonderful, and she married that boy, only he was posted to Guam the next spring and died four days before Hiroshima.

There are so many different ways lives work out, so many stories, and every one of them is precious: full of joy and heartbreak, and a fair amount of situation comedy. Every life is a movie that starts in color. They just all end in black and white.

Don gathered up his kit and we headed inside. The dead girl turned as I came to the door. She was pretty, in an old-fashioned way, but her blind eyes did not see me and she ran across my path in a burst, hands clutched tight to a little black purse. I had to hop to one side to avoid bumping into her. The familiar ice-water tingle of the dead splashed over me: a sucking cold that ran up my arm as she brushed by. The bullet hole in my chest stung badly, then settled down to a dull ache that slowly faded in the warm lobby of the Pasadena Gun Center.

Don was looking at me. 'Qué pasa?'

'Soy muy bien.' No swearing, no drug jokes, no acting crazy, I told myself. Just *don't screw up*.

'You sure you're okay?'

'Let's blow shit up,' I said. *Fuck!* – no swearing, damn it. 'I'm a Caped Crusader, man. I am a highly paid superhero.'

The front display counter, which had once been filled with Goobers and malted milk balls, now had boxes of bullets packed together like shiny brass-colored candies. It also featured a handsome array of Buck knives and guns in assorted calibers, with hand-written price tags tied to the trigger guards. More exotic weapons were mounted on the wall behind the display case: a fully functional replica of one of the rifles used at the Alamo, an Uzi submachine gun that could fold up to the size of a loaf of raisin bread, and a Japanese samurai sword in a bamboo sheath.

Behind the counter, a three-hundred-and-twenty-five-pound concessionaire in a checked shirt was thumbing through an issue of *Guns and Ammo* that rested on the swell of his gut. Two large signs hung over his head: on the left, NO BLAZER AMMO ALLOWED; on the right, MACHINE GUNS FOR RENT.

'For *rent*?'

'Well, let's say you're taking a trip to one of those mugger-infested Yankee towns,' Don drawled.

83

'To fire in the lanes,' the concessionaire said witheringly. He didn't bother to look up. His hair was shaved so close to his pale scalp that his head looked like a dirty cauliflower. 'And we only rent to some folks. Not necessarily you. I turn the lights off at 7:50,' he added. 'Consider yourselves warned. I don't care if you're in the middle of a round. I'll let you out when I come in tomorrow morning.'

It was 6:58, according to the clock hanging just above an AK-47 with a 'Used In Afghanistan!' sign below it.

'Ten to eight,' Don said amiably. 'We hear you, JP'

''Cause I'm not going to be in here late again.' JP paused to scan a bow-hunting ad. He licked his fat thumb and turned the page. 'I told the boss he can come in himself if he wants the place open after hours. He's a friend of mine but he don't understand what some of you sons of bitches are like.' He put down his magazine and stared at me. Five-o'clock shadow stained his cheeks like a bruise. His eyes were watery blue. 'Don't say I didn't warn you.'

He pushed a clipboard across the counter. 'Sign in, gents. That'll be ten dollars. Lanes six and seven.'

I paid with money I had borrowed from Lee. I wondered if I could call this a business expense and whether I should ask for a receipt.

'Any magnum ammo, you fire in lane seven.' From beneath the counter JP drew two sets of red industrial ear-guards and shoved them over, staring at me. 'Has he ever fired a gun before?'

Don just grinned down at the clipboard, printing his name and phone number.

'Has he ever *held* a gun before?'

'I watched a whole hour of COPS once,' I said. 'And I saw *Red Dawn* on the big screen when it first came out.' With the help of two hits of acid, one of the great movie experiences of the '80s, in my humble opinion. I know some prefer Bergman. Call me a patriot.

'Can we have some targets, JP?'

JP reached under the counter, still staring at me. 'Silhouettes or bulls-eyes?'

'Bad guys.' Don smiled affably as JP drew out a sheaf of silhouette targets. 'Will here's thinking about a carry concealed license, JP Don't go scaring off your *bidness*. Come on, Will,' he said, ambling for the theater doors.

JP's voice rose as I trailed after Don. 'Done any good reading lately, my friend? Like maybe the CONSTITUTION OF THESE UNITED STATES?'

I remembered Hanlon talking about getting recruited in Brussels. *They're always looking for patriotic single men.*

Beyond the doors, we found ourselves in a dim concrete passage where the back row of seats had been in the theater. The floor was littered with thousands of spent shell casings, glints of brass that clicked and rattled underfoot. The smell of brick dust and concrete reminded me of Hanlon's garage. It felt hot.

The shooting lanes were separated by a series of quick and dirty concrete walls, each ten yards long and brightly lit. Each lane had a cheap Formica countertop for resting your spare guns and ammo. Beyond the walls was a dim empty space, and then another featureless concrete wall where the movie screen should have been.

Don hefted his Nike tote bag onto the counter in lane seven and began to unpack it. 'Ammo, ammo, ammo,' he murmured, pulling out boxes of cartridges in various calibers and a handful of preloaded clips from his bag. 'Did the cops tell you what kind of slug you took?'

'Thirty-eight.'

'There's a lot of cheap guns in the world these days. Probably like a .380 ACP from Phoenix or Lorcin or some such piece of junk.'

Spring-loaded Walther PPK.

'Worked okay on me,' I said.

85

A flush of heat spilled out from the bullet hole in my chest and trickled over my skin like hot water. I felt light-headed and a little sick – that shaky feeling you get selling men's wear at four o'clock in the afternoon, when the coffee wears off and you realize all you've eaten that day is six packets of non-dairy creamer and a bag of peanut M&Ms.

'You okay, Kennedy?'

'No problems.' Fuck you, army boy.

No swearing. No acting crazy.

I took a long slow breath and the giddiness passed off. I wondered if my chest wound had become infected. Better check under the bandage later on. Man of Steel, I told myself. A real w-w-w-wild child. The smell of the brass shell casings and the faint whiff of cordite was in my head. I could feel memories crowding in on me like ghosts, little black-and-white pictures of me putting together Uncle Walt's service pistol and taking it apart again. The turn of a bushing wrench at the barrel end. Springs rolling slowly across a table.

I shook my head to clear it. 'Let's lock and load, dude.'

'Will, don't ever say that to someone who was in the Forces, okay? It actually means something.' Don pulled out a big hand-gun with a heavy stock and a long silver barrel. 'Twenty-two caliber target pistol. And this *here* is a thirty-eight special. They say the cops first ordered these "to bring down a crazed buck nigger trying to rape a white woman." God bless America.' He tapped the cylinder with his forefinger. 'Notice that this is a revolver, not an automatic. Automatics take clips. With a revolver you have to load the bullets yourself.'

He put the .38 on the countertop and reached into his bag again like a militiaman's Santa Claus. '.357 Magnum,' he said respectfully, holding up a big black revolver. '"Magnum" means there's more powder in the charge. Hits like an Aggie linebacker shot from a cannon.' Don pulled out a blocky, businesslike weapon without a hint of the Wild West about it. 'Ah – the nine millimeter Glock,' he said with satisfaction. 'Best all-around

86

handgun in America, the Austrian-built Glock 17. Good sight, good grip, never jams, good stopping power.' Next he lifted a squat, evil-looking black gun from his bag. 'Forty-four caliber short-nosed Magnum. Not very accurate, but the firing mechanism is highly reliable and you can stick the gun in your pocket with ease. Leaves an exit wound the size of a grapefruit.'

I imagined a grapefruit-sized splatter of my back and lungs blasted across Hanlon's basement steps. The hot-water feeling swept over my skin again and I started to shake, as if my body were terrified of something I couldn't see. Hair prickled on the back of my neck, and on my forearms, and in tingling random splotches on my legs. I felt hot and faint again, worse this time. I jammed my hands into my pockets so Don wouldn't see them trembling. Shell casings clattered and clinked on the floor as I rocked back and forth, back and forth. Listening. Waiting.

Hang in there, Will. This is just part of getting your shit together. This is part of being a Caped Crusader.

Don said, 'I'll fire off a quick round just to show you how it's done.' He picked up the chunky automatic and gave it a quick kiss. Two sets of wires hung from the ceiling, running down the length of the shooting lane like washing lines. Don clipped one of the silhouette targets to a fat metal peg and hit a switch on the wall. Wires whirred, carrying the target jerking and fluttering down the lane. 'Now, I know you'll want to be an ecologically responsible gun user,' Don said. 'So we're going to boil up all the targets we shoot today. The ones we don't eat ourselves, we'll give to the food bank.'

I pretended to run a hand through my stubble. My forehead felt hot. So did my hand. When I blinked my eyes felt like hot marbles.

A ghost can't actually hurt you, can it?

Don ran the silhouette out a good thirty feet, then checked the clip on his Glock. 'Put your ear-guards on.' He lifted his gun two-handed, sighted, and squeezed the trigger. There was a tremendous BLAM, much louder than I expected. I couldn't stop myself from yelling. Don squeezed the trigger again and again. Hot brass shell casings sprayed out of the automatic, bouncing off his shirt and face, tumbling to the ground, the noise lost in the gigantic BLAM of each new shot, and I was back in Hanlon's basement, the dead girl grabbing at his coat, the bullet hammering through my chest. Fire bursting everywhere.

I came back into a humming, buzzing silence. Don's last shell casing ricocheted off his shoulder and spun ringing to the floor. The air stank of gunpowder and hot brass. Don put his gun down and hit the wall switch. The ragged silhouette target whirred slowly up to us. I counted seven holes in its face, the rest scattered down its neck and chest. I wondered what Josie saw in Don that she hadn't seen in me.

'I've got this .38 right here.' Don picked it off the table. 'Why don't you do a little unto others like they already did unto you?' He showed me how to flip the cylinder out and I put in six bullets. 'Your hand's shaking,' Don said.

'Right arm gets tired.' I rocked back and forth. The gun felt like an anvil in my hand. 'Slug kicked the crap out that shoulder.' Shit – did 'crap' count as swearing?

Just don't screw up.

'You sure you want to do this today?' Don asked.

'I think JP is gonna grease my – my rear end if I try to come in here again. Now is the time, my man.' I shoved the last bullet in and switched the gun over to my left hand. That was a world better.

'There's going to be a little kickback.' Don unclipped his shredded paper target and replaced it with a fresh silhouette. 'Okay, Will.' He positioned me in front of the Formica countertop and made me bring the .38 up in a two-handed grip. His big fingers closed over mine. They felt like ice. My arms were shaking from holding the gun out. There was no way I should be doing this. The gunpowder smelled like gasoline. I should tell Don I was sick. No big deal. I had taken a slug three weeks ago, for Christ's sake. More than he had done in four years as a Marine.

Don stopped the target less than ten yards away. 'All right. There's your capitalist oppressor. Waste him.' I raised the gun two-handed like a cop on a TV show and fired. The kickback jerked my wrists around and twisted the ragged muscles in my shoulder. The shot went off with a deafening blast and a big flash of blue flame spat from the muzzle. The stink of gasoline swept over me, and I remembered Hanlon burning as if he'd been napalmed.

'Not much of a shot,' the salesman said.

I whirled around. Hanlon was standing right behind me, still wearing his raincoat and his black leather gloves. Heat pulsed from him. As I stared, the pale skin of his forehead turned slowly black, like newspaper held over a naked flame.

CHAPTER SIX

You missed the whole damn target, buddy.' Hanlon shook his head. 'Hardly Special Ops material. That's what I wanted to be. Of course, I was only a mule. But I was a good one. If I had stayed in Europe, they would have given me bigger jobs. The Euros always liked me. Any line of work, if you've got good people skills, you can get the job done.'

'What are you looking at?' Don said.

Hanlon was standing right between Don and me. A char line reached his left eye and his lashes curled into ash. The air stank of burning hair. 'Most folks think secret agents shoot people,' he said. 'Steal top-secret military blueprints. James Bond stuff. Hell, I thought the same thing when I was a kid. But in real life, it's all about people. Which reminds me, Will – I went to see your daughter today. Megan.' He looked at me. 'She sure is a *pretty* little thing.'

I raised the .38 in my shaking hands and swung around and pulled the trigger. Don grabbed my arm and smashed me into the wall. The gun roared and concrete chips blew out of the wall and went rocketing through the litter of shell casings on the floor. 'Son of a *bitch!*' Don yelled.

The skin on Hanlon's charred forehead split, showing bone underneath. A blast of furnace heat sucked the air out of my chest as he leaned into me. 'You think you can just kill me and walk away, Kennedy? Is that what you think?'

'What the *hell* are you doing!' Don twisted my arm up behind my back and drove me to the ground. I screamed at the agony in my shoulder and ribs and dropped the gun. Spent shell casings gouged into my face. 'You nearly *shot* me, mother-fucker!'

Hanlon knelt beside me. 'This guy's screwing your wife, and you missed him, buddy. A killer like you! And I thought you loved her.' His breath smelled like gasoline and meat burning. 'You shouldn't ought to kill your kin, Will. You start messing with family, where's it going to stop?'

'Please,' I whispered.

'I'll see you in hell,' Hanlon said. Then he disappeared.

The dizzy fever vanished with him. Don had me on my knees with my left arm hammer-locked behind my back. Every few words he would crank it like a pump, driving my head into the floor. 'Would you *mind* telling me what the *fuck* you were *doing*?'

'Ghost!' I screamed and thrashed helplessly on the concrete. Shell casings and concrete scraped my face as Don mashed me into the floor.

'What ghost?'

'Hanlon! Fuck, please! The guy I whacked.'

Don let my arm down a fraction of an inch. 'Where?'

'Gone. He's gone.'

'Well, isn't that convenient.' Don cranked my wrist again, and I begged him to stop. He leaned down close to my ear. 'You know what it looks like, Will? It looks like I just got shot at by my wife's pathetic ex-husband.'

Forty minutes later Don's minivan rolled to a stop behind my building. 'I don't want to see you around our house,' he said.

Pain shot through my shoulder as I undid my seatbelt. No

cussing, no drugs, no acting crazy. 'Jesus, Don, you've got to believe me.' I backed awkwardly out of the van. 'This wasn't about Josie—'

'You need some professional help, Will. You need some discipline in your life. You are going down, but I will not let you take my wife or daughter with you.' Don leaned over and slammed the passenger door closed, leaving me to drag my sorry ass inside.

It was deep dusk in the courtyard behind my building. Neighborhood kids were shooting baskets at a hoop nailed to a tree. The gloom reduced them to flickering silhouettes – a scuff of white sneakers, the angle of an arm crooked against a kitchen window. Kid laughter rustled like bluejays in the live-oak leaves. I trudged up the iron back stairs, clank, clank, clank, and let myself into my kitchen. Needles of pain stitched through my back and shoulders.

This guy's screwing your wife, and you missed him, buddy.

'Fuck you,' I said out loud. 'I am a fucking Caped Crusader, Tom.' Empty words. Hanlon had followed me to the firing range. Hanlon had tricked me into shooting at Don. What if Don tried to get my visitation rights cancelled?

Crap.

I took off my sweatshirt and turned it inside out to check for bloodstains. Sure enough, some of my scars had ripped, leaving little red spackles on the cloth. I spent ten minutes in front of my bathroom mirror trying to stick a big gauze Band-Aid onto the back of my right shoulder, until I swore and threw the goddamn thing into the toilet. Then I stood there, knowing it was going to block the drain. I sighed and hunkered down on my knees in front of the bowl. I reached into the toilet water with my left hand, pulled the blood-splotched bandage out, took it to the kitchen garbage and washed my hands. I put on a crappy old Flaming Lips T-shirt that was pretty much in rags already.

You never realize how much movement it takes to put on a shirt until you've been shot through the shoulder blade.

I took my last two codeines, and then I went through my whole apartment looking for matches. Results: one box of wooden safeties for starting my stove when the pilot light went out, and three books of paper matches picked up in various bars. I threw them all in the trash.

No naked flame. Fire was a road for cousin Tom. He could follow it. He would find me.

Gritting my teeth against the pain in my back, I pulled my stove out from the wall and groped around behind it until I found the gas valve and shut it off. I checked the two lamps in the main room to make sure their cords weren't frayed. They looked okay, but I decided to unplug them anyway. I fished the matches out of the garbage and ran cold water over them at the kitchen sink until they were soaked and then put them back in the trash.

I opened the kitchen door and clumped softly down the iron stairs behind the building, carrying my garbage bag and its cargo of wet matches out to the dumpster. The basketball players had all gone inside, leaving the courtyard to me and the mosquitoes. The night was soft: warm, damp air spilling in from the Gulf. My feet squelched as I started across the common area to the dumpsters. The sewage pipe must be leaking again. A couple of years ago, Parkwood Apartments had actually made it into the *MMWR* when authorities found mosquitoes in our commons carrying both malaria and viral encephalitis. Mom hadn't been thrilled about that.

If you ever want to see something amusing, in a low-slapstick kind of way, shoot a guy through the shoulder and then watch him try to heave up a dumpster lid.

Back in my apartment, I double-checked the gas line to the stove and then unplugged my VCR. I wanted to test the smoke detector to see if it still worked, but I couldn't find anything to light under it, so I gave up. I put R.E.M.'s *Murmur* on the CD player and hunkered down on my couch to wait out the night with 'Perfect Circle' on Auto-Repeat.

94

I still think that song is the most beautiful melody, the most perfect and heartbreaking tune they ever wrote.

Just past three in the morning an ambulance went down my street. Lights flickered in my window, red and white and blue and red and white.

'Will?'

I grunted, with the echoes of my telephone still ringing in my groggy head.

'What *happened* last night?' Megan hissed. I heard crowds moving around her, and the sound of a distant bell.

'Are you calling from school?'

'Dad won't let me call from home. I'm not even supposed to talk to you any more. I heard him and Mom arguing about it. He says you've gone completely psycho.'

I went to see your daughter today. Megan. She sure is a pretty little thing.

Jesus. 'I saw . . . something strange last night, and I over-reacted. There was kind of an accident with the gun.'

I used to be a really good liar, but growing up had put me out of practice.

'Omigod,' Megan said. 'You *shot* at him?'

'No! Sort of. I mean, it was in that direc—'

'*Will!*' A crowd of kids walked by, laughing loudly as Megan reamed me out. Finally she ran down. 'He beat you up, didn't he?'

'Hey, I can hold my own in—'

'It's that Texas macho thing. Though I guess it's a fair fight if you're holding a *gun* on him.'

'I wasn't holding a—'

'At least I know what's going on now. Okay, look,' Megan said, 'you just lay low. Mom and me will handle things here. But for God's sake don't call the house or come by or anything. And we better skip the Sunday visit this time.'

95

'Meg, it isn't your job to handle—'

'Shoot, there goes the bell. I have to go.'

'Wait,' I said. 'Meg, do you guys have a smoke detector in your house?'

'Yeah. Why?'

'You know how to get out of your room in case there's a fire?'

'You itching to burn down another house?'

'No! It's just—'

'No acting crazy, remember?' Meg said. 'I really have to go. Keep exercising that shoulder, or you'll get scar tissue. Bye!'

Click.

Hell of a kid, that one.

I staggered out of bed and took a really long shower, as if I could wash away the whole previous evening: Don and the gun range and Hanlon stinking of gasoline.

When I was done I left the tap dripping in case Hanlon was still scared of water or the dead girl who was following him. I stood in front of the bathroom mirror, taking a good look at my bullet hole. It had closed up pretty well, but the scar was an angry mottled pink. You'd almost think Don pounding the shit out of it had been a bad thing. My chest still ached, and I had a hard cramp in my back.

I put on deodorant, dressed and shaved. I left the tap in the sink dripping too. Back in my front room, I found a message waiting on my machine – Mom asking me to call her back. When I did, she told me my Uncle Walt had nearly been killed.

'What!'

'He had a real bad sour gas knockdown at the Crown plant last night. The other fellow working with him died, and Walt was in a coma until this morning.'

'Oh my God! When?'

'Just after nine o'clock.'

Less than two hours after Hanlon came to gloat over me at

the gun range. 'Shit,' I breathed. Tom, don't.

You shouldn't ought to kill your own kin.

'Language, Will. Listen, I'm just headed up to the hospital to sit with Patty. I'll call you later on.'

'Bye,' I said. She had already hung up.

You start messing with family, where's it going to stop?

Three days later my Uncle Walt was starting to improve, and I earned my first ever paycheck for seeing the dead.

It turned out that Lee's girlfriend, Vicky, had been talking to a cousin of hers named Johnson Del Grande. (God only knows how he survived junior high with a name like that.) Del Grande had seen the piece about me in the *Chronicle*. He got my number from Vicky and called me up with a very peculiar problem.

Del Grande was a realtor, very well known in Houston's affluent Hispanic community. He'd gotten a great price on a house in the Montrose at an estate sale and had fixed it up to resell at a handsome profit – only to find that word had gotten around to his usual Hispanic clientele that the place was haunted.

Enter Captain Underground, stage left.

'If I take you there,' he explained over the phone, 'you can see for yourself that the house is fine. *Casa muy bonita*, sweet little bungalow in the Montrose, by the Rothko Chapel. Fabulous location. *Bueno* – I show my clients the *Chronicle* article about you, and with that, a notarized affidavit on your letterhead guaranteeing the house is 100 per cent ghost free – and bingo!'

'Bingo!' I said, trying to imagine what my official Dead Kennedy Office letterhead was supposed to look like.

The whole scheme was frankly bizarre: but Del Grande was offering to pay me my, um, standard rate of a thousand bucks, and by the time he picked me up in his maroon Lincoln Town Car, I was pretty damn geeked up about the whole thing. As Lee pointed out, this was my dream gig: a guy with money to burn who wanted to pay me serious jack *not* to see a ghost!

97

Except there was a ghost. Of course.

The house in the Montrose was one I actually recognized from when Josie and I had lived in the neighborhood. It was a nice little bungalow from the 1920s, still in pretty good shape. Back when we had lived nearby it had belonged to a gay sculptor named Oskar, who had built the pieces for a hot pink greek temple the size of a garden shed with delusions of grandeur and then toppled them carefully around the front garden to create a Very Ancient and Extremely Gay Ruins Effect. I hadn't been sure about the whole thing when he did it, but in the years since I'd seen it last, monkey grass and wisteria had crawled over the smashed pillars, the pink paint had been weathered by sun and rain and hydrocarbon-laced air, and the ruins were looking better and better. By which I guess I mean the whole place looked like something that could never happen in Deer Park.

The last time I saw Oskar, it was outside the punk club that would later become the Empire Café, and he was explaining why there were so many gay people in Houston. 'Predator pressure. Man, if you grew up gay in fucking *Waco*,' he'd said, tracing lines in the air with a clove cigarette, 'you'd get the hell out too. You got to join up with the herd. 'Cause there's always a few good ol' boys ready to, you know . . .' He took a drag. '. . . pick off the stragglers.'

I think he was already dying by then, but the ghost inside was a woman, thin and drunk out of her mind, a Jazz Age hottie who played Tin Pan Alley classics on a black baby grand in the front room. She finished 'Funny Face' in a burst of drunken giggles and then lurched unsteadily from the piano stool. She gave me a peck on the cheek with her freezing lips as she passed through the foyer, nodding to various invisible dead guests, then tottered up the curving staircase to the second level of the house. She leaned out to wave an extravagant good-night to us all and pitched over the rail, breaking her neck in the middle of the tiled entryway. Then the whole thing started over again, like a tape stuck on Auto-Repeat.

There may be a stranger way to spend an afternoon than watching someone die, over and over again, while you try to convince an unhappy real-estate agent that he has put down a third of a million dollars on a haunted house, but it went to #1 on my Weird Shit-O-Meter. It was very important to Johnson Del Grande, sweating unhappily in a nice linen suit, that I understand the exact details of how this house deal was screwing him until well into the dead girl's third reedy rendition of 'Hold That Tiger.' I finally offered to cut my fee in half just to get out of the house before she went tile-diving again.

Del Grande wrote out my check with sad dignity.

'You couldn't just *lie*?' Vicky asked that night, scowling as she doled out a helping of tamales.

I remembered the sick crack of the dead girl's neck hitting the Spanish tile. 'Not that well,' I said.

On the bright side, that was five hundred Big Gulps and change – enough to pay the good folks at Southwest Bell before they cut off my phone, with money left over for the gas company and part of my rent and a thank-you six-pack of Dos Equis for Lee. Still, that left the rest of the rent and the fine people at the Visa corporation, not to mention Megan's college education and my Caribbean retirement; so I bit the bullet and decided to answer some of the least crazy-sounding people who were still crazy enough to want me to talk to their dead. It was late in the afternoon when I finally drank enough courage to call Norma Ferris, she of the recent divorce and possibly haunted house. She seemed calm, and she said she understood I couldn't promise to make any ghosts go away. She just wanted confirmation on whether her place was haunted or not. I was very careful to ask whether she owned a gun, and she said she didn't. She made it clear that she made a good living and intended to pay me for my services. That didn't hurt either, as Parkwood Apartment

Management had sent me a nasty note about falling behind on my rent.

Uncle Walt had come out of the hospital and Mom wanted me to visit, so Ms. Ferris and I agreed I would come over the next day after work. I hung up the phone feeling like I'd just gone through a brutal job interview, and had another beer or two to steady my nerves while waiting for my ride to Aunt Patty's house.

Everyone in my generation knew AJ's dad as Uncle Walt, but the older folks all called him Thunder, on account of he was born the day of the Texas City explosion. 'The nurse picked me up to paddle my bottom like they do,' he was fond of saying, 'but when I opened my mouth to holler, all Hell broke loose.' Walt is my mom's oldest brother, both of them brought up by Mamaw Dusty and Grandpa Jay Paul.

Texas City is a little refinery-and-dockside town built at the mouth of the Houston Ship Channel, looking across the bay at Galveston Island. Back in 1947, the SS *Grandcamp*, bound for France, caught fire at the Texas City docks after taking on a big load of ammonium nitrate. In peacetime, ammonium nitrate is a fertilizer, but in war it's what you mix with TNT to make demolition charges. This is the same stuff Timothy McVeigh used to blow up the Murrah building in Oklahoma City.

On April 16, 1947, while Thunder was trying to squeeze out of his mom's birth canal, his daddy, Jay Paul Smithers, left the delivery room long enough to check in at the Monsanto plant where he worked. He had just paused at a window to watch the *Grandcamp* burn when it exploded. He raised his arm against the flash, which saved his eyes when the windowpane blew in, but the glass churned his right arm into hamburger, dicing his nerves so his hand never did work right again. Jay Paul got bitter and drank.

My family is pretty high on Thunder. As mean as his daddy was, he could have turned into a real son of a bitch. But though he was tough enough to play varsity middle linebacker and serve in the infantry at Hiep Duc Valley, Thunder never had an unkind bone in his body, and he never hit a woman.

I was expecting my dad to pick me up, but when the knock came on my door it was my sister Fonteyne standing there instead, still wearing her check-out-girl uniform from Kroger's, complete with name-tag. I was talking on the phone with Megan at the time. 'Hey, Sis,' I said, surprised. 'I'll just be a sec.'

'I've got Vi in the car, so hurry up.' Fonteyne stumped back through the hot gym-sock smell of my hallway and down the stairs.

Meg and I said our good-byes and hung up. She had taken to calling from the school pay phone every couple of days just to make sure I hadn't poisoned myself with my own cooking, or fallen down a well, or contracted leprosy, all of which would probably happen in a heartbeat if I wasn't carefully monitored. At first the calls embarrassed me, but Lee said it was all part of Megan's Journey into Puberty. 'You're the middle step between a doll and a boyfriend,' he explained, which on reflection I thought was pretty damn smart. I figured I'd missed out on doing the usual Helpful Dad things – passing on life wisdom, teaching her how to hot-wire her car in case she lost her keys – so I might as well let Megan boss me around a little. And frankly, Nurse Megan was easier to deal with than Bored Eye-Rolling Megan.

I hung up and hurried down the stinking stairwell after Fonteyne.

The biggest difference between me and my sisters, growing up, was how my grandmother treated us. Mamaw Dusty had come to live with us when Jay Paul went into the nursing home. Mamaw had furry red slippers and a red velour bathrobe with shiny spots of wear on the bum. Even now, my earliest memory is of her sitting with her feet up in the La-Z-Boy in the rumpus room, watching Dialing for Dollars during the Three O'Clock Movie.

Mamaw raised me like I was a small appliance: whack me a time or two if I went on the blink and otherwise ignore me as long as I didn't interfere with the TV reception. This was OK. She would lounge around in her robe and slippers doing the laundry, or smoking Virginia Slims while working word-searches in front of the television. I was pretty much free to amuse myself as long as I obeyed a few basic rules: No Loud Noises (the kind you make when you put a bag of marbles in the dryer), No Food Play (like swirling green food coloring into the Miracle Whip), and No Pestering the Animals (e.g., sticking Scotch tape to the cat). To my irritation, this last rule also protected little sisters.

Things were different with Paris and Fonteyne. Mamaw loved them to death with little attentions, lots of hugs and kisses and candies. By the time Fonteyne came along, it had been ten years since Mamaw had to live with Jay Paul, and she had mellowed considerably.

Mamaw Dusty knew that all men will hurt you if you give them enough time. She lived in that second Texas we boys never see up close, that soft, bitter, sticky conspiracy passed on from mother to daughter in stuffy rooms filled with cloth flowers and family photos. It's a Texas of women who cry and plot and sympathize, who never complain out loud and never forgive. We men all feel it, like the flip side of a thousand dumb wife jokes, but it's nothing we have words for, any more than, 'I guess Sue-Anne's fixing to go back to her momma's house.'

Maybe it was because of how Jay Paul treated her, but Mamaw Dusty was that way: always working on my mother, always grabbing hold of my sisters, sticky as honey. Nothing my dad could do but disappoint her.

The summer I moved out and married Josie, Mamaw got throat cancer. It took her three years to die, and she went out like syrup, sweeter and stickier by the week. She held on to the girls like stuffed toys and told them there was nothing wrong and begged them to stay awhile longer in her knick-knack-littered room, and, oh, here was a present she had bought with her social-security check, a tiny glass bell with a yellow rose painted on the outside, or a china kitty-cat that was just the cutest little ol' thing you ever did see.

Then Mamaw finally died, and I didn't see her again until I was thirty-two.

I was over for Sunday dinner, the first big family meal after Fonteyne brought her baby home from the hospital. Fonteyne stuck Violetta in a bassinet on a card table in the kitchen, swaddled like an Indian princess. From there Vi watched us eat with a goggle-eyed amazement I thought was totally appropriate. Fonteyne was into her third retelling of how she had worked the cute anesthetist for a quick epidural when I happened to look back and saw Mamaw leaning over the baby and chucking her on the chin.

Vi blinked. 'Hey,' I said. Mamaw ignored me and bent closer. She was black and white. She took a drag on her cigarette and then whispered something into the baby's ear. Wisps of smoke curled up around Vi, and she sneezed. 'Hey!' I pushed my chair back. 'Leave her alone.' Mamaw looked up and fear went through me like a dose of rat poison. Her eyes were hard as little black pebbles. She put her hand on Vi's cheek.

I jumped up. Mamaw disappeared. Mom was staring at me unhappily. Fonteyne asked what the fuck I thought I was doing. Vi sneezed again.

I kept my mouth shut for the rest of dinner. Afterwards, I waited until the rest of folks were washing up and got Fonteyne alone for a second. I told her she better get the hell out of our parents' house or Mamaw was going to get her hooks into Vi, like an evil fairy godmother. Fonteyne blew me off. She told me I was crazy and asked how exactly she was supposed to afford an apartment of her own, especially when she was between roles. I made the mistake of telling her that for her kid's sake she might consider busting her ass to get a promotion at Kroger's instead of waiting for Hollywood to discover her. We fought, which did Vi absolutely no good.

But that's the real reason Fonteyne never came to visit me in the hospital.

Today Fonteyne was driving Mom's Buick. I leaned into the back seat to say hello to Vi. She looked pretty good to me. She was five months old now, and her head was getting steadier. I waggled my fingers in front of her. She stared at them as if they were the most stupefying thing she'd ever seen. Then, cautiously, she stuck out her chubby arm. Her little fingers curled slowly around my pinkie, until she had my finger wrapped up tight in her sticky fist. She looked up at me, incredulous. Suddenly her whole face gaped into an astonished smile, and she gave a great wheezing screech of delight.

I sank into the deep blue plush upholstery of the Buick's front seat and buckled up. Back when Megan was this age, I worked out that for every hour I spent with her, Don got fifty-three. I hope he was a good father.

'Got another job yet?' Fonteyne asked.

'You sound just like Dad.'

'I'll take that as a No.'

I could have told her I was going to visit a depressed middle-aged lady the next day to see if she was haunted or just crazy, but somehow it didn't seem like something to brag on.

'Since you're, uh, *between jobs*, you better figure on helping Mom out a whole bunch on this reunion thing,' Fonteyne said. 'She wants to change back to the Little Blanco site.'

'Oh, man.' I had a flash of hours on the phone arguing with caterers and trying to rent barbecue equipment and, worst of all, trying to talk various feuding Smithers into bringing all their guns and knives to one place for a happy family get-together.

'Josie was asking after you,' Fonteyne said. 'She called the house a couple of times.'

'Oh?' Josie had left two messages on my machine since my

disastrous trip to the gun range with Don. I had erased them unplayed, worried that she and Don were going to stop my visitation rights. I just couldn't hear that right now. 'I've been busy,' I said.

I remembered Hanlon saying he had gone to spy on Megan. *She sure is a pretty little thing.* A tight, hot feeling slid under my skin in patches, stinging around the bullet hole in my chest. We lapsed into silence. After a while the hot feeling under my skin slowly faded and it got easier to breathe.

Fonteyne hit the 610 onramp. 'Did you ever hear of such a thing as a guardian angel?'

'What?'

'A guardian angel. Ever hear of that, Mr. Doom and Gloom?' She stomped on her accelerator and swerved into the fast lane. 'You could have told me Mamaw was looking out for Vi. A guardian angel for my baby. But instead . . . It was so mean, Will. And now I think about it all the time. What you said is so wrong, it's so stupid to think Mamaw would be bad for Vi, but you put this stupid idea in my head and I can't get it out. I cried myself to sleep for three days over that.'

'Fonteyne, I know damn well you didn't –'

Fonteyne looked at me. I was shocked to see tears standing in her eyes. She crushed her voice down to a whisper, as if she didn't want her daughter to hear us in the back seat. 'You think I want my baby to be sacking groceries all her life? You think I want Vi to grow up like me?' Fonteyne's mouth turned down, open and ugly around her buck teeth. Dad had been real short of cash when the dentist said she should have braces. He asked her if she wanted them and she said no, because the other kids would make fun of her. Now I wondered if she had known Dad needed her to say that.

'She's Vi's godmother,' Fonteyne said.

'What?'

'Mamaw. I was in labor, there wasn't any Daddy there for the baby. It hurt. It hurt so bad, Will.' Fonteyne was sniffling. 'And

I was like, I must be doing this wrong, I'm going to hurt the baby or I'm going to die. And then they finally gave me the epidural, and right when it started to kick in I could *feel* her, I could feel Mamaw in the room with me. And I told her in my heart, I said if I don't make it through, you got to watch after my baby.' She wiped her nose on her shirtsleeve. 'Violet was Mamaw's real name,' Fonteyne said. 'That's why you saw her looking at the baby. She's the godmother.'

'I am so sorry. I didn't mean . . .' I fumbled with the radio. Mom had left it on a Christian music station.

I was seeing Fonteyne and Paris when they were six and four. They wanted to play Princesses and had come to me for help. I found some safety pins and pinned dish towels around them to make princess skirts. Back then they were still beautiful, and none of us knew the Handsome Princes they were waiting for would turn out to be sleazy useless Deer Park boys who would knock them up and leave. Even I didn't know that. Even seeing dead people all the time doesn't prepare you for the ways life can disappoint you.

'There was this time,' Fonteyne said, 'in sixth grade this guy, Brett Mayne, he kept looking up my skirt and snapping my bra, and you came by the school one day during PE. The teacher tried to throw you out but you ignored her, and you told Brett, you said, "I know where you live, you little shit. And if you ever bother my sister again, I'm going to pour gasoline on your fucking dog and set him on fire."'

'I did that?'

'I was so . . . I felt like the queen of the playground, you looking after me like that. But of course you don't even remember.' She laughed, not happily. 'Do you even remember when you were picking fights with those soldiers?'

'Yeah.'

'Did you even know it was because of Don?'

Flashback: check out the comical look on this one jarhead's face. He's got a fistful of fishhooks in one hand, blood streaming from his nose, and he's blinking at the sight of my forearm coming in. Objects in your fucking *eyes* are closer than they appear, cocksucker. God, I hit him hard. Pure glee whining though me.

Fonteyne wiped her nose on her shirt again. 'Mamaw said you got that from Jay Paul.'

'Grandpa Smithers?'

'We were talking about you. We were all worried you were going to get beaten up, or thrown in jail, and Mamaw said, "Honey," she told me, "that's the way men are. Jay Paul, he could get so mean and never even know he was mad."'

I didn't know what to say.

I don't like to think about the past. What's done is done, there's no point dwelling on it. But ever since Hanlon shot me, I was having a hard time keeping my eyes front and focused on the future. Memories kept seeping out, wet and sticky. As if that bullet put a hole in me, and my yesterdays were bleeding out.

Fonteyne and I stopped at Gabby's Barbecue to pick up dinner for everyone. Someone had nailed a wooden cross to the telephone pole in front. In the last ten years these shrines have started popping up all over Houston. Tokens of the dead, they're like ghosts that even normal people have to see. If you pass one near a schoolyard, you know someone there's been hit by a car or capped in a drive-by shooting. On a tenement roof, probably an OD. Cross tied to the fence of a freeway overpass, definitely a jumper.

Under the cross, a picture of a young blond guy was stapled to the telephone pole. A memorial for some high-school kid, probably shot to death when someone tried to rob the Gabby's. No way of telling whether he was the clerk or the perp. Dead for less than fifty bucks either way.

By the time we got to Walt and Patty's place it was deep twilight, but the air was still hot and damp; getting out of the

Buick was like stepping from a refrigerator into a sauna. Walt's concrete back patio looked much the same as ever: the gas barbecue grill, the chin-up bar and rusting set of weights AJ's brothers had used when they were on the high-school football team. Scattered along the back wall lay the pieces of a disassembled sidewalk edger, a fishing rod with the reel cracked open for autopsy, and a cat-food bowl with a few chunks of dog food and a dead cricket in it.

The sad sense of vanished children was everywhere, most of all the aching absence of Walt and Patty's oldest daughter, Julie-Anne, who had lived long enough to become a stranger to them but died before she could get beyond her rebellious years and come home. 'Walt's tough and Patty's a Christian,' my mom said after AJ's boyfriend shot her to death. 'If anyone can make it through, they will.' But how could anyone survive a murdered child? Sure, they kept coming to the family reunions, they didn't get divorced or turn to drink. But a part of them had died with AJ and was never coming back.

I pulled on the glass patio door, sliding it open with that rolling *Star Trek* swish. My mother was setting out a bowl of jellied salad. 'Patty's showing Thunder some slides,' Mom said softly. 'Help me get the dinner fixings on the table.'

I followed her in and Fonteyne came behind me, quickly shutting the door so as not to let the cool out. On our right, in the dim living-room, Aunt Patty was working a slide projector, throwing pictures onto a small white screen she had set up in front of the TV. 'This here's Bryce,' she said brightly, as a picture of their youngest boy flashed up. 'He's doing real well at A & M this year. He's pitching on the baseball team.'

'Got a curve ball?' Uncle Walt asked, smiling.

'You taught him on his twelfth birthday.' There were tear-tracks on Aunt Patty's face, and for some reason I remembered the drip, drip of the tap in Hanlon's garage. Sadness is a wet thing. Rain and creeping water.

'Ah.' Walt's shoulder's sagged. 'I never did believe that hurts their arms, if you teach it right.' He looked and looked at the young man in the picture, as if he would recognize that handsome boy if only he stared long enough.

'Thunder can't recall where he left his feet, let alone his kiddos,' Mom murmured. 'Sour gas takes them that way sometimes. The doctor says he'll most likely get his memory back, but not for certain. He can't stand the light, neither. Will, are you hungry? I worry you don't eat enough.'

On the dining-room table, Mom set out plastic cutlery and a stack of paper plates, which she always did when she didn't care to fuss with washing up. Barbecue smells steamed up out of the Styrofoam containers, brisket and ribs and sausages, as well as one pound each of potato salad and coleslaw, the creamy sweet kind with raisins in. Cornbread she had made herself, because even Gabby's had started putting too much sugar in.

'Food's on the table,' Mom called. Uncle Walt's big torso tensed as he struggled to get up from his La-Z-Boy. That was a hell of a thing to watch, my inexhaustible Uncle Walt so weak he had to fight to get out of his recliner. Dad grabbed his arm and helped him up.

'Thank you kindly,' Uncle Walt said. He moved in little shuffling steps, like an old man, leaning on my dad's forearm. 'I'm sure I ought to know what to call you, but since I got out the hospital, I'm having a hard time putting names to folks.'

'It's Jimmy, Thunder. I'm married to your sister Sue.'

'Your body's still recovering from trauma,' my mom said briskly. 'It doesn't have the energy left over for recalling things. Plus you hit your head pretty good when you fell. You'll be your own self directly.'

Aunt Patty pulled Walt's chair out for him. They had a matched dining-room set of chairs with fancy-carved backs and cushy black vinyl seats that looked almost like leather. Walt's thick hand trembled on his chairback as he eased himself into his usual place, looking across the big dining table into the shallow curve of the bay windows. By this time it was pretty much full dark and there wasn't much to be seen in the windows except for our own bright reflections, and humped behind them, indistinct, the dim mass of trees in the yard.

Aunt Patty fixed Walt a plate of brisket and cornbread.

There was a grandfather clock in the front room of their house. I had a sudden dizzy memory of hiding in its case at the age of four, or maybe five. Impossible, that almost thirty years should have passed. If AJ hadn't been shot, she would be closing on forty. I was nearly halfway through my three score and ten. In a few years Megan would be off at college and forgetting to call Josie. I would never hear from her. Nobody would care about my bands any more; the music Josie and I fell in love to would sound dated and stupid to them. My parents would die, and then friends would start to go, not burning out in firecrackers of drugs and stupidity, but guttering down from cancer and heart disease. I felt a sudden rush of sadness in my chest, real as a drain emptying out from under my breastbone.

'I fell off a scaffold,' Walt said. He turned that concept over like a broken engine part. 'How'd I come to do that again?'

'They asked you to unbolt a flange in a six-inch pipe.' Aunt Patty dipped him out a little hump of coleslaw and plopped it down beside his cornbread.

'Was I putting in a blind?' Uncle Walt asked.

'I guess. Anyway, there was sour gas in the line.'

'They didn't purge the pipe?' Uncle Walt said, surprised. 'I wouldn't have gone up there if they didn't say they'd cleaned out the line.'

Aunt Patty poured him a glass of Diet Dr Pepper. 'The Brown & Root foreman said he thought the Crown guy said they'd cleaned the line.'

'Crown foreman's gonna cover his ass like a pair of jeans,' Walt grunted. No amount of brain damage will drive the scorn for Crown Petroleum out of an East Houston roughneck. To hear Aunt Patty tell it, Crown lawyers had been over Walt like flies on cowshit even while he was still lying dazed and stretched out in the hospital ICU.

My uncle's hands shook with the effort of cutting up his brisket.

Just before nine o'clock on the night Hanlon spooked me at the Pasadena gun range, Walt and his assistant, George Nogales, got orders to unbolt a flange in a six-inch pipe and install a blind – a metal plug supposed to block the flow of anything toxic coming down the line. The pipe was running twenty-five feet off the ground, so this would be scaffold work, with Walt and George both breathing through air-hoses in case of any leaks in the line. They had a stand-by man to watch them from the ground, another Brown & Root guy named Forrest Deese. (A lot of Aunt Patty's information came from Forrest.) The Crown plant had just been through a lengthy maintenance shut-down, and everybody was pushing hard to get it up and running again, since an idle plant burns freight-cars of money for every hour it's out of commission.

According to Deese, the Crown foreman said the line had been purged of H$_2$S and would be running at no more than three to five pounds of pressure. But in hospital, Aunt Patty saw the work order, which both Crown and the B&R foreman signed off on. It said, 'There may be some hydrogen sulfide present, and workers should be given fresh air with egress standby.' Deese said he and Walt figured that meant fresh air on the scaffold for Walt and George, delivered through hoses, while the 'stand-by man,' Deese, would have a free-standing backpack air supply. The Crown lawyer, though, said that because the air hoses wouldn't reach all the way to the ground from the scaffold, the permit meant Walt and George were supposed to carry 'egress bottles' – stashes of air they could use if they had to clear out of the area in a hurry.

The job wasn't supposed to take more than twenty-five minutes.

As per good practice, Walt broke the flange away from him,

and then George handed him the blind. All very routine, until a distant alarm went off. When Walt and George scrambled to get off the scaffold, their air hoses wouldn't reach. They had to crack the seals on their masks to breathe.

The second they took off those masks, they must have smelled the sour gas and known they were in trouble, but by then it was too late. Hydrogen sulfide stops respiration – not in the lungs, but in the cells. A single deep breath with a high enough concentration of H_2S can put a man into coma. Walt was halfway down the last scaffold when the gas dropped him. George, hesitating, was still twenty feet up. He pitched off the scaffold, fracturing his skull. Deese had told Patty he'd been afraid to move George, in case of a neck injury, so he dragged Walt out first, calling for help. By the time he got back with another Brown & Root man in full air gear, George Nogales was dead. The coroner and the company lawyers might know if it was the fall or the gas that killed him, but they weren't telling.

Tonight the plastic knife and fork looked tiny in Uncle Walt's huge hands, which were horny and thick-fingered and rough with scars. His gut overhung his lap, kept from smothering it by a massive bronze belt buckle, but he still looked small somehow. Lost inside a body he was no longer big enough to fill. I wondered if he remembered his dead daughter, or maybe just felt the loss of her like a hollow place inside.

A rush of grief bubbled up in me like cool spring water, rising from somewhere deep underground. I didn't understand why the dim, stuffy sadness in Walt and Patty's house was getting to me so bad. I pushed back from the table. 'Excuse me.' I blinked fast, my eyes so wet my family was only shines and blurs around the table. 'I'll be back directly.'

I made my way to the bathroom, where I put my head down, staring into the sink. The sad, helpless feeling kept spilling through me, stronger and stronger, and suddenly a flicker of movement caught my eye. I looked up.

My cousin AJ was in the mirror, watching me.

CHAPTER SEVEN

Half the time dead people are nearly blind, groping around with underground eyes. Not AJ. She was watching me, amused, like a big sister having fun at my expense. She was wearing her little round glasses, of course, and a white halter-top, thin cotton held on by spaghetti straps. There were two bloodstains like roses on her shirt; a little one at her waist, and a larger one blooming between her small breasts.

I closed my eyes and counted to ten before opening them again. She was still there when I looked up.

I see you, DK.

I see you.

I see you.

I see you.

I couldn't look away from her. I thought of Hanlon lying awake in the middle of the night, mouth dry, heart pounding. People think ghosts must be like cartoons, like illusions. They aren't. When they're in the room, they're more real than you are.

My expression must have been pretty comical. AJ quirked a smile and let one eyebrow arch. Then she stepped back from the surface of the mirror. One deliberate step, slowly, holding my eyes.

'AJ?' I whispered. 'Holy shit. What do you want?'

Watching me over her shoulder, she backed toward the bathroom door. I followed. Still holding my eyes, AJ walked past the edge of the mirror and disappeared.

I could breathe again. It hurt. I missed her.

Then she was back. She was deliberately standing at the edge of the mirror, looking over her shoulder at me. Slowly, this time, she stepped beyond the frame and disappeared. I followed her into the laundry room and stopped. No sign. Back in the bathroom, the mirror was empty.

I stepped out into the hallway. At the far end of the corridor, Aunt Patty kept a vanity with knick-knacks on its marble top, and above them a tall mirror. AJ was dwindling there, all but invisible in the dim light, walking with her back to the mirror as if she were heading into the living-room.

I hurried after her.

The front foyer opened up to my right, imitation marble tiles and a front door with a cut-glass window in it, the glass carved and frosted to be opaque. As I tried to catch up, I could just see AJ's jumbled shadow pass erratically through the imitation crystal. Flashes of black hair and bloody cotton. She was heading for the dining room.

'Will?' Mom called from the table. 'What was your favorite event from the family reunion?'

Truth: watching *My Name is Trinity* while absolutely incandescent on a double hit of Orange Sunshine LSD the last year I was bunked in with the rest of the cousins for the Kids Lock-In Night. I had kept the young 'uns enthralled with my non-stop patter on the Biblical symbolism of Mr. Eastwood's Really Big Gun.

'Watermelon-seed spitting contest,' I said.

'Me too,' Fonteyne said around a mouthful of cornbread.

Now AJ was a full-size reflection moving through the bay windows in the dining nook. She grinned at me.

'These last few reunions that Mabel Rae organized have

114

been real nice, of course, but it seems like the same folks come every year. We ought to get everybody. Get Chase up from Brownsville. Get Billie Mac and Darlene and Great Aunt Norma. Will? Aren't you hungry?' my mom said. 'Try a little slaw.'

AJ opened her mouth in a laugh I couldn't hear.

I would never claim I used my teenage years wisely, but one thing I did learn was how to act straight in front of my parents, no matter how stoned or freaked out I might be. 'I've already had a bunch of potato salad,' I said. 'Ribs too.' AJ was walking fast across the bay window. When she stepped from pane to pane, her body would split and stretch across two sheets of glass for a second, then snap back together. When she came to the last window, she jumped for the kitchen and disappeared.

I found Mom staring at me. 'I'm going to get me some ice,' I said. As I rooted in the freezer, I picked up a flash of movement over the kitchen sink. I backed out of the fridge. AJ was waiting for me in the kitchen window. Our eyes met. Cold water dripped inside my chest. AJ looked down at the sink: then back to me: then back to the sink. I followed her eyes. Hanging over the tap were a pair of latex dishwashing gloves. AJ looked significantly at the gloves, waiting for the light to dawn. It didn't.

'There's ice tea in the fridge if you want it, honey,' Aunt Patty said.

I reached out and touched the gloves. AJ disappeared.

I found Uncle Walt staring at me – or rather, looking past me at the window where his daughter's ghost had been.

Aunt Patty put a hand on his arm. 'Is there something you forgot?'

'Yeah,' he said.

We left Walt and Patty's house about nine. Fonteyne and the baby headed home with Mom in the Buick. I was going to take the bus, but Dad wouldn't hear of it, and bundled me into his

'93 Caprice, a retired police cruiser he'd picked up at an auction. If you looked close, you could kind of see the Pasadena Police Department crest underneath the cheap civilian paint job. Dad liked the idea of wheeling around in a cop car. Whenever I rode in it with him, the Batman jingle would start circling in my head.

We bombed through Refinery Row, the miles-long corridor of pressurized tanks and crackers and polyethylene reactors that lines Highway 255 as it runs between Deer Park and Houston proper. When you're holding Contents Under Pressure, you can't have many corners or straight edges; as a result, big refineries have this bulbous, science-fiction architecture, all tanks and spheres and pipes and udders. The buildings are covered in a spiderweb of metal ladders, lit by red and blue and amber lights that give the whole thing an atmosphere exactly halfway between Christmas and Hell. Every part of Refinery Row (excepting whichever buildings have just recently blown up or burned down) is painted white, and the whole huge complex feels somehow unreal, as if someone had built a *Battlestar Galactica* theme park by the side of the road and then abandoned it after the show was cancelled.

'So,' Dad said, ever so casually. 'How's the job search going?'

'Oh, great.' *Nuh Nuh – nuh nuh – nuh nuh – Nuh Nuh . . .* 'Yeah, I start tomorrow actually. Gonna be a Caped Crusader.' *– Batman!*

'I hear there's a lot of money in that,' Dad said drily.

'Thousand dollars a day. First job tomorrow.'

'You going to be armed?'

'This is a very normal-type lady. She won't be packing.' I could see Dad wasn't convinced. 'At least she's not a Smithers,' I pointed out.

He smiled. 'Thank God for that. So you're going to . . . ?'

'Check her house. See if it's haunted. I did one like that already, actually, for this real-estate guy.'

Dad glanced over. 'Did you write him a receipt?'

116

'I guess it didn't seem like—'

'Got to write a receipt! IRS needs a paper trail.'

'It's only a few hundred bucks—'

'A thousand dollars a day? That'll add up.'

'The first guy was actually only five hundred dollars,' I said.

'Did you set aside any of it for taxes?'

'I was busy paying rent, actually.'

'Social Security? Unemployment? You realize you have to double-dip on those deductions if you're operating as a small business.'

'Wait a sec!' I was beginning to feel a little panicky. 'How much of my five hundred dollars do I get to keep?'

My dad shrugged. 'Maybe three hundred bucks?'

'Three hundred dollars!'

He looked over at me, grinning. 'Welcome to the wonderful world of small business.'

Forty minutes later he was still explaining things to me over coffee at the IHOP on Greenbriar. 'So you're like a consultant, basically, and *normally* that would mean a sole proprietorship.' He wrote the words *Sole Proprietor v Inc/LLC* on a napkin, and underlined <u>Sole Proprietor</u>.

'Normally, but not this time?' I squirted my fourth plastic thimble of half-and-half into my third cup of coffee. Josie used to do this thing where she would dunk the creamer under the coffee until the glue holding the paper top began to weaken, so she could squirt out the cream without ever having to tear back the top. I never had the patience for that.

'Well, the problem is liability.' My dad had taken a pair of reading glasses out of his shirt pocket and was peering over them at me, tapping the Sole Proprietor napkin with his pen. 'Say Granny Bilgepump has you in to talk to the ghost of Papaw Bilgepump. Papaw comes back from beyond the grave and says, 'You got bony knees, old woman, and I always liked your sister Mabel better than you.' You pass this along, not being the sharpest tool in the shed, and Granny has a heart attack.' He looked meaningfully at me.

I looked blankly back. 'So?'

'So the Bilgepump kids are going to sue you into the next county.'

'*Sue me*?' I spilled coffee on the vinyl tabletop.

'Negligence. Infliction of emotional distress. Lost earnings.'

I realized I was starting to wipe up my coffee with the Insurance and Overhead napkin. I stashed that one in my pocket, along with IHOP napkin guides to Cash Flow Projections, County and City Taxes, and Obtaining a Business License. 'Granny Bilgepump had lost earnings?'

'She made heirloom quilts to sell every Easter at her church yard sale and used the proceeds to put her grandkids through college.'

'Must have been a hell of a quilter.'

'The best,' Dad said. He sipped his decaf.

'So you think I should incorporate?' Dead Kennedy Investigations. Captain Underground, Incorporated. Jesus.

'Probably not. Probably you should just get some very specific insurance. But it's something to think about.'

'Dad?'

'Yeah?'

I grabbed the napkins on How to Find a Good Accountant and Home Office Tax Deductions. 'I'm not scamming anyone.'

My father settled back with a creak of vinyl, regarding me. 'I never said you were.'

'Yeah, I know. I just – do you even believe me? About seeing ghosts? You must just think I'm crazy.'

My dad took off his reading glasses, folded them up and put them in his pocket. His hair had gone salt-and-pepper over the last few years, and his shoulders seemed rounder. 'Your mother says she can truly feel the loving presence of Jesus in her life. Now I guess I believe in God, but I never had that. But am I going to call your mother a liar, just because I haven't felt Jesus in my heart?' He took a little more coffee. 'It doesn't matter what I think or believe. My job is to help you out any way you'll let me.'

'Oh,' I said. I was touched, and ashamed – me with the busted marriage and the shitty jobs – of all the time I'd spent looking down on him, while he'd been looking out for me. 'Okay. Thanks.'

It was after midnight by the time Dad dropped me off. I climbed up through the stifling heat of the hallway and let myself into my apartment, only to find that the A/C was broken.

You can't sleep in Houston when the A/C doesn't work. The wet air stays hot all night long – hours after midnight the thermostat in my living-room said it was eighty-eight degrees. I soaked my head in water, trying to cool off. I went over to the Kroger's to see if they had a receipt book in their stationery department, but they didn't, so I went back home. I spread Dad's napkins out on my kitchen counter and tried to imagine myself as a small-business owner. It didn't much take.

The night stretched on forever. I put on some CDs and listened to old bands, the Stranglers and Shriekback and Exene Cervenka, lying on my mattress in the sweltering dark, thinking about family, and the dead.

Ghosts are like the poor in the Third World countries. You teach yourself not to think about them. You can't deal with all that need, all that grief. Even me, I try to stay uninvolved. Because if you start noticing, where does it stop? There's rivers of grief out there, floods of it. You'd drown. Anybody would.

But I think once the first ghost catches you, others can feel it. They can find you. We're alive; we burn like candles in their darkness. Even the blind ones come groping for our heat. Lying there in the hot dark, I figured maybe meeting Uncle Billy was my first big mistake. If I hadn't stumbled across him, if he had never spoken to me above the dark mutter of the bayou, maybe the other ghosts wouldn't have found me either.

But that wasn't the way it happened. Billy had seen me, he had known who I was. Maybe – it suddenly occurred to me – maybe it wasn't my mother who was reading Bible verses to me in the hospital. Maybe it was Uncle Billy at my bedside that night. *I baptize you with water for repentance, but He who is coming will baptize you with the Holy Spirit and with fire.*

Billy had found me first, and now the rest of them were clustering in on me, thick as moths around a light, Tom and Mamaw and AJ . . . a regular family reunion.

I got up and went outside for a walk. Three o'clock in the morning, pacing into the pretty neighborhoods around Rice University, thinking about my dad and Mamaw and AJ in her daddy's bathroom mirror.

Just past Roberts Elementary, a part of Addison had turned into a ghost road. The Lincoln Town Car in front of the corner house was black and white; the roses beside the front walk had blooms as gray and felty as old newsprint.

There was a shrine under the stop sign at the corner. It was new, a small cross beaten into the dirt, wreathed with white flowers and bearing a candle on each arm. A framed picture of a little boy leaned against the bottom of the cross. It looked like one of those stiff smiling portraits from Sears. You could tell the kid had been dressed up for the picture in uncomfortable new clothes. It was such a normal street, nice big middle-class houses; the kind people live in on TV. Hard to believe someone's child could have died here. The flowers were fresh and the candles were lit, two tiny tongues of white flame, flickering in the dusk. The road stretched back in black and white, that dead boy's shrine before it like an open door.

It would be good to walk down this quiet gray street. I felt cool and calm. The sleepy promise of release was in me everywhere. I knew in my body that going down the ghost road would be like sleeping; the sweet blood-deep surrender of putting your head on a pillow and closing your eyes. Letting darkness run into you like rain.

And then, quite suddenly, I remembered I had gone down a ghost road before.

I was little, playing with a squirt gun on the patio behind our condo. The third time I went to load my gun at the bathroom sink, Mamaw Dusty had yelled at me for dripping water in the house, so this time I squeezed through the scratchy dead hedge behind the patio and trotted over to the swimming pool. It was hot and quiet, the drowsy middle of the afternoon. All the grown-ups were at work and all the big kids were in school. Only old people and babies left, everybody inside, watching TV in air-conditioned gloom. I can remember the A/C unit chugging away against our back wall. Water from it creeping down the bricks like a sweat stain. Me hunkered on the concrete, prying out the plastic plug on my squirt gun and sticking it into the swimming pool. The smell of chlorine in the air. Light glittering like broken glass on the water.

The silent sunlight closed around me and I could barely breathe. It felt like the afternoons Mamaw made me pretend to nap and I wrapped myself up in my sheet as if I were a mummy until the cloth was tight and soaked with sweat. Time opening up, the hours stretching into years of boredom. Time measured in Mamaw's slow cigarettes.

A little Mexican girl in a polka-dot swimsuit ran by, hopping on the balls of her feet as if the hot concrete were burning her. Her wet hair was stringy, and her tummy bulged and jiggled as she ran. She was black and white, like someone in an old movie. I knew that meant she was dead. Her eyes skipped right through me. I watched as she ran down one of the little sidewalks that disappeared into the complex. Eight of these concrete paths snaked out from the pool, but this one was black and white, with a gray hedge lining it and a scrawny cedar tree to one side. A spray of gray needles shook where the girl had brushed against it.

I jumped up and trotted after her, not quite running. I didn't want to spill the water out of my gun. I was still fumbling to get the plug back in when I hit the ghost path. Daylight bent in front of me, then popped like a soap bubble; and then the whole world was black and white. Ahead of me the little Mexican girl turned a corner by an abandoned BigWheel and disappeared. I followed her. The condos around me were gray and shabby. It was lovely and cool and the pavement no longer burned my feet.

There was something wrong with my eyes. Whatever I looked at seemed to slip out of focus, coming clear again just as I looked away. I slowed to a walk. A sewing machine stopped and started inside the apartment beside me. I looked at its glass patio doors, but they were dark and I couldn't see inside. The sewing machine stuttered and stopped, stuttered and stopped. Air-conditioners churned and beat like hearts.

I reached the corner where the little girl had turned. She was slapping on an apartment door with her open hand and yelling something in high-pitched Spanish. A Mexican opened the door. He had thick brown arms and an Astros cap. He was scared. He reached out with one hand, feeling the air like a blind person, but the fat girl slipped around his leg and disappeared into the dark apartment.

A deep quiet fell.

'She went inside,' I said. The Mexican in the Astros cap couldn't hear me or see me. 'Hey!'

He closed the door.

Nobody could see me. On the ghost road, I was invisible.

I could creep into people's houses and they would never know. I could see what TV shows they watched after the kids were in bed, sneak anything I wanted out of their refrigerators, take cookies out of their cookie jars. Be a super-spy. I always loved to hide, to burrow into the laundry basket and then shout Boo! when Mamaw discovered me. Once I crept into the dryer and stayed there for an hour while she looked all over the house.

But here, down the ghost road, nobody would ever find me. 'Will!'

It was Mamaw, faint and far away, as if she were calling to me out of a TV set. 'William Kennedy! You come back here this second or I'm going to whup you within an inch of your life!' Her angry voice so thin and powerless.

I crept back around the corner from the Mexican's house and looked up the ghost path. All was gray, except over the pool, where I could see the regular colors of the real world: a thin strip of smoggy blue sky, winks of light from the swimming pool, glimpses of Mamaw's red stretch polyester shorts between the needles of the cedar tree.

'All right,' Mamaw said. 'I'm going to call your mother.'

That froze me. I imagined my mother hanging up the phone and having a quick word with nice Dr. Jeffers, who had gray curly hair in his nose. Then she would have to flush and apologize to Dr. Boseman, who was young and thin and mean.

'I'm going inside now,' Mamaw said. She turned and headed heavily for our condo, thighs wobbling.

It was much harder going up the ghost path than it had been to come down it. Tiring, as if I were walking uphill. When I got to the cedar tree the air thickened, holding me in. The sewing machine chattered angrily at me. Air-conditioners throbbed and beat. It was hard to walk back into the harsh bright heat. So much easier to stay here, in the cool, quiet black and white. I almost gave up, but then I thought of my mom, how worried she would be, and I kept trudging forward.

The air broke and I was back in the Texas sun, with the concrete scalding my feet. I screwed my eyes tight against the glare and the noise of traffic and the smell of chlorine.

Mamaw was just picking up the phone when I slid open the heavy glass patio door and trudged inside. 'There you are, William Kennedy.' She jabbed at me with her cigarette. 'How many times have I told you not to go outside like that? How many times I told you not to play those hiding games?'

'Seventeen?'

'Don't you sass me. Don't you think you can run out on me, William.' She started to put the phone down, then thought better of it. 'You know, I believe I'll call anyway,' she said. 'I believe I'll tell your momma that you're lost, and I can't find you. Then you can wait here and see how she feels about that.'

'Hey!' I said, outraged. 'I comed back!'

Mamaw took a drag on her cigarette. 'Do you know what your momma would do if you ever did get lost? Do you?' She leaned forward through a haze of blue-gray smoke until her fleshy face loomed over me. 'I'll tell you what she would do, Mr. Will. She would go get one of your Uncle Walt's guns, is what she would do.' I couldn't look away from her face, thick with foundation and eyeshadow. 'If you went missing, Will, her only sweet little baby, she'd take that gun and she'd put it in her mouth like this.' Mamaw made a gun from her pointer finger and her thumb. 'And then she would blow her own head off.'

'Would not!'

'Then I imagine your daddy would come home and find her and he would do the same thing.' Mamaw nodded as I broke down and started to cry. 'What else do you think they live for, kiddo? I've known your momma all her life and I guarantee that's what she'd do. She's very sensitive.'

I saw my mother slumping down in black and white, like a dead woman at the start of an Ellery Queen episode.

'You better cry,' Mamaw said with satisfaction. 'It's about time you learned to think about somebody besides just me, me, me. Hiding, hiding, hiding. You think it's a joke to run off on us, do you?' She leaned back and took another puff on her cigarette.

'I hate you! I hate you!' I was crying uncontrollably. I lifted up my water pistol and squirted Mamaw and waited for her to grab me and jerk me over her knee and spank me.

She just looked at me, smoking her cigarette. 'Well, I love you, kiddo,' she said at last. 'We all do. That's the point.' Mamaw paused to cough. 'You better remember it.'

'I hate you! I hate you I hate you I hate—'

Mamaw made the little gun out of her fingers again and stuck it in her mouth and yelled '*BLAM!*'

I ran into my room and jumped under the covers and wrapped myself up as tight as I could. I was still crying when Mom got home. She was mad at me for disobeying the rules and making her come home from work. I never said anything about Mamaw and the gun.

And then for almost thirty years I forgot the whole episode. The gray cedar tree, the sewing machine, the little dead girl disappearing around her father's leg. The smell of chlorine.

And maybe ever since that day a part of me had been lost down the ghost road. Maybe that was the reason Mamaw liked Fonteyne and Paris better than me. Maybe that was why my dad never settled down and my mom seemed so worried all the time. Because they could tell, I'm sure they knew they had lost part of me already. And they were always waiting for the moment when I would leave for good.

CHAPTER EIGHT

The next day I saw AJ at my local Kroger's. It was four o'clock in the afternoon, another unbearably muggy August day, and getting only a couple of hours of sleep made the heat feel worse. I was heading to the store to pick up a can of coffee. I needed something to wake me up; I was supposed to go to Norma Ferris's house in less than two hours on my first business call as a Caped Crusader, and I didn't want to yawn my way through it.

I saw AJ first in the supermarket parking lot, gliding over the windshields of parked cars. My heart revved in my aching chest. She looked at me and winked. I ran to catch up and found her loitering in the supermarket's glass doors, waiting for me. I stepped on the pressure-sensitive mat. The door swung open and she vanished inside.

For the next ten minutes I lost her completely. I tried the big glass panels in the frozen-food section, expecting at any minute to see her drifting in front of the frozen pizzas and bags of Mixed Oriental Vegetables. But she wasn't there, or lounging over the fried chicken at the deli counter, or hidden in a thicket of water bottles in the beverage section.

I stopped trying to guess and went systematically up and down the aisles until I caught a flash of AJ's blue jeans in

Kitchen Wares, reflected on the bottom of a stainless-steel skillet. Peering around the section, I made out a twist of blood-stained cloth in the curving edge of a Pyrex measuring cup, and part of her neck – white skin, a strand of straight dark hair – showing in the bottom of a shiny aluminum pie plate.

At just the height of the bullet holes in AJ's shirt hung a display of latex dishwashing gloves.

East Texas has four great natural resources: heat, oil, mosquitoes, and cousins. They all have their complications, but they have their uses too. I called my cousin Andy the second I got back to my apartment. When we were little, Andy was a scrawny, hyperactive kid a few years younger than me, destined for Refinery Row. Then his mom stuck him in Boy Scouts, where a merciful God revealed unto him a Tandy 2000 computer. His Computing Badge had turned into an obsession, the obsession became a gig with a local software company, then a promotion, then a move to Austin, where he now had a title like Vice-Pope of Remote Server Access and an imported Yankee wife who didn't much care for his redneck relations. As Uncle Walt once put it, 'Sonia's got him on a tight collar and a short leash.'

'Andy! Howdy! Long time no talk,' I said brightly, gulping down a soothing cup of Gold Key. 'Hey, this is your cousin Will. Yeah, that Will. Listen, I need you to do a little computer research for me on hydrogen sulfide disasters and rubber gloves. Or could be latex gloves. I don't know if that part matters.'

'Shoot, I'd like to,' Andy said, sounding as if he'd rather deep-throat a weed-eater. 'But we have a big crush at work just now, and, um . . .'

'No problemo. Say, did you know my mom is organizing the family reunion this year?'

'We're really not supposed to do personal phone calls at work. Oh, here comes my boss—'

'So we'll just put you and Sonia down to head the Entertainment Committee.'

The sudden silence was gratifying. Entertainment Committee means running the dominoes tournament. Bad blood had been simmering since last year's scandal in which Uncle Chase and Aunt Betty were found to be using under-the-table signals to pass bidding hints to one another.

'You wouldn't,' Andy hissed.

'Try me.'

'Will!'

'All righty then, you have a good day at work. Don't want you to get in dutch with the boss. Bye now!'

'WILL!' Andy yelped.

'Yeah?'

'Tell me your damn question and I'll look it up for you.'

'That's more like it.'

'"Howdy Andy" my ass,' he said bitterly. 'If I do this, you take us off the committee list.'

'You betcha.'

'And if I find something good, you lose our invitation.'

'No can do, man. I can't lie to my mom.'

'Last year Sonia decided to be brave,' Andy said. 'She ate Aunt Mabel's Cubed Carrot Mousse.'

'That's the melted marshmallow one, right?'

'She thought it was yogurt.'

'Dude,' I said.

'Then she got up the nerve to sit at a different table from me. By Jerome.'

'Uh-oh.'

Jerome is Uncle Billy's younger brother. Before sundown he takes in nothing but fifteen cups of coffee with five packets of sugar in each, which leaves him a tad on the jittery side. He is extremely and sincerely devout, and spends most of his parole time on witness missions. 'Jerome and Tommy Rae started out talking about the finer points of black-powder shooting,' Andy said gloomily. 'They finished with "the biggest animal you ever killed without a gun."'

129

'Who won?'

'Tommy Rae said he dropped out of a tree once and took the throat out of a razorback hog with his Buck folding knife,' Andy said absently. 'The point is, Sonia is from *Connecticut*.'

'I understand.'

'They don't have razorback hogs in Connecticut.'

'I guess not.'

'They don't cook much with Jell-O neither. So no reunion invites, all right? I want to walk out of this a free man, with no grief from my momma.' Aunt Naylene was terribly and loudly embarrassed at her daughter-in-law's coldness, treating her with incredible fake friendliness to her face and ripping her constantly behind her back.

I really didn't want to explain things to my mother if Andy and Sonia got 'accidentally' left off the invite list . . . but on the other hand, I needed Andy's product. 'Deal,' I sighed. Then I explained about Uncle Walt's accident.

'Hydrogen sulfide and rubber gloves. Will, is this another dead guy thing?'

'Sort of.'

'My mom e-mailed a link to the *Chronicle* article about that guy you blew up.'

'Don't tell me they don't have dead people in Connecticut.'

'No, it's all right. Sonia thought it was kind of cool. Sort of Trailer-Park Southern Gothic.'

'Sonia can kiss my rebel ass.'

Andy snickered. 'I'm Googling your rubber-glove thing, by the way.'

'I thought you had to work?'

'Not as much as I need to get out the reunion. . . . Hey. Hang on.'

Hold music played. With a shock I realized it was 'Waiting for the Man' by the Velvet Underground. The apocalypse is coming. I'm serious.

A click and Andy was back on the line. 'Get ready to lose that reunion invite,' he gloated. 'I tracked down some other sour gas knock-downs. Listen to this: *The McCoys charge that hydrogen sulfide sensors were deactivated – in some cases covered with rubber gloves – so that alarms would not sound and bring work to a halt.*'

'Holy shit!'

'There's more,' Andy said gleefully. '*The day before the accident, they said, H_2S levels near the faulty compressor had pegged a meter designed to detect up to 1,600 ppm – three times what is usually a lethal dose.*'

'Oh my God.'

'So they knew, somebody at Crown *knew* there was going to be hydrogen sulfide in the line. But they didn't want to shut down the plant, so they just covered the alarms instead.'

'Damn,' I said. 'Wish they'd done a better job.'

'What?'

'If they're better cheaters, no alarm goes off. Uncle Walt and the other guy don't try to go down. They don't take off their masks. Nobody dies.'

Andy whistled. 'It's still negligence, though, right?'

'Hell, yes. Mom says Patty and Walt owe forty thousand dollars in hospital bills. Company's got to cover that.'

'Crown? Or Brown & Root? Neither's going to admit a damn thing.'

True. 'Can you look up the names of some heavyweight accident lawyers? I doubt Crown is going to talk to Aunt Patty, but they might talk to Johnny Cochrane, if you know what I mean.' Here in the South, class-action lawyers are what we have instead of unions. Legally speaking, we prefer shoot-outs to sit-ins.

'Aye, aye, sir. Running a search now, Captain Underground.'

'Oh, fuck off,' I said. 'And thanks.'

'Hey,' Andy said. 'It's family.'

*

Then it was five o'clock and I still had half an hour to kill before heading off to my appointment. I hoped Norma Ferris wasn't crazy, suicidal, armed, or weird in any way. I knocked on Lee's door just to shoot the shit but he had already headed out for the restaurant where Vicky was a waitress and he tended bar.

My phone rang and I grabbed it. 'Andy?'

'Will? It's Josie.'

Shit. Should have checked the Caller ID.

She would just be in from work; Megan would be sacked out in the living-room watching TV. 'Hey, Jo,' I said. I figured a twenty- to twenty-three-minute window before Don was due back from his Assistant Mall Manager gig, give or take traffic.

'I've been worried about you,' Josie said. 'Didn't you get my messages?'

'After the gun range fiasco, I figured—'

'Understandable. You don't always like to hear things.' Silence. 'Remember that time we went out for lunch?' Josie asked. 'Me and you and Megan in the Snuggli?'

'Yeah.' Megan had been fourteen months. We'd gone for cheap Chinese at the Chicken and Egg Roll on Alabama, cautiously catching up over ginger beef. Me trying to hide the fact I'd gotten a rib broken in a stupid bar fight the week before. I had smiled a lot, but God it hurt to laugh.

Josie said, 'I knew that day we shouldn't have split up.'

Time passed in heartbeats.

'But by then I was with Don, and there was Megan, and it was too late,' Josie said sadly. 'You know? I would have been making the same mistake again.'

'Josie! Jesus. Megan's home. You shouldn't be . . .'

'Why should I have to do all the hard things?' Josie said. 'You grab my hand and depend on me to pull it away. And God knows I do. I've been a good wife,' she said bitterly.

'I know,' I said.

'Don got laid off.'

'What! I thought the mall was talking about promoting him.'

'They were. Decided to go with another guy and eliminate Don's position. August 31st is his last day.'

I tried to imagine Don getting called into the office of some pot-bellied balding manager and canned. Having to listen to the 'Company is restructuring' speech or the 'Frankly, we've been worried about your work performance' speech. Or my all-time favorite, the 'This is the hardest part of my job' speech, where you sit there thinking, If it's so hard on you, let's trade places and put *your* ass on the street, motherfucker.

'Damn, Josie.' I didn't know what to say. I wished I had gotten more sleep. 'What about your mortgage?'

'I don't know. I guess we'll be all right. I guess Don will find something. He better. I sure can't pay it on my own.'

'If you guys need space to, to strategize, Meg could crash over here for a few days.' I looked around at my grubby walls and the unmade mattress in the middle of my floor. Trying to figure out what could be cleaned and what ought to be burned.

'Don doesn't want you to see her any more. He wanted me to get a court order against you. He really lost it when I said I wouldn't do that.'

'What do you mean, he lost it?' More heartbeats passed. 'Did he yell at you in front of Megan?' Silence. 'Did he hit you?' That's how AJ died. Abusive boyfriend. I thought about the combat knife Don kept beside his table.

Once you start killing family, where's it going to stop?

'I've been calling you, DK, but you wouldn't answer my messages.'

'I'm sorry, Jo. I should have called.'

'It's not like we've lost the house yet,' Josie said. And then, 'We have a past, Will. You're always thinking about the future, about how nothing lasts. But the past is already in the books. It's forever. You can't pull yourself out of my life.'

'Hey, you threw me out, remember?'

'You could have fought it, Will! If you were going to fire a few bullets at Don, ten years ago would have been the time.

What was the point of waiting?' she said, deadpan. 'What's a girl supposed to make of that?'

'I wasn't shooting at—'

'I kept waiting for you to tell me our marriage was worth fighting for, Will. But you didn't. You were relieved,' Josie said bitterly. 'Just like you always are when the ax finally falls. God, you'd be in pig heaven at my house this week.'

'If there's anything—'

'I should go,' Josie said. 'Don will be getting home soon.' There was a catch in her voice. She was crying.

'Jo—'

She hung up.

I have somewhat against thee, because thou hast left thy first love.

I am twenty-one and Josie's ghost is haunting me. I see her everywhere. A cocked hip in the line at the bank, a strand of dirty blond hair seen from the back and I think it's her gassing up her car, or squeezing tomatoes at the market on Shepherd, or coming out of a movie at night. When it's hot, I remember the sweat stains creeping down her tank top. When it rains (and it rains a lot) the rush and patter pulls me into the backseat of her mom's Skylark, parked next to the Cactus Records on Alabama and us fucking under cover of downpour, Josie sitting on top of me, biting her lip to keep quiet, and the incredible lightning flash when I came, the thunder instant and so loud it set off car alarms everywhere around us and we couldn't stop laughing. Couldn't stop.

You love someone, they're in you like a fishhook. Can't just pull them out.

Long unsleeping nights I spent walking down Shepherd, Greenbriar, Alabama, Holcombe. So late my bootsteps were as loud as the traffic. Moonlight through the live-oak leaves, dark water muttering down in the bayous. And maybe Uncle Billy had already been there, barefoot in the foul water, waiting, but

I had passed by at just the wrong time.

Josie was my world. The year after she left me, the city windows were her eyes and the gutters ran with the sound of her crying when she thought I was asleep. She thought I was asleep but I heard it, little catches in her breath. Little trembles in the mattress.

I was lost for months. Couldn't find my way back from yesterday, from the nights I was out listening to bands when I should have been home, from the fight we had about how much the stupid bedroom lamp had cost. I let her make me so mad I grabbed her by the arms and shook her, hard: and something came down like steel shutters behind her eyes. I was trying to get my shit together, but every road was a ghost road; one wrong turn and I was back to the time we were making love and I found her crying under me. No worse feeling than that, unless maybe it's *Will, I want a divorce.*

Time is a dark air you can fall through. That's all being haunted is, really. The falling.

So you don't fucking scare me, Tom. I've been haunted before.

Norma Ferris was renting a bungalow in a nice residential neighborhood off Shepherd. She came to the door wearing a business suit and Naturalizer shoes. She was in her early forties, thick around the waist but not fat, with pretty auburn hair that probably came out of a bottle. She had the controlled manner of a woman who has been Coping Well for way too long. 'The place isn't very homey,' Norma said, opening the screen door to let me in. 'Molly and I just moved here last month.' The living-room was wooden floors, nice rental furniture, and a big aquarium full of worried-looking angelfish. 'Tea or coffee?'

'No thanks.' My blood was still fiercely buzzing with Gold Key and the sound of Josie's voice saying we should never have gotten divorced. I followed Norma into the kitchen. 'What did you want to be when you grew up?'

'Not alone.' Norma reached up in a cabinet for a box of tea,

135

Sleepy-Time Chamomile. As she spoke her voice was calm, but she kept her back to me so I couldn't see her face. 'When I was a little girl I had a big sister named Caroline. Her hair was curly where mine was straight. She would play horses with me and she put French braids in my hair. I worshipped her.' Norma reached for a packet of low-cal sweetener and dumped the white powder into her cup. 'Caroline died the day after Christmas, 1968. She was eight years old. I was five.'

No ghost yet that I could see: no chill tremble in the air, no flicker in my vision, as if I was looking through bottle glass. No cries or muttering. Nothing in black and white.

Like the living-room, the little kitchen felt empty and unlived-in. Norma grabbed a quart of milk from the fridge, which had nothing inside but eggs and margarine and a stick of wilting celery in the vegetable crisper. The sight of those bare refrigerator doors, without BBQ sauce or jam or pickles, seemed to make the loneliness in the little rental house even more crushing.

It's a funny thing, how sometimes you feel other people's pain worse than your own. I don't think I ever felt as lonely in the year after Josie left me as I felt right then for Norma Ferris, exiled into this cold new life. We're armored against our own troubles, I guess. We can't afford to give in to despair. Then you see someone else struggling, and it breaks your fucking heart.

'We moved in here two weeks ago,' Norma said. 'My husband isn't – well, that doesn't matter. Molly – that's my daughter – she didn't sleep well the first night. The family counselor told us that might happen. The next day I went to the mall across from my office for lunch, just like normal, but there was this toy store across from the food court. . . . This sounds pathetic. I must sound pathetic to you.'

'I think you're very brave,' I said. Thinking how Josie must have felt after she left me, living alone in a new apartment, knowing she was pregnant. Knowing that being alone was better than being with me.

The kettle hissed. Norma poured hot water into her little teapot. 'I got Molly a doll. It reminded me of my sister. Same dark ringlet hair. Blue eyes, like Caroline had. Molly liked her all right. Not too much. She's thinks she's too old to like dolls any more.'

She blew on her cup of tea and took a sip. 'Follow me.' We walked along a little hallway and then she opened the door into the only room in the house that truly felt lived in. A girl's room: two shelves of books, with a stable's worth of toy horses on top, and a small aquarium with a couple of feisty-looking goldfish swimming about. A wash of badminton racquets and rollerblades spilled out of Molly's closet, and a cheap silver tape player stood on the bedside table.

'That night I woke up with this feeling in my chest, as if something horrible was going to happen to Molly. Something unspeakable. I got up and came into her room.' Norma opened the closet door and took a shoe box down from a high shelf above the clothes. Her hands were shaking. 'The doll was in bed with Molly. Its eyes were flicking back and forth so hard you could hear them rattling. It was Caroline. And she *hated* me.' Norma's face was white. She handed me the shoe box. 'I don't understand why she hates me. I loved her so much.'

I took the lid off the box. There was a doll inside. It was a little girl about the length of my forearm, with dark curly hair and blue plastic eyes. It looked like a hundred other dolls. I touched its rubber cheek. I moved its arms and legs and brushed the curling brown hair back from its face. It stared up at me blankly.

'Nothing?' Norma said at last.

'I'm sorry,' I said.

'Is it possible she just isn't here right now?'

'I guess it's possible.'

'But you don't think so.' Norma nodded, as if talking to herself. 'No Caroline, then. So maybe I want her? I'm scared but I want her back, because I'm alone? But I don't understand why she hates me so much. Why I feel like she hates me.'

'The dead always hate us,' I said. I didn't even know what I meant by that, but Norma Ferris nodded as if I had said something profoundly true.

She sat heavily on the edge of her daughter's bed. 'So that will mean therapy. I made an appointment to see a psychiatrist last year, you know. He told me I was handling myself really well. That's what he said. I knew he would give me a prescription if I cried for him, but I couldn't make myself cry.' She looked at me. 'I never did want to be one of those girls who cries at every little thing.'

I took the lid to the shoe box and put it over the doll. 'Cheaper just to get rid of this.'

Norma shook her head. 'Molly needs me to hold it together. If that means a psychiatrist, that's what I have to do. I can't afford to be proud.'

'I think you're very brave,' I said again.

Norma took a deep breath, studying the goldfish in her daughter's tank. 'I should probably wait until my next performance review. I'm not doing my best work right now, and the market's soft. If I get laid off and have to switch carriers, I don't want depression on my record as a prior condition. They won't cover the cost of the meds. So it will have to be after my next review. September.' Norma glanced at her watch. 'I'd better write you that check.'

'Screw it. Keep your money.'

She pulled a checkbook out of her purse and rummaged for a pen. 'I knew what I was getting into when I called.'

Ten years ago I might have said something nice about her house, or the clothes she was wearing, to cover the miserable silence while she wrote the check. Now at least I knew to say, 'Molly has a good mom.'

We pretended she wasn't crying as she showed me to the door. I forgot to give her a receipt.

*

138

I had a long wait for the bus. When it finally came it was crowded and stuffy, but at least it was brightly lit with utterly unspooky fluorescent glare. A heavy woman who smelled of talcum powder lowered herself into the seat next to me, squeezing me against the side of the bus. I rode along, trying to find that blank Zombie state most bus riders have mastered, but instead I found myself trying to name all the songs off *Murmur* and getting stuck because I usually play the same two or three tracks. Then I thought about AJ, who was the first person to play R.E.M. for me. She never lived to hear *Monster*. She would have loved that album.

More people crowded onto the bus. Outside in the fading daylight, young thugs would be starting to prowl the streets in their dinged-up Firebirds and Camaros. I thought of them slowing down to pace Megan on her way back from soccer practice. *Hey, baby! Want a ride?*

Want a ride?

The bus got hotter and more crowded. As we lurched to a stop, I tried to slide my window open for a breath of fresh air. There were instructions in English, Spanish, and Vietnamese, but the window latch was broken and wouldn't move. My seatmate got up and pushed for the doors. Someone dropped into the spot where she had been. A gasping oven heat rolled over me, released from the folds of a beige raincoat. 'Hey, buddy,' Hanlon said. 'Long time no see.'

Once the dead find you, they're hard to shake. Your fear is like smoke in the air. They can smell it.

'Her name was Julie,' the dead salesman said. There were bags around his pale eyes. 'I met her in a bar in Düsseldorf. A bunch of Americans had gathered there to watch the Super Bowl.' My cousin smiled. 'Hey, Will. How's it hanging? How's your ex? Josie?' He grinned. 'Surprised I remembered her name? Tools of the trade, buddy. Tools of the trade. When you're in sales, you learn to remember names. Especially kids – people like that. Want to get on a client's good side, say something nice about his kid. Or like your niece, eh? Violetta. Nice name. Italian, isn't it?'

The fight drained out of me like blood.

'The point is, you gotta be likable. The day people don't like you any more, you're finished.' The chummy grin faded from Hanlon's face. 'You're finished.' He was all in black and white, of course. A patch of his forehead began to blacken and bubble, as if I were seeing an old movie and the film had begun to burn. The bus lurched into motion again, swinging out into traffic. 'Where was I?'

'Düsseldorf,' I said.

'Yeah! Right! Julie. So I met her in this bar. We got to talking, I told her about my business. She asked if I had an apartment in town. I said I was based out of Brussels. Turned out she was heading that way the next day. She said she was going to hitchhike. Hitchhike! Can you believe it? I told her she was crazy. Those Germans, I mean, they've been model citizens since we kicked the crap out of them in '45, I grant you, but don't fool yourself. There's some creepy guys there. No sense of right and wrong. I'm not really a Christian myself, but over in Europe . . .' Hanlon scratched at his neck, scraping a char-line under his ear. 'It's like they don't believe in anything.'

I tried shutting my eyes hard and biting my lips. He didn't disappear.

'I gave her a ride. Then she said she'd lost the address of the place where she was supposed to crash. I said she could stay at my apartment.' He grabbed my hand. 'Will, I never made the first move. I swear it. I wouldn't have touched her if she didn't want me to.' His fingers were like burning wires around my wrist.

'I believe you,' I hissed, trying to keep my voice low. The other passengers couldn't see him, of course.

Slowly Hanlon let go of my hand. My wrist was ugly red where he had touched it. 'She came to me in the middle of the night. Said she had a nightmare, and could she sleep in my bed for a while? Will, I was thirty-eight. She was twenty. Twenty years old, standing beside my bed in nothing but a tank top and a pair of panties. What would you have done?'

'Beaten her to death?'

'That—' Hanlon struggled to keep his temper. 'You don't know anything about that.'

I remembered the dead girl crawling out from under the sink in his garage. Her pale face bloated and bruised. Silk knotted around her wrists.

Hanlon's face softened. 'The next two months were the best days of my life. We used to go to this little café every morning and have apple strudels and coffee. She was so young, Will. Her dad was a tax accountant in Wheaton, Illinois. She was just a mixed-up kid. Full of opinions, but she didn't know a damn thing. Daddy sent her to Europe for a graduation present. She threw her return ticket in a trashcan in the Frankfurt airport. Phoned her parents every few months to let them know she was still alive.'

I imagined them at home and the phone call not coming, not coming, not coming.

'Then I got back one day early from a trip to Cologne. She had been using me, of course. Having young guys up to fuck her in my bed while I was on the road. Ran up some pretty good phone bills, too. Oldest story in the book. Hard to believe I could be that much of a sucker. But that's sales, you know? You have to like everybody.'

The lashes over Hanlon's left eye caught fire and crumpled like mothwings, leaving nothing but a thin coil of smoke. It was a struggle for me to breathe. I was panting and panting. I gasped for air. Heads turned to look at me, and I realized that two of them were in black and white. I panicked, staring around the bus. Half the people on it were dead.

'Well, it happens to the best of us, Kennedy. Women have us by the balls, and that's the truth.' The bus paused to spit out a couple of passengers under the glowing marquee of James'

Coney Island. Hanlon shook his head at the wickedness of the world. 'Say, did you ever figure out that Josie was screwing Don before you two split up?'

The bus lurched back into traffic.

'I see from your expression the answer is 'No'. This is what I'm talking about, Will. You think you have the balls to face the ugly truth head-on, but it's just a pose. In twelve years, did it never occur to you that while you were kicking around clubs until three o'clock in the morning, Josie was getting her needs satisfied?'

'You're lying.'

'He had a day job, Will. He had his shit together.'

I thought of Josie sitting across from me on the sand at Galveston Island. No way was she fucking Don already. No way.

'Christ, Kennedy, they got married less than a year after you separated. The divorce papers were hot off the Xerox, buddy.' He leaned closer to me, stinking of gasoline. 'Too bad you missed when you shot at him, Will. It would have saved a lot of trouble in the long run. Jealousy is an ugly thing, DK. It burns, doesn't it? Just the thought – the idea of your woman screwing around. That would get some guys pretty mad.'

I tried to look away but I couldn't.

'Say you had a disappointed guy,' Hanlon murmured. 'Just lost his job, fired by some jackass civilian. And then, let's imagine that this guy got it into his head that his wife was screwing around on him.'

My mouth went dry. 'Josie's been a good wife to Don. She put his name on the birth certificate, for Christ's sake. He's got no reason to think . . .' Except he knew she had come to see me in hospital, right? And maybe she had mentioned about me trying to hold her hand. And then Hanlon had made me shoot at him. And then Josie had refused to stop me from seeing Megan. How must that look to a guy like Don?

'And then,' Hanlon said softly, 'imagine if this man had a gun.'

'Don't. Please.'

'What was the name of that cousin of yours?' Hanlon asked. 'The one whose boyfriend shot her to death?'

'Leave Josie and Don out of this. This doesn't have anything to do with them,' I said. Begging.

'But Will, that's the fucking *penalty*, buddy. That's the price you pay for murdering me.' He grinned. 'This is where I get off.' He stood and made his way to the rear exit as the bus lurched to a stop. The doors chugged open. Hanlon paused in the stairwell, looking back at me. 'I'm going to kill them all, Will, just for loving you.'

CHAPTER NINE

Just after midnight on August 1, 1966 – Don would have been no more than a toddler – another blond ex-Marine, named Charlie Whitman, stopped by his mother's apartment building in Austin. She buzzed him in, and he took the stairs to her apartment. After they talked for a while he strangled her with a length of rubber tubing. Then he stabbed her in the chest with a large hunting knife. Whitman wrote out a confession and forged a note to the superintendent saying she was feeling ill and was not to be disturbed. He locked up the apartment and left, only to return in half an hour to retrieve a bottle of dexedrine, which he had been using to go without sleep for days at a time while struggling through a heavy load of classes at the University of Texas.

Charlie Whitman returned to his own home, where he pulled the covers off his sleeping wife, Kathy, and stabbed her five times. *I imagine it appears that I bruttaly kill both of my loved ones*, he wrote. *I was only trying to do a quick through job.* He then spent some hours going through his diaries, highlighting all the good things he had ever written about his wife.

Semper Fi. That's the Marine motto. 'Always faithful.'

The following morning, dressed in a maintenance man's blue overalls, Whitman rented a trailer and drove to downtown

Austin. He passed through the University of Texas gates and drove to the base of the University Tower, where he unloaded a dolly and his Marine footlocker. The footlocker contained an M-1 carbine, a 12-gauge shotgun, two Remington rifles (a .35 caliber and a 6mm with a 4x scope), a .357 Magnum Smith & Wesson revolver, a 9mm Luger, and a Galesi-Brescia pistol. Charlie took an elevator to the 27th floor, and then dragged the dolly and locker up three flights of steps to the 28th floor observation deck. There he clubbed the receptionist, Edna Townsley, in the back of the head with the butt of a rifle. He dragged her body behind a couch, where she would die some hours later. Then he took up position on the Texas Tower observation deck. He picked up the scoped Remington first.

It was 11:30 in the morning of August 1st. The temperature had climbed over ninety-five degrees.

Charlie's first target was Claire Wilson, an extremely pregnant eighteen-year-old girl. The bullet passed through her abdomen, fracturing her baby's skull. Her walking companion, Thomas Eckman, had just turned to ask her what was wrong when Whitman's next bullet went through his chest, killing him instantly. His body toppled over hers. Over the next ninety minutes, Charlie Whitman would kill fourteen people and injure dozens more.

Semper Fi.

Don could do that. Hanlon could make him.

While I was talking to Hanlon, the bus had passed the Astrodome and gone under 610, taking me outside the Loop. I waited three stops past the one where Hanlon had gotten off and then jumped out and started walking home with his gasoline stink still clinging to me. I was wide awake now, wired and walking fast. The neighborhood around me was working-class poor: body shops and gas stations, walk-up apartments, old black people and young Latinos. White guys with Gulf Coast

146

Angler's Association bumper stickers. Back fences made from cinderblocks, front yards with tire marks in the grass or a low-rider up on blocks. The kind of place nobody comes from, but a lot of people end up.

The kind of place Megan could be living in a year.

That's what Hanlon would be saying to Don in the middle of the night. *You're out of work with a mortgage to pay and a kid to raise. Not even your own kid, but something your wife caught from a toilet seat. How are you going to put her through school? Six months out of work, a neighborhood like this might be all you get for your years of service, soldier-boy. After they repo your car, you'll have nothing left but your guns, and then what, Don? Then what?*

Ghosts don't do things to you. Ghosts make you do unspeakable things to yourself.

Heading home, I stuck to the biggest streets I could find. There were more ghost roads than usual. These I hurried across, staring straight ahead. Houston was thick with the dead that night, old drunk Zombies in doorways or preaching on street corners, one Cobain chick fixing a rig for herself while staring up at a third-floor apartment. Suicide by smack, was my guess; hoping her body would be found in the doorway of some guy who had dumped or betrayed or just never noticed her. Look at me! Look at me! You'll be sorry. Why didn't you look at me? You'll see me this time, and you'll be sorry.

It was nearing twilight by the time I came up the west side of the Astrodome, past the peeler bars and liquor stores to the big Target on OST, the rush-hour traffic thinning at last. I found myself wondering if Uncle Billy was standing in the darkness of Braes Bayou, waiting for me by the black water.

I thought of Don's gun collection, spread out on the counter at the Pasadena Gun Center: the .357 Magnum and the short-nosed .44, the .22 target pistol and the .38 special and the 9mm Glock automatic, 'the best all-around handgun in America.'

Imagine if this man had a gun.

147

I walked the last few blocks along OST, past the Marine base where Don had probably been stationed years ago. I passed the Kroger's where he and I had both bought coffee and fried chicken. I turned up Cambridge. The dusk had deepened and the lights along my street had come on. Tinted amber and buried in live-oak leaves, they didn't shine so much as leak, dripping yellow light into the dim humid air. I remembered Josie visiting me in the hospital, the feel of her hand under mine. *Don wouldn't like me being here.* The shock of seeing her face gone dead, the color of wet cement.

That's the fucking penalty, buddy. I'm going to kill them all, Will, just for loving you.

I ran upstairs just long enough to get my jacket with the fishhooks, and then I caught a bus for Woodland.

It was full dark by the time I got to Josie's house. I stood on the sidewalk out front, trying to decide what to do. I didn't have a plan. I just needed to peek through a window and prove to myself that everything was okay. Probably no bad shit would actually be happening inside. The sick panic in my stomach would quiet down, and I would grab the next bus back home, feeling stupid but reassured.

A car rolled by, one of Don's neighbors. His headlights picked me up, and he began to slow. Like a spy in enemy territory, I started walking fast down the sidewalk, knowing I couldn't get caught loitering around Don's front yard. The car hesitated and then picked up speed. As soon as it turned the corner, I doubled back and snuck into Don and Josie's back yard. It was dark. Their sprinkler was running. The water caught me once as I made my way onto the back porch, but the night was warm and I didn't mind getting a little wet. I crept up to the kitchen window and peered in.

Once upon a time there had been a future with Josie and me in it together, but now she lived with Don in a suburban cookie-cutter house: linoleum counters faked to look like marble tile, and a magnetic calendar on the fridge with the name of their insurance agent in big letters at the top. The Josie I had taught to love Bauhaus and Tom Waits had ended up so ordinary, somehow; and I was even less than that. I was a ghost. All I could do was stare in at her from the wrong side of the glass.

Don and Josie were arguing. Megan pushed back her chair and slipped out, leaving her dinner half-eaten. Don was almost yelling; long rolling sentences. Anger danced over his face like firelight. Josie stared grimly back at him, bitter, not saying much. We used to fight the same way, me doing all the talking. Don stood up and threw his napkin on the table. I had a sudden image of him stalking out to the gun safe in the garage, coming back with the Glock 17 and making flowers on her shirt. One, two.

Very slowly, Josie turned black and white. First her skin went dead, color draining out of her like blood from a terrible wound. Then her eyes flickered like candles and went out. My first love.

And once Don left Josie slumped on the floor with two wet roses on her chest, he would come for Megan. That's what Hanlon would want him to do. *Imagine if this man had a gun.*

I couldn't let that happen, so I knocked on the door.

Everybody froze. Don saw me there on his back porch. Knew I'd heard them fighting. Knew I had been spying. He jerked the door open and started mouthing off. Josie stared at me in shock, but what I noticed was the smell of her tuna casserole. We used to live on that fucking casserole, back when we were nineteen. Five dollars a day, that's what we budgeted for food. Noodle soups, oatmeal, lentil curry, peanut butter, tuna casserole: no-name brand tuna bought by the case from a warehouse store and broad egg noodles and generic cream of mushroom soup. She probably used Campbell's these days, I thought. The smell of that casserole in the air was like having to watch them fuck.

'Tuna casserole,' I said. 'Man, I haven't had that in years.'

'*Jesus*,' Josie said. She was still black and white. 'This is not a good time, Will.'

'Josie, take Megan upstairs.' Don started to roll up his sleeves. His forearms looked as thick as my legs. 'Will and me need to talk.'

Well, that was one way to break up a domestic tiff. If it came to fighting, I figured Don had me by about six inches and seventy pounds, but to tell the truth, I was feeling better than I had in a while. My head was clearing up fast. There's something wonderfully focusing about the immediate prospect of getting your ass handed to you. At least this time, I wasn't busy talking to a ghost while Don beat the shit out of me.

'You want to dance?' I said.

'You bet,' Don said. 'I'm a hell of a dancer.'

'Josie and Meg? Are you okay?' I kept my eyes on the top button of Don's shirt. When you first start fighting, you tend to get caught looking at guys' hands. The chest gives you a truer read on when they're going to break for you. I was thinking Don sure was a big guy. Your responsible gambler would probably give the points and take the favorite. Either I was going to win this fight dirty in the first fifteen seconds or get the crap kicked out of me.

'Knock it off, both of you,' Josie said.

'Hold on, honey,' Don said. 'This will only take a—'

I kicked the door at him as hard as I could, knocking him into the dinner table. Then I jumped for him. A dish of mashed potatoes went over and smashed on the floor, followed by a salad in a loud metal bowl. Little frightened cherry tomatoes scurried around on the dining-room linoleum.

'Eat shit, you sonofab— *ULK!*'

Don braced against the table and shot his foot out in some kind of fancy karate kick he must have learned in the Marines. It smacked me like a cinderblock in the chest. I went flying into the screen door, fell backward off the stoop and rolled awkwardly down into their back yard. It was pretty wet down there, thanks to the fucking sprinkler. It was one of those ones that attaches to a hose and makes a slow rainbow of water go back and forth across the lawn. Soggy grass squelched under my hands.

Don stopped to examine a bulge where the mesh in his screen door was all out of shape. 'I just fixed this damn screen, Will. After I kick your ass until your hair falls out, I am going to call a lawyer and I am going to put a restraining order on you so the next time I catch you within a mile of my house, or my wife, or my daughter, the cops are going to throw your ass in jail.'

'A lawyer?' I said. 'What are you going to pay him with? USMC blow job? Or had you forgotten you're out of work?'

Don's face twitched. 'Who told you that?' He raised his voice, ugly with anger. 'Who fucking told him about that?'

Josie grabbed his arm. 'Don, leave it alone.'

'I don't feel like leaving it alone. You feel like leaving it alone, Will?'

'Me neither.' The waterline from the sprinkler passed over me, pattering on my leather jacket. Water ran down my face, and I found I was grinning. '*Semper Fi*, big guy.'

'There, see?' Don jerked his arm away from Josie. 'So why don't you get the hell back inside and let me and Will talk this over?'

My heart was a trip-hammer. Got to get in close, got to clinch. Fucker's jab would kill me if we stayed at range. Don stepped onto the grass and we circled in the dim back yard. Got to get him to grab me, get some fishhooks in those big meaty paws –

I tripped over the hose. I stumbled in the wet grass, got my balance, turned around and blocked Don's fist neatly with my face. My legs went all scrambly underneath me and I would have fallen over, but he held me up for an extra second with a left to the stomach. The next right was like being clubbed with a brick. My face hit the wet lawn and I tried to get up, coughing grass and snot and blood out of my nose. 'Come on, you pussy,' I said thickly. Just grab the jacket, motherfucker. Don reached down. That's it, shit-for-brains, get a good handful –

'Watch out!' Josie yelled. 'Don't touch the jacket!'

Don backed off.

The sprinkler sprayed up into my bloody face. '*Jesus*, Josie,' I said. 'Who the fuck's side are you on, anyway?'

'Oh yeah – the fishhooks,' Don said. 'I forgot about that.' Then he kicked me in the head.

I grabbed his foot, but he just stood on my hands so I couldn't cover myself while he bent over to pop me in the face. I twisted onto my front and wiggled away. He kicked me in the thigh as hard as he could with his shiny black assistant mall manager's shoes. I swore and kept crawling and he kicked me again, taking his time, and then I felt the garden hose under my hands. I made like I was about to lunge away. Don leaned down toward me and I jerked around with the hose and hit his face as hard as I could with the sprinkler.

Don stood dazed and swaying, blinking blood out of his eyes. 'Holy shit,' he said.

I spat out some blood. 'No *cussing*, motherfucker.'

Josie gasped. 'Don! Oh my God. Are you okay?' she said, with such obvious concern that I had to hit him in the face with the sprinkler again. This time he dropped.

We lay side by side in the wet lawn, curled up and twitching. The stupid-ass sprinkler didn't know any better than to keep trying to water us, like two big ugly shrubs. There was this horrible gurgling sound, as if Don was breathing through a mouthful of blood and broken teeth, except then I realized the sound was coming from me.

Megan marched into the yard holding a cordless phone. 'I'm calling 911,' she said.

Don and I yelled, 'No!' at the exact same time.

I heaved myself up to my feet. My right leg buckled, but I caught myself and steadied up. In a strange way, I felt more clear-headed than I had all day, as if Hanlon had been in me like a drug, and Don had smacked me sober. I spat out some more blood. Josie ran down into the yard and knelt next to her husband. She was still black and white. 'Gonna be okay?' I asked. My lips were fattening up and it was hard to talk. She ignored me.

'We'll be just *fine*,' Megan said sarcastically. Don was trying to sit up. 'I think you better go.'

Twenty minutes later I was swaying heavily inside a phone booth in front of the Woodland Public Library, trying to find exact change. I pulled a handful of coins out of my pocket and blinked at them through the blood that kept trickling into my eyes. A couple of nickels, a dime, a jingle of pennies. Blink, blink. A fat drop of blood dripped onto another dime, splashing over Franklin D. Roosevelt. I let my bruised and swollen face rest against the Plexiglas for a moment, then fed a random selection of coins into the payphone and called Lee. He picked up in two rings. 'Gulf Coast Bail Bonds. If you've got the dime, why do the time?' He thinks this puts off phone solicitors.

'Good evening, Mr. Bonds. I'm calling on behalf of the Sorry Motherfuckers tonight. Can I assume you will be making your' – I paused to swallow some blood –'usual donation?'

'Will?'

'Mostly.'

'You sound funny. You have the chit again, don't you? Are you drunk?'

'No, I'm okay. It's just my mouth is swollen and I think maybe I broke my nose.'

Pause. 'You want to *get* drunk?'

'Good plan.'

I heard a woman's voice in the background. 'He broke his nose,' Lee said. 'Vicky wants to know how you broke your nose.'

'Fell down.'

'Into someone's fist, by any chance?'

'Mm.' Your classic Caped Crusader deals with his sidekicks on a strictly need-to-know basis. It makes them less attractive prey for scheming supervillains. I noticed that the spot where I had let my face rest against the Plexiglas was smeared with blood. Gross. 'How about a ride?' I said.

'How about an ambulance?'

Sure. Like I had a few thousand more dollars lying around. 'I don't feel emotionally ready to go back to hospital. People take you for granted if they see you all the time. I gotta limit my exposure. Celebrity, man. Look at Spiderman.'

'Superman did interviews, I think.'

'Who's cooler, Superman or Spidey?'

'Good point. Where are you?'

'In a pay phone outside the Woodland Public Library.'

'Woodland?'

'It's not what you're thinking,' I said.

'*Will.*' Okay, it was exactly what he was thinking. 'We'll be there in thirty minutes,' Lee said. 'Forty-five if we get pulled over.'

'However much I'm paying you, double it.'

'Woo hoo.' Lee hung up.

Having successfully summoned my sidekick, I slid to the bottom of the pay-phone booth for a little nap. My Spidey-sense was aching like anything.

A flicker of movement caught my eye. AJ was in the glass, looking out at me. She hid her face behind her hands, and then slowly split her fingers and peeked out at me, ruefully taking in my swollen knuckles and bloody face. 'I fell down,' I said. She rolled her eyes. 'Hard,' I said.

AJ laughed. She held out one hand, pressing her palm flat against the glass of the phone booth. I uncurled my aching fingers and did the same. The glass between our hands was cold, cold. I felt cool water spill down my arm and in through the bullet hole in my chest. AJ looked at me with love in her eyes. For the first time in years, I felt forgiven.

*

The first time I had sex was after AJ's funeral. Josie and I had stayed up long past midnight, talking over milkshakes at the Denny's. It had been an open-casket viewing, AJ looking nothing like herself in a white prom dress, hands crossed on her chest. I was humming like a live wire and Josie grounded me. Two o'clock that morning found us tangled together, all skin and elbows, trying to be quiet, lying in her bed at home. Her dad was in jail at the time. Her mom had zonked out with her usual nightcap, a screwdriver and a joint.

Sixteen years ago. Exactly half my life.

Ten minutes later Lee drove up in a classic Texas car, a Mercury Marquis he'd bought from his mom when she got tired of it. People make fun of Texans for driving big cars, and it's true we like lots of shock absorbers and upholstery softer than a fat woman's ass, but in a state where Grandma will routinely make a six-hundred-mile round trip to drop in on family for the weekend, the rolling sofa is a perfectly sensible choice of vehicle. The Marquis' interior was plush burgundy – emphasis on plush. I lowered my aching body into the backseat, trying not to bleed on the upholstery while Vicky mothered me. She and Lee had come equipped with Tylenol and a Kroger's bag full of ice-cubes and a box of Winnie-the-Pooh bandages raided from my bathroom. Also, two little airplane bottles of tequila. I dry-swallowed three Extra-Strength Tylenols and tried to sit still while Vicky clucked and fussed over me.

I like the Mexican girl, AJ said. She was in the passenger side window. When she laughed, the corners of her eyes crinkled up. In black and white, I could see every freckle on her pale face, and the tiny silky hairs on her cheek, and the seams of her T-shirt.

'Pay attention!' Vicky frowned, leaning over the seat back to dab at my cuts with the tequila, which stung and made me smell like a bum. She closed up the cuts on my forehead with two Eeyore Band-Aids and a butterfly-shaped Piglet. When she was done I slumped back into my seat, holding a bag of ice gingerly to my bruised face.

Lee mentioned that he was still all excited at the idea of running me into the Emergency Room at Methodist, but I managed to convince him I had no major injuries. 'You don't want to go to a hospital,' Vicky said darkly. 'They're full of sick people. Last place you want to go if you can help it. They got drug-resistant TB, they got everything in there. Boy, you wouldn't catch me in a hospital.'

'Vicky had a year and a half of nursing school,' Lee explained. 'You hungry? I'm hungry,' he said. 'Man, you are lucky I had the night off.'

'Hospital's the *last* place you want to be, 'specially if you're sick. You want to be at home, let some nice girl take care of you, Will.'

In the window, AJ smiled at me, so close we could have kissed. *Be thou faithful unto death*, she said, *and I will give thee a crown of life*.

They took me to a Thai restaurant Lee liked, the Nit Noi in Rice Village. I hobbled across the parking lot, wondering if maybe I did have some broken bones after all. AJ was waiting for me in the smoked-glass door. Age before beauty, she said, sliding along the glass as I pushed the door open. And pearls before swine. She laughed and disappeared inside, a glimpse of bloody halter-top flickering across the cutlery and bending around glasses of ice water.

A tall, sour-faced Thai waiter came to take our orders. He was one of those men whose life hadn't worked out. You could tell he was working in his rich cousin's restaurant against his will and resenting every minute of it. His high forehead was marked with liver spots, sallow skin stretched tight so you could see the ridge of his eyebrows and the bones of his skull. 'What you want?' he asked, with the air of a man expecting to be disappointed. I didn't feel like doing anything with my teeth as risky as chewing, so I ordered the Hot and Sour Soup and a Dr Pepper. The waiter turned to Lee and Vicky, and I rooted surreptitiously in my wallet, thinking I might not have enough money to cover my dinner.

'Dude,' Lee said, 'there's nobody there.'

I looked back at the waiter. Shit. He was black and white, obviously dead, but somehow I hadn't stopped to think about it. 'Sorry,' I said.

Lee waved it off. 'Hey, it could happen to anyone.'

The dead waiter sniffed. 'You want wait, okay with me,' he said disdainfully. 'You wait for Trin, it be awhile.'

Our waitress showed up – the live one – trotting out from the kitchen and walking straight through her dead uncle to take our orders. He glowered down at her rump, which was currently taking up the space where his left thigh should have been, and then moved irritably out of the way. She was an absolute hottie, maybe twenty-two, with round cheeks and laughing eyes. Her shirt ended just above the waist of her black work pants, so I could catch a glimpse of her flank when she leaned over the table to refill Lee's water. Her breasts would just cup nicely in your hand. I would have given anything to kiss her.

AJ whispered, Isn't she beautiful?

'My name's Trin, and I'll be your server today.' Her accent pure Gulf Coast Texan.

I repeated my order. Lee went for the Chicken with Lemon Grass and Basil. 'How's your Masman curry?' Vicky asked.

The old dead waiter wrinkled his nose.

'Great!' Trin said. 'That's my favorite.'

Uncle made a gagging face.

'Bueno,' Vicky said. 'I'll have that and a Thai Ice Tea.'

Trin bounced off with our order. The dead man watched her go. 'Hope you got no hurry for dinner,' he said. A busboy zipped by, walking a platter of dirty dishes through the old man's head. He pursed his mouth, sighed, and followed Trin through the door into the kitchen.

Around us, people talked and ate, most of them living, a couple of them dead. Vicki made me drink lots of water, and lectured me about getting into fights, and complained about the rowdy boyfriend she'd been going out with before she met Lee. I sipped my soup, wincing at the sting of vinegar and hot sauce on the cuts inside my mouth. I prodded my wiggly teeth gently with my tongue. In my experience, loose teeth will usually recover (if they aren't actually broken), but you have to treat them gently for a few days and let your gums get their confidence back.

'I figure we've earned at least a play-by-play description of you getting your ass kicked,' Lee said, twirling some noodles around his fork. I gave them a ghost-free version of the story up to the part where Don kicked me out the back door.

Lee winced. 'Gotta watch those supervillains, dude. Why didn't you get him with the old fishhooks?'

'Josie warned him.'

'Now, that's cold. And she used to like you, too.'

Vicky shook her head when I told them about dropping Don with the sprinkler. Lee whooped and we went high five/low five, which hurt my shoulder but was worth it. I sipped another mouthful of soup, letting the clink and chatter of a busy night at the Nit Noi wash over me. 'You know, I've had the shit kicked out of me before—'

'Now there's a surprise,' Vicky said.

'—But I have to say, I'm enjoying this time more than most.'

Lee poured another couple of fingers of Sapporo into my glass. 'Because I'm buying the dinner?'

'Because I normally don't have anyone to dust me off afterward. So, um, thanks.'

Vicky laughed. 'Let's just bond over beers next time.' She paused to lick a splotch of curry off the side of her mouth with her narrow pink tongue. A sudden wave of hopeless, despairing jealousy rolled over me. I wanted a pretty Mexican girlfriend of my own so badly I couldn't breathe. Like if I could never lift up a heavy ponytail of sleek black hair and kiss a woman on the neck, my life was a waste of fucking oxygen. I might as well be black and white.

These bullets of loneliness used to get me all the time, the first six months after Josie left me. You just learn to let the feeling roll by you, like you're standing in the Gulf surf and a wave goes by over your head; just hold your breath and wait, wait, wait until you can breathe again.

I sat there looking like a damn fool, staring blindly at the corner of Vicky's mouth while the dinner crowd buzzed and clattered around us.

Hey, DK. AJ was watching me from the curving side of the water pitcher on our table. The curve made a hideous distortion of her face. I'm always here, she said.

'Will?' Lee said.

I squeezed my eyes shut. 'Sorry. Headache.' Also toothache, leg ache, face ache. Heartache.

I pulled my shit together. You can't make a revolution with silk gloves. You can't go crying over a buddy's girl.

True to his word, the dead waiter was always back at our table before Trin. When she forgot the day's dessert special, he added it acidly, rolling his eyes: Mango and Sticky Rice with Sankhaya Custard.

Then dinner was over and it was time to go. Lee and Vicky got up to use the bathroom. The dead waiter was weaving busily between tables, doing his surly best to avoid bumping into people who showed him no such consideration. I bummed a pack of matches from the hostess, paper ones with the restaurant logo on the outside. I pulled a dollar bill out of my wallet and rolled it up like a cigarette. I caught the dead waiter's eye. When he came over to the table, I set the bill on fire in the middle of my plate.

That's good, AJ said.

The bill caught quickly, unrolling and burning with clear pale flame. It had a different smell from regular paper burning

– a businesslike chemical tang, like dry-cleaning. It didn't crumble into ash; mostly the fire passed over, leaving a gray and flimsy shadow version of the dollar behind. I could still read 'n God we tr' above the afterimage of the pyramid. At the charred black edge of the bill, thin emberlines still gleamed and glimmered. The money made a quiet, precise sound as it burned, a steady crack and rustle.

I looked up at the dead Thai waiter. 'Tip,' I said.

His mouth gave way to a tight smile. He reached forward and held his hand over the bill. Grey streamers of smoke curled and twisted around his fingers.

A middle-aged black woman leaned over from the next table. 'Excuse me, young man,' she said disapprovingly. 'But this is a *non-smoking* section.'

Lee and Vicky took me home.

Just after my sixteenth birthday, I filched enough money out of my dad's wallet to buy two tickets to see The Gun Club live. The ticket was for Anita, this Tex-Mex girl I dated before Josie. With the benefit of hindsight I can see Anita was just killing time with me, waiting for a real guy to come along, but I was crushed when she dumped me for the school meth dealer. I went to the gig anyway, scalped the other ticket in line for five bucks more than I had paid for it, and thrashed my way through a set that would turn out to be one of the hottest Gun Club bootlegs of all time.

Afterwards I turned the wrong way trying to get out of the club, found myself talking to their front man, and ended up going for drinks with the band. A few years later Jeffrey Lee Pierce would die of a brain hemorrhage after destroying himself in the approved rock-star manner, but at the time he seemed like the best kind of drunk, funny and charming, and he was so interested in what I had to say about the band's music that he bought me a round. Nobody even asked to see my ID. By four o'clock that morning I was at somebody's apartment getting a discreet handjob from a mischievous blonde in leopard-skin pants who was laughing and smoking at the same time. She had a voice like velvet tearing and her fingers were soft and warm.

Three hours later I was walking home along a drainage culvert watching the sun rise, and this incredible sense of peace descended on me, because I was small and the world was big: and I felt in my heart that everyone, everywhere, could be forgiven.

Lee and Vicky stopped on the way home to pick me up an economy-sized bottle of ibuprofen. My whole body had started to stiffen while we were sitting in the restaurant, especially the big bruises on my legs. My face was aching, swollen and hot. Naturally, Parkwood hadn't gotten around to fixing the A/C yet. Looked to be another bad night for sleeping. Lee and Vicky helped me hobble up to my door and said good-night. I shuffled into my bathroom, fighting with the childproof cap on the bottle of painkillers. I nearly gave up, but I didn't want to go 0–2 in my bouts for the night, so I finally battered the fucker into submission.

AJ was waiting for me in the bathroom mirror. Hey DK, she said.

'Are you here because of Uncle Billy?' I asked. 'Did he help you find me?'

No, no, no, Mr. Wolf. She smiled at me over the tops of her glasses, the sly grin I remembered from when she was wearing tube tops and smoking grass and dissing President Reagan.

'Billy doesn't approve of you,' I said.

Take us the foxes, the little foxes, that spoil the vines, AJ said, wetting her lips: *for our vines have tender grapes.*

That used to be her favorite Bible verse, the one that would come out when she was tipsy or starting to get high, and about to do something Deer Park would disapprove of.

The bloodstains on her halter-top still looked damp. Her smile faded. Don't stare, she said.

161

'Sorry.'

Let's play a game, DK.

'Like what?'

You choose. Something we used to play.

It was stinking hot in my apartment. I ran a little more water in the bathroom sink and splashed my face to cool down. Maybe it was a bad idea to notice AJ. Maybe I should just pretend she wasn't there. But my body hurt, and it was hot. I wasn't going to be able to sleep worth shit for the second night in a row, and I didn't want to spend the long dark hours alone. 'I guess tag is out,' I said. AJ laughed.

I shuffled back to the fridge and grabbed a bottle of Dos Equis. I turned on a lamp in the living-room, so the whole room was dimly reflected in the window. AJ was there at once.

Hide-and-seek?

'Okay,' I said.

You're it.

She vanished. I moved things around in the living-room – chair, mattress, speakers – watching the reflection in the window to see if she was hiding behind any of them. I ran a little water in the sink to look for her face. Warmer, she said. I lowered myself, creaking and wincing, to the kitchen floor, and found her grinning at me from the glass window in the oven door.

'Why do I only see your reflection?'

She smiled. Want to go again?

'You bet.' It was nice not to be alone.

The second time I found her looking up at me from the shiny surface of the CD in my CD player. The third time it took forever to find her in the surface of a little shaving mirror I had forgotten about and stuffed in a bathroom drawer. I hobbled back into the living-room and put on an ancient Roxy Music album I knew she liked and told her I was too tired to play hide-and-seek any more.

She hummed along with Brian Ferry. Truth or dare, she said.

'Okay. But I go first this time.'

Okay.

'Were you the one that told Tom Hanlon about me?'

She met my eyes reluctantly.

'Not great at keeping secrets, were you?'

Her fingers settled on the bloody fabric of her shirt. I'm better at it now, she said.

I drank some beer, wishing I felt sleepy. Tired, yes. I was exhausted and hot and hurting. But sleepy, no. I thought of Hanlon again, lying awake night after night, listening for the girl he had killed. I looked at my room, reflected in the window. A ghost version of me lying on a half-real mattress on the floor, AJ crouching next to me, looking through my CDs. *Avalon* playing softly in the background. 'Your turn,' I said.

She abandoned my collection, crawled back across the mattress on all fours and settled down beside me. In the window you could see the mattress give under her, so close her jeans nearly brushed my hip, but beside me the air was empty and cold.

Truth or dare, DK. What did you want to be when you grew up?

That caught me off guard. When I was a kid I guess there were things I thought about sometimes – songwriter, late-night DJ, paleontologist – but the truth is, I never believed in any of them, not for a moment. Couldn't imagine growing up, really. World too full of people already, living and dead. 'I don't know,' I said.

That's a dare.

'No, really, I just can't think of anything.'

AJ scoffed.

'Take another question.'

She rolled her eyes.

She curled up, thinking, with her arms around her knees, hugging them to her bloody chest. It was nice to have company, even if it was only in the window.

Truth or dare, Will.

'Bring it.'

Who was your first love?

She put her head on her knees, smiling at me through her bangs. In black and white her smooth young shoulders were dove gray, as were the ankles below her jeans. She was wearing white canvas sneakers with no socks. AJ never went barefoot, on account of having those toes fused together. Even in the pool she always wore flippers, except one day one of the boy cousins which might have been me pulled off one of those flippers and that was the last time I saw her go swimming.

Who was your first love?

I looked away from the window. 'Dare,' I said.

Silence.

'What's the dare?'

I'll think of something, she said.

Three hours of sleep again, ended by a pair of stupid mockingbirds who had apparently never seen a sunrise before and got extremely excited by the spectacle. I felt like I'd been beaten with a tire iron. My head was throbbing and my faced ached and my eyelids were so gummy I had to stick my fingers in them and rub them around before I could get them to open. The first thing I saw was my legs, which were bruised like a pair of old bananas. The whole experience was like waking up with a stupendous hangover, only without the good parts.

AJ was standing in the window with her back to me, looking at the day.

'My women are usually gone by the time I wake up.'

She glanced back over her shoulder at me, amused. Not me, she said.

She kept her promise. When I woke she was waiting in the window. When I went outside I could see her slip across the windshields of parked cars, keeping pace with me. I went over to the Kroger's once and she walked the aisles beside me. She was sly and funny, like I remembered, and grave too, and it hurt to be around her, and she was beautiful. It reminded me of being with Josie. How nice it was to wake up and have someone there beside you. I was tired of being alone.

A day and a night passed. My body hurt. I kept waiting for Josie to call, or Don, or their lawyer, telling me I wasn't allowed to see Megan again, but time seemed suspended somehow, and it was two days before my phone rang.

You should get that, AJ said.

'What?'

She grinned. Good news, she said.

I picked up the phone. A flood of happy Spanglish burbled out of the receiver. It was Vicky's real-estate cousin, Johnson Del Grande. 'It's the power of positive thinking, *todos*! Last time we talked, for one hour I felt terrible, the worst. And then – you know what I did? Can you guess?'

Mystified, I shook my head, which usually isn't very helpful over the phone, but Del Grande wasn't waiting for me anyway. 'I phoned an ad into the *Houston Press,* that's what. *For Sale: Genuine Haunted House!* – certified by famous local expert, William Kennedy, as seen in the *Houston Chronicle*!'

'Omigod.'

'The *Press* comes out every Thursday morning, yes? You know how many showings I had booked by lunchtime? Eleven. Eleven showings! *Más gente* calling all the time. Not one, not one of them my usual customers. *Todos nuevos.* A whole new clientele.'

'You're kidding,' I said. AJ was grinning at me from the window.

'Now, for you I have a plan. In real estate we hear these things. *Casas frecuentadas. Casas maldecidas.* Ghosts in the insulation. It's always a headache. *Pero ahora*, now, when I hear such a thing, we will go over, you and me. *Si es verdad*, you tell me the house is haunted, I make myself the listing agent.'

'How?'

He laughed. 'You leave that part to me. Every house, you see, it will be a Will Kennedy *guaranteed* haunted house!'

'Wait a second, now—'

'Of course, for this exclusive endorsement, I will give you half a point on the asking price.'

'But I never said—'

'Okay, okay, on the purchase price.'

I wondered what 'half a point' meant. 'I don't—'

'Okay! Okay! One point! *Madre de Dios*, you want to ruin me? On that place we saw two days ago, that's four thousand dollars for twenty minutes work! Isn't that enough?' he said beseechingly.

In the long silence that followed, I worked out that whatever a 'point' was, you could buy a shitload of noodle soups with one. 'Deal,' I said faintly.

'*Bueno*! I will send you a check by the end of the day, four thousand dollars against the sale of the first house. But this is an exclusive, okay? Just you and me.'

'Exclusive,' I said dutifully.

When Del Grande signed off, his voice was popping with glee.

Megan called. 'Hey,' she said.

'Hey yourself.' I could hear the buzz and murmur of kids around her. Calling from school again. 'You okay?'

'Nobody kicked the crap out of *me*.'

'Good point.' I took a deep breath, which hurt. 'Listen, are they talking about not letting me see you?'

'Yeah.'

Fuck.

'Nothing's settled yet,' Megan said. 'Dad thinks you should be locked up. Mom says you could just as easily press charges against him.'

'They fighting?' Silence. 'Sorry. None of my business,' I said.

Which was a lie, because I had loved Josie once and Tom Hanlon was working on Don and I knew it and it was my fault: but obviously I wasn't going to say any of that to Meg.

'So me and Trish and Fonda were thinking of going to Six Flags this Saturday,' Meg said blandly. 'I already cleared it with Mom and Dad. They're gonna use the time to argue about money and throwing you in jail. Want to come?'

'Don't you think you'd have more fun with your pals?'

'Haven't seen you in a few Sundays. And Trish . . .' Carefully. 'Sometimes they aren't totally reliable. Like, sometimes they just don't show up when you think they will.'

You're not getting it, AJ said, looking at me from my living-room window.

Oh. The light dawned. 'These buddies of yours. Are they the kind of teenagers who would, like, lie to their parents about where they were? Cover up for each other? Stuff like that?'

'Kids these days,' Megan said. 'It's scary.'

Trish and Fonda had already disappeared into Six Flags before I got there. They had been fully briefed, according to Megan, on what they were to say should any parents call. Meanwhile, we painted Six Flags red, Megan and AJ and me, courtesy of Norma Ferris's thousand dollars. I had meant to start paying off my hospital bill with it, but . . . what the fuck.

It was a fabulous day. The weather had cooled a fraction and the air had dried out a little too. Don was at work all day and nobody had to worry about him. It had been days since I had seen any sign of Hanlon. Best of all, my kid still liked me.

We started on the big roller coaster, the Serial Thriller™. About the time we got to the first awesome peak, I remembered that roller coasters scare the pee out of me. Megan shrieked with glee as we started the terrifying plunge down. Personally, I could barely breathe. I just sat there gripping the rail so hard I thought my fingerbones would snap. Finally the little car rolled to a stop at the end of the ride and Megan bounced out.

It was all I could do to keep my knees from buckling as I staggered across the platform after her. 'Awesome!' she crowed.

'Awesome,' I said. I licked my lips. 'Let's do it again.'

'All *right*!'

We did the Thriller again, and the Texas Tornado, and the
230-foot Dungeon Drop. What the hell kind of engineer wakes
up one morning thinking to himself, You know what I bet
would be fun? Falling off a twenty-story building! I found it
helped to scream. A lot.

By eleven o'clock, the temperature had climbed into the
mid-nineties. AJ and Megan both wanted to ride the water
slides. We climbed slowly toward the top of the Tidal Wave™
and paused, teetering at the top of the park. I dangled my hand
in the water sluicing around us. Bright water-drops were scattered in Megan's hair like wet sunlight. Our seats began to tip
forward. Lying like a drowned girl under the water next to us,
AJ reached up and brushed my fingertips with hers. Imagine
how beautiful this would be, she said, if you knew you were seeing it for the last time.

We plunged toward the concrete far below. Faces shot out of
the cement toward us and then disappeared with a huge smack
and splash of spray and I was drenched and Megan was laughing and I had money in my pocket and I was laughing too.

I bought Megan a milkshake with lunch, and I bought her
a Republic of Texas T-shirt. Megan wanted a pair of cool
purple sunglasses, but I balked. She put her hands on her hips.
'We read this book for English class and the girl's parents get
divorced and they get into this competition to, like, buy her
love.'

'Your point being?'

'Try harder!'

I bought the sunglasses. When Megan put them on, AJ was
waiting for me in the dark round lenses.

Megan was supposed to meet Trish and Fonda at 2:30 and
get a ride home from Fonda's mom. She made us stop and buy

balloons on our way out: a big Tigger-shaped one for her, and an Eeyore-shaped one for me. 'We'll each write down a wish and tie it to the ribbon and let the balloon go, and our wishes will come true.' She made it sound very scientific.

We strolled out the exit to the parking lot and stood sweating in the smoggy Houston air. Megan took the little pen out of the Swiss Army knife I had given her on her eleventh birthday. I got some napkins to write our wishes on. I tried to think what I would wish for, but my mind was blank.

Nothing, AJ said. Nothing could be more perfect than this.

Meg finished and handed me the pen. My hand shook. I pretended to scribble something on the back of another napkin. Then I rolled it up, still blank, and tied it to my ribbon.

Megan cut the weights off our balloons. 'One, two, three, GO!' she said, and we let go. Up they went, Eeyore and Tigger, faster than I had expected, carried on the thermals rising off the hot asphalt. About a hundred feet up the balloons began to drift apart, bumped by little flukes of wind, still speeding into the sky. We stood there for a long time in the parking lot at Six Flags, watching our wishes getting higher and smaller, higher and smaller, hard to see against the bright sky.

Brief bright glitters, untouchably high. And then they were gone.

After I got home, I went walking along Braes Bayou. The afternoon clouds had thickened and the wind had picked up, restless and uneasy. The bayou was running faster than usual over its concrete bed. Big mottled catfish hung in the stream, waiting for whatever the current would bring. AJ's reflection paced me in the dark water.

'Why did your boyfriend kill you?' I asked. 'What did you do?'

That was a long time ago.

'I'm not saying it was right. But you don't kill someone for nothing,' I said. 'There must have been a reason.'

I turned off the asphalt walkway and crouched down beside the bayou. The warm dishwater smell of it filled me up. I thought about how the sound of burning and the sound of running water are almost the same. I stretched my hands over the stream as if reaching for AJ's reflection. My fingers hung just at the surface of the water. One by one, the long dark bodies of catfish came unstuck from where they were hovering, slipped and drifted down to me. Blind and gaping they jostled under my hands. Unclean. I felt the wet trailing touch of whiskers. Bump. Bump. The gurgle of water.

'You must have done something to him,' I said.

The phone was ringing when we got back to the apartment. 'Will! Guess what!'

It was Josie.

My stupid heart banged away inside my chest. 'What is it?' I said. 'What has Don done? Are you okay?'

Josie laughed. 'Nothing, it's fine. Everything's fine. But we're moving. Not just changing houses, we're leaving Houston.' I could hear a TV playing in the background. Megan watching *The Simpsons*. My kid.

'This buddy of Don's from the service offered him a manager position in a town called Santa Rosa, California. It's somewhere north of San Francisco. He says it's really beautiful, lots of trees. He and Don used to talk about going camping. Now he's got a big sea kayak. He goes kayaking nearly every weekend. So I think it's going to be really good for him,' Josie said. She paused. 'The thing is, Will, I need you to write a letter saying it's okay for us to go.'

'What?'

'The lawyer says that under the terms of the custody agreement, I have to have your permission to take Megan out of Harris County.'

'Take Megan.' Holding the cordless phone in the crook of my shoulder I grabbed some Tylenols from a bottle on the kitchen sink and dry-swallowed them. They stuck like stones in my throat. 'Christ, Josie.' *No, you can't fucking move to California!* Jesus, no.

AJ watched me sadly from the living-room window. My apartment was pathetic, of course: one big room, a mattress without even a box spring underneath it. Grime on the walls I had never bothered to clean. You might excuse a twenty-one-year-old for living like this, but anyone over thirty had clearly fucked up.

'How do you feel about getting dragged up there?' I tried not to panic. Jesus, no. 'It's going to kill your mom, being so far from Megan.'

'She can visit. Will, I know I'm asking a lot.'

I imagined Josie on the sidelines of a soccer field surrounded by gigantic redwood trees. Aging hippie dads with tie-dyed T-shirts and graying ponytails would be arguing with the refs. Healthy snacks at half time, banana nut loaf and orange slices. Megan's ponytail bobbing as she swooped in to score a winning goal. 'Great,' I said.

'I was blue last time we talked, but I know this will be good for Don.' I remembered standing next to Josie at her daddy's funeral. Promising her I would never be a fuck-up like him.

Josie said, 'If Don can just be happy, we can be too, Megan and me.'

'Sure.' In my mind's eye I saw Josie sitting next to me at twilight on the beach at Galveston. The curve of her throat and how it felt to know I would never kiss it again. That sick endless drop in my stomach. 'How far away is Santa Rosa from here? Two thousand miles, maybe?'

'I do love him, Will. I know it's important to you to think he's just some jerk, just a stupid ex-Marine, but that's not true. He's a smart guy. He's—' Silence. 'He's not always fighting himself, Will. He doesn't get in his own way.'

'Sounds like a real find.'

Josie laughing in the darkness, taking a swig of red wine

from my thermos cap. *Will, I want a divorce.* Your life can turn on you like that.

'Semper Fi,' I said.

'What?'

I am a ghost.

I am a ghost.

'What?' Josie said.

'Nothing. Sorry. I was thinking of something else.'

And how funny it was, how hysterically amusing, all the times I said I would never come back after I died. Because the joke was, I was already dead. I had been dead for twelve years. Not my body – my body was still alive. But in every other way, I was nothing but a drift of smoke. Untouchable. Dead.

'Will?'

'I can't drive a car, Josie. It's two thousand miles, and I can't drive.' Megan with her drug-store sunglasses. Her little feet drumming against the back of a bus seat. No more bus rides now. *The thing is, I need you to write a letter.* Megan standing next to me in the parking lot at Six Flags watching our balloons stream into the sky. Mine with no wishes on it. Sailing up and up and up.

'I'll send her down. Maybe during summer vacation she could visit you for a week or two.'

'Don's never going to let her come here. You know that. You're taking her away, and I'm never going to see her again.'

'Will—'

But of course she was Don's kid. And she had always, always been. He and Megan were alive, after all. You can't expect the living to be loyal to the dead.

'That's just great. That's just great fucking news, Josie. You have a great time. Send me your new address when you get settled in. Or don't,' I said. Dead man talking.

'Will? Will, it would mean so much – Oh, shit. Here he comes. I better get off the phone. He doesn't like me talking to you.'

She hung up.

I listened to the dial tone for a while. 'Good-bye,' I said.

I grabbed the jewel case for *Murmur* and popped it open. 'Radio Free Europe,' 'Pilgrimage,' 'Laughing,' 'Talk About the Passion,' 'Moral Kiosk,' and 'Perfect Circle' – the first half of that album – it remembers. It's haunted. Great music to get divorced by. I listened to it every day in the year after Josie left me.

Even on my bad days, my numb days, I always loved music. It's not like I never cared about anything.

The business side of a CD is a perfect circle, a shimmering silver mirror with a hole in the middle. My face had aged a lot since *Murmur* came out. My hairline had receded and my buzz-cut had a few gray hairs mixed in, coarse wires the color of cigarette ash. My eyes were hollow and beaten down. Dead Kennedy. Never loved a woman enough to kill her.

I thought of AJ, facedown on the sidewalk, trying to crawl away from her boyfriend's second bullet. Now she was watching me from the living-room window. Behind her, in the vast Houston sky, heavy-bellied clouds were building, wide thrones and towers of them. I wondered what she had done to make him shoot her.

Who's your first love? she murmured. Truth or dare.

'Dare,' I said.

For some reason I had never actually broken a CD, so I squeezed *Murmur* in my hands, looking off to the side in case it splintered. I didn't want to take any shrapnel in my eye. The CD bowed and then snapped with a surprisingly loud pop. Not as loud as a gunshot, but louder than I had expected. It came apart into six pieces, two big ones and four smaller splinters about the size and shape of the blade on Megan's Swiss Army knife. The big pieces were smooth, but the little ones were webbed with cracks, like a car windshield after a collision.

I broke a few more, and this seemed to be a pretty regular

173

pattern. There were never fewer than three pieces, and only once did I get more than seven; my trusty old copy of *Rum, Sodomy, and the Lash* burst apart in a shower of splinters. Trust the Pogues.

Getting more methodical, I proceeded alphabetically. The first time I cut my hand (Butthole Surfers, *Locust Abortion Technician*), I thought about fussing with a Band-Aid, but it wasn't worth the bother. By the time I got to Tom Waits's *Rain Dogs*, there was blood running down my palms, streams of it over my wrists and up my forearms. The funny thing was, I was getting that same feeling of lightness that had come over me after Josie said she wanted a divorce. That same empty relief expanding in my chest, lifting me up and up and up.

The phone rang. I headed for the living-room and reached to pick it up.

Leave it, AJ said.

I stopped with my hand touching the receiver.

Ring.

Time to go, she said gently.

Ring.

I flexed my hands, which were stiffening up from all the little cuts covering them. I should pick up the phone.

AJ said, Are you lonely, Will?

Rin— Too late.

I am, she said.

I walked through crackling drifts of broken CDs to the bathroom. I opened the mirrored door to the medicine cabinet and groped on the top shelf until I found the aspirin bottle with my wedding ring inside. I opened the childproof lid by feel and shook the ring out. It felt surprisingly heavy for such a little thing. I stood over the toilet and opened my hand and let the ring slide into the bowl. Splash-clink! Then I flushed.

AJ was waiting for me in the bathroom mirror, blood spattered on her chest. Kind eyes. My first love.

174

'I fucked up so bad,' I said. 'You don't know. I didn't take care of Josie when I had her, and I hated her when she left. I sat on Megan like a dog in a manger, just to piss off her dad, probably. I threw away twelve years of my life on *nothing.*'

AJ touched the bloody front of her shirt with two fingers. She lifted them up, dark and wet at the tips, and touched them to her lips. Then she held them out to me.

I headed back into the front room. She came with me, bloody cotton winking and flashing across the splintered CDs on my mattress. A strand of black hair, one eye, two fingers. Then her face, whole again in my living-room window, looking at me, full of love.

I checked to make sure all my windows were closed. I humped the stove out from the kitchen wall and turned the gas back on. I got a little cup full of water and knelt down on all fours in front of my oven. The pilot light gleamed in the darkness. I reached in with my splash of water and put it out.

Then I turned the oven on, and the broiler, and the burners. No light this time, just the calm, steady hiss of gas. After that I went back and settled down on the mattress in my dark one-room apartment, looking at the window. I pushed aside the broken CDs and tried to get comfortable.

They say that no love lasts forever.

Sometimes it does.

CHAPTER TEN

The goddamn phone rang.

Ring.

Well, let it ring, I thought hazily. My head was aching and my tongue was fat in my mouth.

Ring.

It's not going to be Josie.

Ring.

It's not going to be Megan.

Ring.

It's not – Oh, fuck it.

I groped my way across the mattress, poking myself on shards of broken CD, and grabbed the receiver. 'Who the hell is this?'

'Will! Finally! I've been trying to reach you all day! Look, I need a really, really big favor. I put in an application to the Grande Vista theater program, so now they want me to come audition, only it's during the day and Dad and Mom are working. Could you possibly, possibly baby-sit Vi for me? On Friday?'

'What?' My head was pounding. 'Is this Fonteyne?'

'It would only be for an hour. Two hours, tops.'

The room stank of gas and I felt loggy all over, as if my blood had been replaced with pancake syrup. And my eyes –

something was wrong with my eyes. Everything was black and white. My phone, candy-apple red when I bought it, was now gray – gray handset, gray coil of cord, gray cradle. The sheets on my mattress were gray, spackled with little spatters of shadow that must be my drying blood. There were bits of broken jewel cases all over my bed, and a litter of CD booklets. But all the cover art and band photographs had gone black and white, as if replaced with Xerox copies. I looked out the window. AJ was there, so close I could kiss her. Behind her, the whole world had gone black and white: trees, buildings, sky. A dead blue jay darted onto a branch outside my window and cocked its head at me. The leaves around it were soft charcoal coins shivering in the afternoon breeze.

'Will? Are you stoned?'

'No. Sort of.' Christ. My head hurt too much for me to be dead. 'Just – wait a minute.'

I dropped the phone and crawled over to the living-room window and heaved it open, accidentally erasing AJ's body so only her head was showing above the sash. An eddy of sultry Houston air spilled into my apartment, smelling of asphalt and distant lightning. AJ looked scared. Watch out, she said. She was looking behind me. I turned around.

Tom Hanlon was standing in my kitchen, patting his pockets as if looking for something. The stink of gas was everywhere. 'Hey, buddy,' he said, 'got a match?'

'Will?' Fonteyne said tinnily from inside my phone.

"S'minute,' I croaked.

'Or a lighter,' Hanlon said. 'A lighter would do.'

I stumbled past Hanlon to my stove and turned off the gas. Oh, Jesus. A stray spark in my apartment would have blown the whole building apart. 'Don't give me that look,' Hanlon said. 'I'm not the one who told you to gas the place up.'

I looked back at AJ, then at the litter of smashed CDs on the mattress. And the bloodstains. I remembered the hiss of gas seeping into the apartment.

Aren't you tired of being alone? she said. I am.

She stepped down from the window, flickering to me across the broken CDs on my bed: a pale eye, the shoulder of her T-shirt with a bit of tanned arm showing underneath, a hand passing through the jewel case that had once held my ancient Joy Division compilation disk. I won't leave you, DK.

I started shaking, scared and furious. I imagined Lee getting home from work, he would smell the gas and find me dead in my crappy little apartment. That would not be the spirit that won the fucking Battle of Stalingrad. Because then Josie would have been right all the time, and she would look down while someone shoveled dirt onto my coffin, and it would be Don standing there beside her. And she would say, 'Thank God I didn't stay with *him*,' and every soccer game I had gone to and every box of fucking Christmas Gift Wrap I had flogged would have been for nothing.

'Will?' Fonteyne said. I grabbed the phone. ' – Will?'

'Yeah, I'm here.'

'You're creeping me out.'

'Sure, Fonteyne, I'll look after Vi for you,' I said. Because sooner or later even Dead Kennedy has to commit to something. *Semper Fi*, baby. *Semper Fi*. 'Look, can I call you back in a few minutes? Are you at home?'

'No, I'm at the Ice Capades. What do you think, moron?'

'Great. That's just great. I'll call you right back, okay?'

'Will—'

I hung up.

God, my head hurt so bad. I'd barely slept for days. My body felt bruised and hot. Fucking Parkwood still hadn't fixed the fucking air-conditioning.

Got to look out, AJ said. Got to learn how to see in the dark, DK.

'Screw you.' I pulled the blinds down over the living-room window.

Hanlon yawned. Heat beat at the back of his mouth. He

179

opened a cabinet and made a face at the bare cupboard inside. 'Show some self-respect,' he said. 'You never get a second chance to make a first impression. If you *look* like a loser, people will *treat* you like a loser.' His face was shadows. 'And if they *treat* you like a loser, you will *be* a loser.' I was sick from gas poisoning and couldn't seem to breathe. 'You didn't pick up the phone,' Hanlon said.

'What?'

'The phone. It rang while you were trying to kill yourself. You didn't pick it up.'

Right. I remembered. I had been kneeling on my mattress with blood running down my arms. The phone had rung, and AJ had said, *Leave it.*

'You should have gotten that,' Hanlon murmured in the darkness. 'It might have been *news*. It might have been something you needed to hear. It might have been something you needed to hear a long time ago.'

'Who was it?' I was afraid.

The salesman studied his hands, stretching out his fingers. Limbering up. 'Time for me to go to Josie's house.'

'No. Don't.'

'You know, there's a guy who's just gotten some news,' Hanlon remarked. 'Some very disappointing news.' He glanced up at me. 'After I drop by Josie and Megan's place, I think I'll go back to that nice little condo in Deer Park and do the family too. Mom and Dad and your ugly sister, Fonteyne. And her kid, what was her name?' Hanlon paused. 'Vi. Violetta. Pretty name. I've always been good with names,' he said. Then he was gone.

In the gloom I could just make out the glowing display on the Caller ID box. I had missed one call.

It was from Don.

Shit, here he comes. I better get off the phone. He doesn't like me talking to you.

Click.

180

Dread spilled under my skin. I imagined Don watching Josie as she put down the phone. He would try to act casual. 'Who were you talking to, J?' But he knew Josie was a cheater. He would know that better than anyone. Once a cheater, always a cheater. That's how he would think.

I opened more windows, trying to get the gas out of my apartment. I felt drowsy and terrified and my head was pounding. *Imagine if this man had a gun.*

Lee was at work. It would be hours and hours before he got home. I found my copy of the key to his apartment and let myself in. The Frankenterrier met me, looking up to see if I was bringing food. I found the shoe box with Lee's disassembled .45 inside. I brought it back to my apartment and spilled the pieces out on my kitchen table and sat there, not moving.

Maybe Don had been calling me to bury the hatchet. After all, he needed my signature to move to California and start his wonderful new life. Maybe there was nothing more to it than that.

There's a guy who's just gotten some very disappointing news. I'm going to kill them all, Kennedy, just for loving you.

'I really wish I hadn't heard any of this shit,' I said out loud. I could pretend I didn't know. For fuck's sake, Josie hadn't been my problem for twelve years. She was a big girl. She had chosen her bed and now she might as well lie in it, like she'd lied in mine.

It was hard to find an excuse for leaving Megan in a house with a haunted man with a gun.

I started picking through the pieces of .45 on my table. I pulled out the slide, then the frame, then the barrel and the barrel bushing. Recoil spring, slide stop, recoil plug. Five years old again, playing in the hot silence of Uncle Walt's back room, working the puzzle. Faint smell of machine oil.

I kept waiting to see in color, but it didn't happen. Something had gone wrong with my eyes, like the two times I had suddenly seen Josie in black and white. Only this time it was everything. This time the whole world was dead.

I called Don's cell phone. No answer. 'Out of use or out of

range.' I called the house phone. No answer there either. Probably there was a simple explanation.

The .45 clip felt light when I picked it up. Five bullets inside. I ran my thumb over it, the whole thing smaller than a Hershey bar, dotted with little perforations. Walt always said he should have made AJ take a gun when she moved out of the house.

There was a bushing wrench in Lee's shoe box. I wondered if he even knew what it was. Probably not. Just another part of his daddy's awkward gift. He would be at work for hours and hours. If I took the gun I could get to Woodland and back long before he got home. I could make sure Josie and Megan were okay and nobody would ever know.

It's pretty easy to strip and clean a Colt .45 service pistol. It has to be. If you're going to set a task that every sad mother-fucker in the United States Armed Forces will be required to perform, you better set the bar low.

Houston air is like gun oil, sticky and damp and it smells like metal. Anything you leave out gets coated in this grime that is not like the dust in other places. Imagine powdered grit and motor oil sprayed out in a fine black mist, so you can dust anything left lying out and the paper towel will come up black. There was a lot of this crap on the pieces of the old gun. I cleaned them all with a rag while I sat there trying to figure out what to do.

Seemed like even if Lee never put the Colt together, he ought to clean it once in a while, out of respect for his father who loved him.

I picked up the pieces and tried to put them together. It didn't matter that I couldn't see in color, but it was hard when I started because I was staring at them with thirty-two-year-old eyes, on the other side of my whole life. I knew I should put the barrel in the slide and the slide on the frame. Snap the clip into the butt. My mind raced in my throbbing head. Hard to blank out the image of Josie with her blouse blown open and her white skin spattered black. Hard to stop seeing Megan with blood dripping from her mouth. She would try to hide up in her bedroom. That's where I would find her.

I got myself under better control and put the slide group together, barrel and recoil spring and so forth. With each component I cleaned, it was as if I could wipe away a few more years of grime. I set the forward sight and my hands got more sure, moving back to the years when I was out fighting Marines in bars and meeting the nice cop with the arugala salads. I fixed the mainspring housing and mainspring cap and trigger assembly, back to the end of my marriage. I looked down the barrel, peering through the iron sights at my wedding.

If Don was at the house in Woodland and there was shooting to be done, it wasn't going to work out well. I knew that. Even if I didn't turn up in the black-and-white type of the next day's obituaries, even if I killed him before he killed me, that would still be a one-way ticket to Huntsville. I remembered the letter Lee had read me from the inmate at Huntsville and wished I had written that guy a really, really polite letter back.

Slide stop plunger, hammer strut, hammer pin, hammer. Snap, click.

The Colt 1911A .45 caliber pistol is so named because they first started rolling off the assembly lines in 1911. It's amazing how little they've changed since. Good reliable machines, Uncle Walt used to say. Basic machines. Of course, they're made to do a basic job.

Back even further in time, I remembered AJ showing me a stash of *Playboys* she'd found in her daddy's closet. The magazines were hidden behind the toolbox where Uncle Walt kept his gun. Like a schoolteacher she had said, 'And here we see some extremely large boobs. Don't look, DK. You're too young,' she added teasingly. I was twelve at the time.

I screwed the trigger back together and seated it on the frame and ran the slide back in and locked it down. Last of all I took the clip with its five bullets – should be enough – and slid it into the stock. I sat back, five years old again, almost happy:

the pure pleasure of seeing all the jumble and mess click together into one clean and simple thing.

Then I called a cab.

After I hung up I remembered I had burned my last dollar bill as a tip for the dead waiter in the Nit Noi, so I went back to Lee's apartment and went through his clothes until I found a twenty and two ones and seventy-three cents in change. Even though the evening was hot, I put on my jacket with the fishhooks, partly for luck and partly because I needed a pocket to stash the gun in. Then I went down to the curb in front of my building to wait. The amber streetlight overhead had gone black and white too, shedding a thick gray light. A few drops of hot rain fell.

My taxi pulled up. It was supposed to be yellow, but it was dead. The upholstery was a dapple of grays. Every little patch of wear showed a different shade, from the sun-bleached seat-tops down to the dark, wet-looking wells where the seat belts were socketed. In black and white my eyes saw with such *tenderness.* The scuff-marks on the belt buckles, a crumpled Wendy's cup, the stubble smudging the driver's chin: everything pressed into me as if I were wax. The world was more beautiful in black and white.

My head hurt and hurt.

The cabbie was a chubby black-and-white Pakistani named Abdul with strong opinions and ex-wives who were a trial to him. We sympathized with one another. From my apartment, the ride out to Woodland is forty-five minutes at one dollar per. I got him to stop a block away from Josie's house so he wouldn't know exactly where I was headed when I stiffed him. 'This is all I've got,' I said, handing him my $22.73. 'I'm sorry.'

'You're fucking sorry! You pay up, you son of a bitch, or you stay in the car while I drive you into the fucking police station.'

'I'm sorry, I can't. It's life or death.' I swung my door open and he started to drive forward and I had to draw the Colt. 'I've got a gun,' I said.

Abdul stopped and looked at me, hurt and offended. 'You and me got along so good!' I apologized again, but he wasn't paying attention. 'I mean, I got a gun too, this is fucking America, eh?' he said, and I realized he wasn't kidding – his left hand was on the steering wheel, but in his right he held what looked like a pocket cannon, some stupendous piece of Wild West hardware like a Peacemaker Colt, with a barrel about as long as my forearm and a mouth that looked as wide as a billiard ball. He waved it around at the sad state the world had come to. 'I mean, you try and fuck me, I leave you so much hole you can put your head up your ass,' he said, in a melancholy tone, 'but *that's* making a shitty day, you know?'

A spatter of rain hit the windshield. A second later came another, and then the rain started in earnest. Abdul flipped on his hazards with one fat thumb. Finally he shook his head. 'So here's what I do. I give you my card, and you give me my moneys plus ten dollars to teach you not to be waving these guns around.' The muzzle of his cannon traced a line across my chest as he leaned over the front seat at me for emphasis. 'Jesus, you can't just be scarings everybody.'

I took the card. His hands were beautiful, the fingers plump, the nails sharp and clean. 'Deal,' I said. I really, really liked him. 'Thanks. And sorry again.'

He looked at me sadly. 'And we were getting alongs so good.'

I scrambled out of the cab, sticking Abdul's card in my back pocket, and watched him drive away, still shaking his head at the wickedness in the world. Then I took a breath and ran through the rain, hoping I wasn't too late, hoping I hadn't missed my one chance to do Megan some good while I sat in my apartment trying to make up my mind.

I pounded down the sidewalk. Rain was drumming down. It got in my eyes and made my jacket cling to my elbows and shoulders. The gun in my pocket bumped against my hip. I couldn't shake the image of Josie blown open. It made me so fucking *angry*, here I was thirty-two years old and I was still looking out for this fucking woman. I wished she had never come to visit me in the hospital. I wished I had never seen her face go suddenly black and white. It would have been easier to believe in happy endings. But not every ending is a happy one, for Christ's sake. That's life in the real world. *There is a fountain filled with blood.*

There was a lamp on in Josie's living-room. Dead light spilled through the big front windows into her yard. I wished my eyes would work right. I jogged up the sidewalk and rang the bell. My heart was beating so hard it hurt. It hurt and hurt. Finally the door pulled open and there was Josie in jean shorts and a T-shirt. I couldn't tell if she was alive or dead. Nothing between us but the glass and wire of the screen door. So close I could kiss her.

She looked surprised to see me. Not happy. 'Will? What are you doing here?'

I saw AJ in Josie's living-room window, shaking her head. She looked scared. I wondered again about AJ's boyfriend. He must have loved her, in his way. You don't kill someone unless you love them very much.

My hand was on the gun in my pocket. I pulled it out. 'Oh, Jesus,' Josie said.

Hanlon was beside me. 'Do it,' he said.

And I thought maybe I would.

And right then I realized that sometimes a guy is haunted for a really good reason.

CHAPTER ELEVEN

Hot outside, and dark. Maybe nine o'clock. Rain running down, running down. Oil-streaked rivers of it in the gutters. Woodland is planted out with evergreens, big blue spruce and Scottish pine; the heat and the rain brought a faint smell of resin in the sweltering gloom.

I was surprisingly calm and alert. Like an interested specta-tor, watching the whole scene from behind a pane of glass. There was a lot to watch. There was me, obviously, standing there with the .45 Colt automatic that Lee's granddaddy had carried at the Battle of the Bulge. It was a good reliable gun. Tom Hanlon stood beside me, smelling of charred meat and gasoline. He looked impatient. Our mutual cousin, AJ, looked out at us from Don and Josie's living-room window. It was a regular family reunion. AJ's chest was a mass of blood and her face was sad, sad. And of course standing in the doorway was Josie, the only woman I had ever loved enough to kill.

I was the guy Hanlon wanted to murder her. Not Don. Looking back, it was so obvious. Say you had a disappointed guy, just got fired, Hanlon had said. And this guy got it into his head that his wife had been screwing around on him. And then, imagine if he had a gun.

As good as Josie looked alive, she looked better in black and white. People's faces settle as they get older; the years crust over them like Mamaw Dusty's pancake make-up. But fear had wiped ten years off Josie. It was good to see her this intensely, to remember how her eyebrows slanted slightly down, so that even relaxed she seemed serious, on the verge of frowning. She still had the six rings running up the side of her left ear, and I remembered with an ache in my fingertips how it felt to turn those little gold hoops while she lay drowsing in bed next to me. We had a box spring then. As broke as we were, Josie would never, ever sink to sleeping on a mattress on the floor. I felt a great rush of tenderness for her; the fond, distant affection you feel looking back at someone who died a long time ago.

All this time I was examining Josie's beautiful dead face: but the middle of her body was a bigger target and that's where the gun was pointing. My blood was still thick with gas from my apartment. My head was pounding and pounding, but the Colt felt light and my hand wasn't shaking at all. It was steady as a rock. I felt like I could hold that gun forever.

Josie said, 'Will?'

Hanlon shifted impatiently beside me, giving off little eddies of heat, like an open oven door. 'Do it, DK.'

I wasn't ready yet. 'Don home?'

Josie wet her lips. 'Yeah. He's in the workroom.'

'You're lying,' I said. 'You think I don't know what you look like when you lie? He's out. He's out with his buddies some-where having a drink to celebrate his new job. He's out cele-brating Northern California.' In the living-room window, AJ was looking sadly at me, but I didn't give a damn. I felt okay. Tight as a drum. Alert. 'Go ahead, Josie. If he's in the work-room, go call him. Go on. Call him.'

'Will,' she said. 'Please.'

'*Call him*, dammit!' She didn't. 'You shouldn't lie to me,' I said.

'I talked to your mom tonight,' Josie said. 'She told me what you did for Uncle Walt.' She kept trying to look at me, but her eyes slid back to the gun as if magnetized.

'Come *on*, DK,' Hanlon said impatiently. 'What are you waiting for? Don't you love her?'

I did. I still loved her. I had tried to stop but I couldn't. I couldn't stop. That's the part I hated. The fucking fishhooks were in me and I was going to spend my whole life loving this woman no matter how much it hurt. She would go away, or she would die, and it would never help, it would never stop hurting because I couldn't stop loving her. I would always be faithful. What kind of lousy deal was that? Why wasn't I allowed to get over things? Everybody else lived in color. They changed. They forgot. But the dead – we remember. We know what we know and we never forget.

Semper Fi.

'Will, you're scaring me,' Josie said. *Will, I want a divorce.*

'You abandoned your first love,' I said. A trickle of heat ran out of the bullet hole in my chest and spilled across my skin. For the first time I felt a little less calm. 'You were fucking Don before we broke up, weren't you?'

'Are you going to believe anything I say?'

'Probably not.'

'Then I guess we're both screwed, aren't we?' Josie said. 'I mean, you just want to shoot me now, it doesn't matter what I say, does it?'

'If you *dare* sound pissed off, I will fucking kill you,' I said. 'If you get smart with me, if you act all hurt or God help you *angry*, I will shoot you where you fucking stand.'

My calm self, the one watching from behind a pane of glass, was amazed to hear those words come out of my mouth. Still, I obviously meant it. I could tell from the steady way I was holding the gun that I wasn't going to take one ounce of shit from her. Not one fucking ounce. Not after everything.

Movement in the living-room window. AJ touched her fingertips to her bloody shirt, brought them up wet and wrote NO on the glass. 'I don't trust you any more,' I said. Josie saw me

189

looking at the window and asked who I was talking to, but I ignored her. 'I could have told your folks where to find your birth-control pills or your microdots, but I never snitched you out. I never told on you.'

'Bitch,' Hanlon added.

AJ's eyes snapped over to him. *Hey, mister*, she snarled. Her pretty dead face was suddenly hideous. Her voice was dark and ugly as water running down a sewer. *You want a fucking ride?*

Hanlon jerked back. You could see flames dancing in his wide, frightened eyes. I remembered the dead girl in his garage, her lips black around her gag.

I'll give you a fucking ride, AJ said ferociously.

'It's Hanlon. He's here, isn't he?' Josie said. She was talking really fast. 'He's here and he's telling you to do things, but he's the killer, Will. Not you. That girl. He tied her up and then he beat her to death, that's what you said.'

'She was screwing around,' I said. My headache was so bad I wanted to cry. Pounding and pounding. I felt a little off balance. 'He trusted her. He was nobody and she made him real but it was just a lie.'

For some reason my hand had started to shake.

'Do it!' Hanlon said.

But I found myself looking at Josie, and then at AJ. I remembered AJ taking me to visit that classmate of hers in the hospital. The girl who got broken and would never be fixed, the white plastic bracelet around her thin wrist. AJ lecturing me in the elevator afterwards. *Someday it's going to be you in that closet, DK. So don't be a jerk.*

Out of nowhere I found myself imagining what it would be like to shoot AJ instead of Josie. I imagined how the front window would explode and AJ would burst apart in a rain of glass. AJ pattering down in pieces, facedown on Josie's hardwood floors. The big ugly bloodstains on her chest hidden. Just two little holes showing in her back. I wondered what she had done to her boyfriend to make him do that.

From somewhere upstairs, Megan yelled, 'Mom? Who is it?'

It was like a bullet through Josie's heart. You could see her face die. 'Nobody,' she called. Her voice with the panic crushed out of it. She had sounded like that the day she found her father dead on the toilet with a needle dangling from his arm.

Tell Megan to come down here, I meant to say: but my body had started to shake. My hand especially was shaking and shaking. Also there was a gun at the end of it. Something was coming up inside me, coming up really fast. Some terrible bullet was tearing through me, drilling up through my guts and my lungs and shattering my ribs, and I knew if it reached my head I would die. I saw Josie lying murdered on her floor, two red flowers on her chest. So beautiful.

There was a gun at the end of my hand.

'Do it!' Hanlon yelled. 'Do it! Don't you love her, for God's sake? Can't you love anything?'

'Is that Will, Mom?'

'You can't let Megan see you like this,' Josie said.

The gun sagged in my hand. Here it comes, AJ said sadly. Truth or dare, DK.

The glass between me and what I was doing blew out, and suddenly I could feel everything. I was like my grandpa Jay Paul, caught standing in front of a window when the *Grandcamp* blew: a thousand needles of glass exploding into him. That's the way men are. Jay Paul, he could get so mean and never even know he was mad.

'Oh my God,' I whispered. 'Josie, I came here to *kill* you!' I looked at her, horrified. 'I wanted to kill you as soon as I saw you in the hospital. That's why you turned black and white. Oh my God.'

Devastation. Devastation.

'I loved you so much,' I said. Bewildered. Just now, too late, I was beginning to make sense of things – now that I had crossed a line that could never be uncrossed. I looked down at the gun in my hand. I wasn't just a failure, I was a monster. I wanted to die.

I would have given anything for another chance. If it were just an hour ago, or a month, or better yet thirteen years. If I could be nineteen again, I could do it all right. Knowing what I knew now, it would be *easy* to be a better husband, a better father. Not perfect, maybe, but good enough. It would have been easy.

But life doesn't work that way. You never get a second chance to make a first impression. I would have sold my soul in a heartbeat, I would have done anything, if only I could go back to a time before I failed Josie and Megan and Mom and Paris and Fonteyne – everybody. Before I let everybody down. But there was no way to go back, there was nothing but the prison of a future in which everything was already ruined and would be forever. No way out.

Hush, AJ said. It's all right, DK. You'll be okay.

Hanlon grabbed my wrist and pointed the gun back at Josie's chest. '*Do it, Will!*' And I wanted to. I wanted to make flowers on Josie's shirt and ask her why she didn't love me any more and wait forever for her answer. Forever and ever and ever.

But I didn't. Crying, I pulled the gun out of Hanlon's grip and pointed it at the ground, because I was a goddamned Caped Crusader, and good guys don't kill people. Because I had never, *ever* abandoned my first love – and however stupid that might be, I'd be damned if I was going to screw up my perfect record by shooting her. Because I was not Tom Hanlon. Because I was not AJ's boyfriend. Because I was not dead, not yet.

Hanlon sighed and kicked moodily at the ground with his burning Florsheim shoe. 'For Christ's sake, DK,' he complained, 'even with a hell of a product, you still have to close the sale.'

Megan's footsteps came down the stairs. 'Get rid of the gun *right now*,' Josie said. There was a little splinter of color in my world again: in the middle of Josie's white face, one of her eyes was denim-blue and running with tears. 'Don't let her see, Will.'

I threw the gun in the flower bed underneath the living-room window. In the glass, AJ sighed with relief.

'Why won't you just tell me who it is?' Megan said, stomping into the hallway and glaring at her mom. She caught sight of me. 'Jesus, Will, what are you doing here? If Dad gets back, you're going to be in trouble.'

I couldn't think what to say to that.

Meg squinted at me. 'Are you drunk?'

'Not yet,' I said. Then I threw up.

'Oh, gross,' Megan said. 'He is drunk. I'll get a towel.'

When the heaves finally subsided, I wiped my mouth on my jacket sleeve. I felt bruised and hollow inside. The rain had stopped and the hot night steamed around us. I could see some color again. Whatever I looked directly at was still black and white, but around the edges color was creeping back – a flash of yellow from Josie's T-shirt, and red letters on the living-room window where AJ had written with her bloody fingers. NO.

No.

No.

No.

I was twelve when Hurricane Alicia crashed into Houston, and of course I thought it was a blast – putting masking tape over the windows, packing the refrigerator with extra ice. My dad pulled the mattress off the master bed and used it to make a lean-to for the kids, propping it sideways in a corridor so we would have some protection from falling debris in case the condo roof collapsed. My job was to keep my sisters from freaking out, and I can still remember when they both finally started to snore. I know the wind was strong, there was hail and driving rain, but what I remember is creeping outside the next day into an utterly trashed city. Branches in the street, and palm trees with their heads snapped off sticking up like broken spears. Broken glass everywhere. The stink of mud. A Winnebago was stretched out on its side on our neighbor's lawn, with a solemn line of white egrets perched on it. Later on, there would be distant sirens and the sound of chainsaws, but in the very early morning there were no cars moving anywhere, and the world was held in a strange and eerie silence.

That's how I felt, washed up like a piece of wreckage on Josie's sidewalk. Trashed inside. Weirdly quiet.

Megan clattered down her porch steps and handed me a wet rag. I took it and cleaned up. The taste of gas was finally gone from my mouth. I felt tired but cleaner.

'Sorry about the mess,' I said to Josie. 'I've been sick. Really sick. Look, if you have those papers, I'll sign them. About taking Meg out of Harris County. That's probably a good idea,' I said.

'I think you have to do it in front of a notary.'

'Really?'

'I think so.'

Megan took back the washcloth, holding it gingerly by one corner. 'You have to get out of here before Dad gets back.'

'Yeah. Listen, kiddo, I need to talk in private with your mom for a sec.'

Megan looked at me, offended. 'Fine. I'll just take your spew rag to the laundry, why don't I?' She turned and marched back into the house.

I looked at Josie. 'I need the gun.'

'What?'

'It belongs to this friend of mine. It was a present from his dad, it's got sentimental value. I should . . .'

'*Fuck you!*'

'Okay, no, you're right. Okay, how about I tell you how to drop the clip out and you can unload all the bullets and *then* give me the gun?' Josie eyed me steadily. 'Or I could walk out to the sidewalk and you could throw me the gun and then lock your door.' I was really tired. 'Or you could hold on to the gun as evidence until the cops arrived.'

'That's a good idea,' Josie said.

I started to say, 'I'm sorry,' again, but bit it back.

Josie stared at me. 'You bastard,' she said.

'I know.'

'Sentimental value. You bastard.' She came down off the porch and got the gun from the flower bed. 'How do I get the clip out?'

'There's a button, on the side – there you go. Now just – right.' The clip slid out into Josie's hand. It occurred to me how lucky I was to be dealing with Josie here instead of someone like Andy's wife, Sonia. I'm not sure they understand about the sentimental value of guns in Connecticut. I dunno. Maybe that's an unfair stereotype.

Josie asked me how to get the bullets out of the clip and I told her. She shook them out like bright brass candies and put the clip back in and tossed the gun onto the lawn. I picked it up and put it in my pocket. 'So I'll sign those papers whenever you want.'

'Okay.' We both knew we were probably never going to see each other again. 'Give your mom my love.' Josie's way of saying good-bye.

'Take good care of Megan.' I wanted to say 'my daughter,' but I couldn't. Not right now.

I thought I had emptied out every tear in my body, but my eyes starting getting wet again and I could feel another wave of grief coming up on me like the heaves, so I turned my back and walked away from Josie and my daughter. I was pretty sure that in another sixty seconds I was going to feel more miserable than I could imagine, and the only ambition I had left was to get the hell away from Josie and Meg before I contaminated another second of their lives. If there was nothing else I could do for them, at least I could disappear. I could promise never to say another word, or ask another favor, or call on the phone or write. I could at least be dead for them.

I picked up my pace and started to walk faster.

'Will?' Josie called. The effort of turning around took years off my life. She was standing in her doorway, exasperated. 'Do you need bus fare?'

'Oh shit,' I said.

When I got back to my apartment, the lights were off but the door was standing open. The only illumination escaped out of the refrigerator, which Lee was holding open while pawing around inside. 'You're out of beer,' he said.

'No, I've got two bottles of Dos—' I saw the empties on my kitchen counter.

'I said you're out of fucking beer. What the hell is this?' Lee straightened up, holding a jar, and squinted down, trying to read the hand-written label.

'Jalapeño jam. My Uncle Chase puts it up.' My insides were bombed out and I was so tired I wanted to die.

'He's the one in Brownsville?'

'Yeah.'

Lee considered. 'I hate Brownsville. And I hate fucking jalapeño jam, and I hate fucking Dos Equis anyway, and what the fuck kind of friend only has two fucking beers in his fridge on a night like this?'

In the dim light of the apartment I actually couldn't tell if Lee was in color or black and white, but he looked like shit either way. Rumpled and unhappy. In fact, he was crying. 'Oh my God,' I breathed. 'You've got the chit.'

'You bet your ass I have the fucking chit,' Lee said.

But –

Lee's lip trembled. 'Oh man, I feel really bad.'

I couldn't believe it. I had just pulled a gun on my ex-wife, and Lee had the chit. Some days, you just can't win for losing.

I took a breath. 'Fired?' I asked, 'or dumped?'

'Dumped for sure. Fired maybe. Vicky, can you believe this shit, walks in while I'm pulling dollar Lone Stars for the eight-ball league and says, Lee, I can't take this any more. I'm standing

196

there with the goddamn tap in my hand. People at the bar looking at me. But I play it cool. I lay Melanie's tray, turn back to
Vicky, and say, Can we talk about this later? No, she says, we're
always going to talk about it later, and I've had it with you and
your future tense.'

'She said future tense?'

Lee nodded. 'Then she just said, It's over, Lee. I can't do this
any more. She walks out, and I'm standing there with an empty
mug in my hand, and I reach under the bar and pour myself a
generous three-quarters of a mug of Shiner Bock, and then I
walk out the back door.'

'In the middle of your shift?'

'I guess.'

'So fired is maybe tomorrow.'

'It wasn't real busy,' Lee said. His shoulders stiffened and his
mouth firmed up. 'Time to drive, amigo.'

'No!'

The last time Lee got dumped he loaded up on a fifth of
Bacardi and then drove to Disneyworld in Orlando, Florida, for
reasons he couldn't recall after he sobered up. 'Lee, no driving.
You already smell like a frat-house carpet. Where are your
keys?'

'Bracs Bayou. But we can find 'em,' he said, starting for the
door.

'Or – we could get more beer from Kroger's.'

Lee slowed up. 'Okay,' he said. 'That works too.'

Half an hour later, we were sitting on the iron fire escape behind our building, drinking Tecates. Lee was sitting on the
landing propped against my kitchen door, talking. I was two
steps down from him, with my back against the warm brick
building and my bare feet up on the warm iron rail. It was
sometime between eleven o'clock and midnight. The one light
over the courtyard behind the building had burned out last
November, and Parkwood hadn't gotten around to replacing it

yet. The green area was dim dusty ground and big shadowy trees nailed up with rope swings and basketball hoops. It was dark, but that was okay. It seemed right to travel by touch and smell. Walking in an old dim country without so many words.

I was slowly peeling the label off my bottle of Tecate. The communal washing machines across the courtyard thumped and churned. Farther away, steady traffic hissed down Fannin and OST. Every now and then, a distant siren. When my sisters were little, I used to tell them that those far-away sirens were like shooting stars, and if you heard a faint one you had to say *Shhh!* and make a wish.

One time when I was ten, AJ turned off every light in her room and then lit a single candle and told me to stare at my flickering reflection in her vanity mirror. She said that if I looked long enough I would see my future, but I drained out of myself instead, until the face in the mirror looked like a stranger to me. Scared the piss out of me at the time, but tonight I was more than willing to let my edges run. I didn't need to be Will Kennedy on this disastrous August night. Better to be something less definite. Just a scatter of connected memories, rocking on a dark sea.

Also, the beer helped.

'Fuck,' Lee said. 'It's probably for the best.'

'More time for movies,' I said.

'I could read some of the great books. Relationships take time, man. And let's face it, Vicky is not an intellectual.'

'Also, there's *Smackdown*.'

'Exactly! Women hate that.' Lee drank more beer. 'The things that do not kill us –'

' – Make us bugfuck.'

'Amen.'

Lee made that pensive sound you make by blowing over the top of a beer bottle. 'And another thing is: I'm not Catholic. Or Mexican.'

'You could convert.'

'To Mexican?'

'Sure. Why not?'

'Dude,' Lee said. 'You cannot learn to like accordion music. It's a gene.'

'Good point.' I still had his grandfather's gun in my pocket. 'Have you heard that narco-corrida stuff? Gangsta-Tejano.' I drank more beer. 'Drug deals with accordions.'

'Wild.' Lee made the lonesome beer-bottle sound. 'But then again, consider the Eagles.'

'*Excellent* point.'

I kept working at my Tecate label, scraping away with my thumbnail. I wished I had thumbnails like Abdul, the cab driver. He could probably pop staples with those mothers. Have to remember to send him the rest of his money.

'Your folks still together?' Lee asked.

'Yeah.' Once, I wouldn't have given that a second thought. Incredible, really. You think the world is durable, dirt and steel and concrete, as dull and solid as Refinery Row. But it's all made out of spiderweb. It can be gone in a flash. Look at Uncle Walt, or AJ. Look at Uncle Billy. Or my cousin Tom, for that matter – single and lonely and okay with that in Europe. Then love hits like a fucking bullet to the heart, and suddenly you're back in your mother's house with a dead girl in your garage.

Look at me. This morning I wasn't a killer. This morning I had an ex-wife I tried not to think about and a kid I saw once every two weeks. Your life can turn on you in a heartbeat. Nothing left behind but silver footprints.

Lee's voice came to me out of the darkness. 'I was real little when my folks split up. My dad never said one word against my mom. She tried hard not to say much about him.'

'Did you like him at all? Your dad?'

'I worshipped that guy. He just embarrassed me, that's all.'

'Yeah.'

Lee wouldn't have been saying this to me if he wasn't drunk. If we were anything more solid than two voices in the darkness.

I wondered when Megan had started wearing a bra. I wondered if the boys in her class snapped her bra-straps like they did when I was in sixth grade.

'My mom always said, there comes a time when you have to say, I don't deserve to feel this bad.' Lee paused to drink.

'Yep,' I said. Good-bye, Josie.

'My *dad* always said, in every relationship you have to be willing to work like a fucking dog. You have to pay the price.'

'Very true.'

'So what I don't get,' Lee said, 'the mystery here is, how do you know which is which?'

Good-bye, Meg.

'I mean, maybe I should be completely freaking out. Maybe Vicky is the *One*, and I should sell my soul to keep it together.'

'Just for the cooking.'

'Right. Exactly. Or maybe keeping it together would be the exact wrong thing. Maybe that would just spin out the fighting and the fucking *exhaustion*, and on top of everything else, maybe the *real* One would go by for each of us, and we would never know it because we were too busy trying to prop up this fucking bitter waste of time.'

A lonely pick-up truck bumped up the back alley and nosed slowly along the length of the tin-covered communal carport, looking for a space. I wondered who was in that truck. How tired he was. Some kid just getting home from a party? Grad student coming back late from the lab? Maybe somebody coming in after a longer drive, back after visiting family in Lake Charles, or Tupelo, or even Pensacola.

'Will?'

'Yeah?'

'What do you think?'

'I think it's all songs.' I drank some more beer. 'I think we each get a CD, three score minutes and ten. And some of the songs are short, and some are long. Some of them have a big fucking beat. Some of them break your heart.' I had the label off my bottle of Tecate. Now I was just rolling the last little sticky bits of glue and paper under my thumb. 'At the end of seventy minutes you get what you get. We'd all like to make *Murmur*, but maybe that isn't what's given to you. Maybe you have to make, I don't know, German Industrial Metal. You don't always get to choose. But the thing is, you should never leave dead space.' I was probably drunk. 'Fill up every fucking minute with music.'

'Amen,' Lee said. 'Did you know she asked me to marry her?'

'Vicky? Holy shit. Tonight?'

'While ago. Day you got fired.'

'What did you say?'

Lee blew a long, slow, sad note on his bottle of beer. 'Thought she was joking.'

'Oh, *man*. So this was coming.'

'For weeks,' Lee agreed. 'Dead man walking.'

'Shit,' I said. 'You really fucked up.'

'Yep.'

Long silence.

'Will?'

'Yeah?'

'You got anything I could try that jalapeño jelly on?'

'Ritz crackers? They're on top of the fridge. Help yourself.' He came back a few minutes later with a plateful, munching thoughtfully. 'How do they taste?'

'Wow.'

I finished my beer. Talking to the darkness I said, 'I noticed something really important about dead people today.'

Lee munched his way through a Ritz. 'What's that?'

'They are so beautiful,' I said.

Lee's cell phone shrilled like a cricket. He scrambled to dig it out of his jeans pocket, dropping his beer, which sprayed briskly over my shirt. The phone shrilled again and Lee swore, trying to flip its little face plate open with his big drunk fingers.

His face was a rumpled mass of panic in the pale amber light of the display. 'Vicky?' he said, through a mouth full of crumbs. You could tell the mere sound of her voice undid a six-pack's worth of resignation.

I summoned every ounce of Captain Underground's beer-enhanced mental powers and willed the conversation to go well. I felt like it would take all my super-concentration to keep Lee from yelling, or groveling, or throwing up. The strain was enormous. I felt my hair turning white, like Dr. Strange.

Vicky finally wound down. 'Okay, yeah,' Lee said, grinning. 'Okay, it's a date. Tomorrow at five-thirty. That'd be good . . .' Pause. His smile widened. 'What the hell do you want to go *there* for?'

It hurt a bit too much to listen to them making up. And I still had some broken CDs to clean up, and a bed to make. I should probably turn off the taps and plug in my appliances. Plus, I wasn't crazy about lolling around in the beer-soaked shirt, either.

I grabbed the iron banister for support and hauled myself heavily to my feet. Lee paused to raise his eyebrows at me as I lumbered up to the landing. 'My work here is done,' I said, stepping deliberately over his outstretched legs. I could still hear Vicky talking a mile a minute on the other end of the phone. Lee rolled his eyes and grinned at me, *Here We Go Again*, but underneath you could see exhaustion and gratitude and happiness. He covered the mouthpiece for a moment with his hand. '*Las chicas*, man. It never ends.'

CHAPTER TWELVE

Six weeks later I pulled a letter from Megan out of my mailbox as I was heading out the door on my way to the family reunion. The 'Santa Rosa, CA' postmark caught me like a spray of buckshot. My eyes were still partly broken. I saw colors around the edge of things, but whatever I looked directly at was dead, so the ink and the stamp and Megan's return address were all black and white.

I stood in the boiled-carpet smell of the apartment foyer. It was the third weekend in September; another month to go before the heat would finally break. Not in Santa Rosa, California, though. There was probably fog curling among giant redwood trees in Santa Rosa.

An impatient horn honked at the curb, and I hurried outside, bringing the letter with me.

'Get in the back with Vi,' Fonteyne said. 'She likes company.'

'Me, too.' I slid into the Buick's backseat and buckled up. Working the seat belt still tweaked my shoulder enough to make me wince. Vi goggled at me from the depths of her car seat and then screeched in a friendly manner. She looked good – strong head, curious eyes. She studied me carefully, taking in my *25th Anniversary Smithers Reunion* T-shirt while slowly trying to jam her folded hand into her mouth.

For the last few years the reunion had been on Lake Conroe, which is pretty close to Houston, but Mom had switched it back to the old Hill Country site on the Little Blanco River, partly so we'd get more people from Austin and San Antonio, but mostly because she knew that was my favorite. These are the little perks that go with being shot.

Up in the front seat, Fonteyne turned the A/C up to a dull roar. She looked good too. New pair of sunglasses and a big grin. 'Everybody ready to hit the road?'

'You're a beam of sunshine.'

'I got a three-day weekend and *somebody* slept through the night last night.' Live-oak reflections streamed up the front windshield as she pulled out from the curb.

Megan's letter made my hands nervous, like it was something I had shoplifted. I hadn't talked to her since the night I had thrown up on her doorstep. I didn't know if Josie had told her about the gun. I had made sure Josie didn't have to see me when I signed the papers allowing Megan to move out of state. I sort of expected to see the cops the next day, but I guess she never called them.

I was getting sweat stains on the envelope.

Fuck it. I was the grown-up here – theoretically – and it was my job to hear whatever Megan had to say. I opened up the letter. It was written in blue felt-tip pen, so the letters were big and blotchy.

Dear Will,

– good start. I looked away again. That wasn't so bad.

I didn't used to be so good about feeling things. Instead of experiencing a whole bunch of different emotions, I was like a broken radio – my volume might slide from Quiet to Really Fucking Loud, but it was always tuned to the same station. The same songs. But ever since the day I nearly killed Josie, I was feeling all kinds of things.

That sounds good, I know. I'm sure a therapist like the one Norma Ferris was probably seeing would say that being able to feel really sad or really angry was a Sign of Progress . . . except the *when* was unnervingly random. I might be riding on the bus and see some black kid wearing a Steve Francis jersey and holding a basketball and all of a sudden I would make up this whole story about him, how he thought he was going to make it in the NBA and he was dominating at the high-school level but he didn't have the SATs to get into a big-time NCAA school so he would try to go the JuCo route, and three months into the season at San Jacinto he was going to blow out an ACL and that would be the end of his career. Six months later he would be working at a Footlocker and everyone he knew would think he was a has-been at twenty-one.

And my eyes would start to tear up, right there on the bus. And then the kid would catch me looking at him and give me the hard stare back like, What the fuck is up wit' *you*?

'I love driving,' Fonteyne said from the front seat. 'I love to drive. On the highway, obviously. I just like to get out of the city and . . . drive.'

'Mm-hmm,' I said.

Dear Will,

How are you? I am fine. Things are OK here except for the kids at school think I'm a freak. They think everyone from Texas has a shotgun and a pickup truck and hates black people, which is pretty funny because there are zero black kids here, except for one girl who was adopted from some-where in Jamaica, but everyone here is real proud of how tolerant they are of all their non-existent African American neighbors. They also think that everyone in Texas lives in the desert which is just ignorant and when I tell them Houston has the most trees of any city in America they think I'm making that up. So I just let them think what-ever. No sense wasting time on fools. Mom really wants me

*to play soccer, but another four hours a week of California
Girls is the <u>last</u> thing I need so mostly I just hang out and
watch TV alot.*

'Damn it,' I said.

'No cussing in front of Vi,' Fonteyne said automatically. 'So,
I had a pretty good thing happen to me the other day.'

'Yeah?'

*So the reason I'm writing this letter is to say I wasn't too
impressed with you. Fighting with Dad and throwing up
and, like, stalking us. Mom and me haven't snitched to Dad
about the last time – so don't worry about 'getting caught'
– but believe me, there's times when I want to. Plus after all
that you couldn't even be bothered to get a lawyer to write
in some kind of guaranteed visitations or anything?*

*All I asked you to do was just Don't Screw Up. I can't
help thinking the big reason we had to move to California
was because you freaked Dad out so much, only now I'm
the one who has to pay for it.*

'So I was in the Galleria the other day, and I saw Richard
Linklater in the food court,' Fonteyne said.

'What?'

'Richard Linklater. He's this director from Austin. You of all
people must have seen *Slacker.*' Fonteyne laughed. Not a mean
laugh. 'Or *School of Rock.*'

Megan quitting soccer was a nightmare. Josie and Don
should force her to stay on a team.

'So anyway, I went up to him and I said, 'You're Richard Linklater, aren't you?' And he said he was, and I told him *Before
Sunrise* was my favorite romantic movie, which it nearly is, and I
also was thinking how more people know him for *Slacker,* you
know, and maybe it would be nicer to hear something good
about a movie that bombed even if it was really good, which it is.'

Vi was tilted sideways as far as the straps of her car seat would let go, leaning toward me and peering down at Megan's letter as if reading over my shoulder. She seemed to be thinking about it really hard.

> And then getting pissed after we had a really good day at Six Flags and barfing all over our yard and freaking Mom out. So I guess why I'm writing is to say, thanks for nothing. If you're just going to screw things up, don't bother. I always used to take your side with Dad, but maybe he was right.
>
> You need help. I guess I hope you find it. Don't worry about us. We can take care of ourselves.

'So he seemed like a really nice person,' Fonteyne said. 'I told him I really liked the way the people in his movies were like just regular people, and he said he liked that too. And then I said' – Fonteyne glanced into the back seat – 'I said, "I'm a check-out girl at Kroger's who wants to be an actress. That's about as regular as you get, isn't it?" I figured he would like roll his eyes and I would die of embarrassment, but he was really nice about it, he just laughed and asked if I had seen *Waking Life*, and I said I had and I thought there were parts I didn't quite understand but I thought it was really cool. Not just, you know . . . Hollywood.'

Don't worry about us. We can take care of ourselves.

I realized Fonteyne was waiting. 'Not just Hollywood,' I said.

Yours sincerely,
Megan Cummings

As in, not Kennedy. Well, it was Don's name on the birth certificate, after all.

The Buick's A/C roared around us. Vi raised her head from the letter and gave me a long look, screwing up her little face like, *Ouch*.

'So what do you think?' Fonteyne asked.

I wasn't sure. I seemed to have lost the tuner on my emotional radio. Maybe in a minute I was going to pick up K-SAD and bust out bawling. *Yours sincerely, Megan* <u>*Cummings*</u>.

Vi burped, and looked down at herself in great surprise.

'Will?' Fonteyne said hesitantly.

Get your shit together, Comrade Will. I tried to remember what she had said. Director, food court, movies. My sister was looking at me in the rearview mirror. There were little worry lines starting in her forehead, and I realized she was waiting for me to cut her down. 'You did great,' I said.

'You really think so?' The pure relief in her voice hit me like a slap.

'I think you played it perfect,' I said. 'Did you, um, did he give you a card or anything?'

'No. That was it, really. I didn't want to push my luck. I figured I'd say something stupid and blow it, knowing me,' Fonteyne said. 'Anyway I had Vi in the Snuggli and she was starting to fuss. So I just said thanks for the movies and walked away. Exit Grocery Checker, stage left.'

I held a finger up in front of Vi. She took her wet hand out of her mouth and grabbed it and screeched happily. She was a very different baby than Megan had been. Vi was all about her hands. Meg had been a looking-around baby. Her hands and feet just spazzed every which way, forgotten. Megan was all in her eyes.

'Sometimes a good exit is all you can ask for,' I said.

'Yeah, well, maybe,' my sister said. 'But just in case, I went and made up a new resumé with a couple of new photographs, and if it's okay with you, since we're going up into the Hill Country anyway, I thought maybe I could drop it off at his office in Austin on our way home.'

'Linklater's?'

'Yeah.' Fonteyne looked at me in the rearview mirror again. Nervous. A little defiant.

'Kid,' I said, 'I hope he makes you a star.'

I am eight, visiting Grandpa Jay Paul in the nursing home. Mom's at the head of the bed, talking. I'm down at the bottom, looking at his feet. There are blue veins spidered all over them. His skin is so white and thin it's almost transparent. Before the strokes put him in the nursing home, he taught me to play pool on the table in the garage. His hands shook so bad he had to use the horse for every shot. He never could get his dentures to fit right, and when he laughed his teeth would wobble in his mouth. Now, in the home, his toenails are the same dull yellow as that old cue ball.

The first couple of weeks after I nearly killed Josie I did all the right things. Cleaned my apartment, for instance. That took three days, by the time I got the bloodstains dry-cleaned out of my sheets and replaced the batteries in my fire alarm. I thought about cleaning up a bit inside too. I went so far as to look in the phone book under Therapist and Psychiatrist, but they were all crazy expensive and I figured that could wait until maybe I had a job and insurance again.

I went out on three calls for people who were haunted: two false alarms and one real one. Ended up making two thousand dollars, plus another three grand from Johnson Del Grande. My dad took me to the city offices and stood in line with me to get a business license. He told me how to get cheap business cards made up at Office Depot and introduced me to this accountant who seemed like a pretty good guy.

I am nine. We're visiting my daddy's folks in Dallas, watching a girls' fast-pitch game. I'm sitting with my Grandpa Chet, watching another one of his grandkids play second base. He likes to watch her glove work, so he takes all his cigarette breaks when her team is batting. I still remember the chigger bites I had that night, the way they itched, and the cigarette smell of his skin.

My apartment was clean, I was finally making some good money, I was still showering every day. In short, I was behaving well . . . but at another level I was just Going Through The Motions. One of the things about being a grown-up is learning how to do that, learning how to act right even when you feel wrong. The one thing I did do with genuine passion – nobody more surprised by this than me – was help my mother organize the family reunion.

A couple of days after I got my business license, Mom asked me to meet her for lunch – she had News, she said. So I caught a bus for the long ride to Deer Park and arrived at the medical office where she worked just before noon.

A little crowd of patients sat in the waiting room. There was a young mom with a snot-nosed little girl who played with the plastic office toys, slathering everything with germs. Next to her sat a middle-aged man, digging his fist into the small of his back. When I was twenty I wouldn't have given it a second thought; now I recognized him as a member of the Universal Brotherhood of Lower Back Pain Sufferers. Across from him, a thin, exhausted black man with bloodshot eyes was paging slowly through a month-old office copy of *Sports Illustrated*.

Mom pushed the sign-in clipboard across the counter, then looked up and saw it was me. She smiled. I sat next to the black guy and watched the fish in the office aquarium until 12:15, when she got to start her lunch hour. We walked out of the cool office together into a sweltering hot day. She was sweating by the time we made it across the street to the local Mexican restaurant. When I was little it was called El Monterrey, and she would take me there for lunch after my doctor's visits, especially if I had to have a shot. I would order the cheese enchiladas, with sopapillas for dessert. The place had changed hands in the '80s; now it was called Taco Loco. Inside, all the old Mexican waiters were gone, replaced by teenage black girls and gangly white boys. They didn't have sopapillas on the menu any more.

I ordered Lunch Special #3, two burritos with Mexi-rice, beans, and a Coke for $5.25. Mom had enchiladas verdes with extra sour cream, a plate of nachos swimming in cheese sauce, and a Diet Coke. A pretty young black girl with 'D'Andra' on her name tag brought us our food. 'I got a call from your Aunt Patty last night,' Mom said.

'About Uncle Walt?' According to Andy, who had been doing more research on the internet, the death of a man often result-ed in the company getting an outrageously small fine from the Occupational Safety Board; maybe a twenty-thousand-dollar slap on the wrist. If you grew up on Refinery Row, it wasn't surprising that a man's life would cost less than a new Toyota, but it was still sort of depressing. Once we got over that, Andy and me figured Crown might as well give Aunt Patty the twen-ty thousand dollars as have it go to some bureaucrat at OSHA.

Mom took a sip of her Diet Coke. 'Crown has decided it's not worth going to court.'

'They're going to give Aunt Patty the fine money?' It made so much sense it was hard to believe a lawyer had allowed it. 'That should help with the medical bills, anyway.'

'I sure hope so,' Mom said, breaking into a smile. ''Cause they're paying out six hundred thousand dollars.'

It was like being hit by a truck.

'S-s-s-s-six hundred grand?'

'Your Aunt Patty went to some hotshot lawyer who's done a lot of asbestos cases and other industrial accidents. She told him the plan, about getting Crown to pay us the OSHA money. He looks at her and he says, "Ma'am, I don't pick up my phone for twenty thousand dollars, and you better believe those sons of a so-and-so know it."'

'*Six hundred thousand dollars?*'

'You said that already, hon.'

'Oh my God!'

'And they owe it all to you and Andy.' Mom grinned. 'You done good, kid.'

We ate. My mother dosed her enchiladas with rivers of Papa Charro's Picante. Six hundred thousand dollars. Unbelievable. Apparently Aunt Patty was going to pay off the house and hire a day nurse to come help with Uncle Walt. Very good news, and thanks at least a little bit to the super-heroing of yours truly, Captain Underground. A happy ending. Josie would like that.

I stirred my fork around in my Mexi-rice for a while. 'Mom? Do you think Josie was having an affair with Don before we broke up?'

My mother paused with a forkful of refried beans halfway to her mouth. 'Now why— ?' She put the fork down and looked at me sadly. 'Oh, Will. You've always been so worried, kiddo. Even when you were a little boy. Your father used to get mad at you sometimes, you were that stubborn, and I always told him, 'He's scared, Jimmy. That's all.' Because you'd never show it. You scowled when other kids would cry.'

Around us cutlery clattered and clinked. D'Andra kicked the kitchen door open and whipped past us with a plate of sizzling fajita fixings.

My mother sighed. 'As for Josie . . . it sounds more like something you would believe than something she would do. But I don't know. You never can see into someone else's marriage. Not even your kid's.'

'Okay.' I stirred around my Mexi-rice some more.

My mother finished her second enchilada, then carefully put down her knife and fork, and wiped her hands. 'When you were one year old, I had an affair.' I looked up in shock. She met my eyes, flushing. 'I guess I had post-partum depression. Your father had quit a steady job the month before I got pregnant. When the test results came back, he was so scared. That first year after you were born, he was working all the time trying to

212

get his own business going. Working all the time.' Mom took a breath. 'And there was a young doctor in the office, he'd been in the Peace Corps and he would see the poor blacks and Mexicans and not charge them so much, you know. And I wasn't heavy back then. And I was so sad.'

The smell of scorched onions drifted from the fajita platter at the table behind us. I coughed.

'We slept together three times.'

'Mom—'

'Of course I knew it was wrong. and I couldn't bear it. I couldn't bear to come home and look your father in the eye. Such a terrible mother. Mamaw would hand you over when I came in the door, and I felt like I didn't deserve to hold you. I still loved your father very much. So I told him.' I thought of my dad, one scheme after another. Scrabbling to put money on the table. 'Your father was shocked. It hurt him so bad. But I told him I still loved him, and he believed me. I have never stopped being grateful for that.' Mom took a sip of her Diet Coke. 'He forgave me, when he never had to. He never asked if you were his child. Which you are, you can't ever doubt that. Not once in thirty years has he ever reproached me. So don't you think that man is a failure. I know his businesses haven't all worked out, but he was there for me. He never let his family down.'

It was hard to breathe, as if another bullet had gone through my chest. 'Jesus.'

A couple of tears spilled out of my mom's eyes. 'I used . . .' She caught her breath. 'I always used to wonder why you saw these dead folks. I used to wonder if it was something about me. Something I did.'

'I don't think so,' I said.

'Nobody else in the family had to suffer with it like you did, you know, and I just couldn't help thinking . . . I don't know.'

'I think it's just one of those things,' I said.

She gave my hand a squeeze and she tried to smile. 'Tell me you still love me, Will.'

'Always,' I said.

When I was young, I remember being bored all the time. I remember hating how ordinary everything seemed. Stupid boring Deer Park, my whiny sisters, my embarrassing dad. Reruns of *M*A*S*H* on TV nine times a week and the Eagles on the radio every fucking hour.

Now I have days when I just don't want any more surprises.

I am thirty-two, thinking about my dead.

So anyway, I was a reunion demon. I called the guys who rented the big pit barbecues, I haggled over motel-room rates, I made up chore lists and coaxed people into signing up for them. I called my Uncle Chase and bullied him into coming even though Aunt Dot was going to show. Chase said she wasn't allowed to talk about her past lives or weight-loss therapies while he was in the room. This I presented to her more as a suggestion than an ultimatum, but she was a good sport about it. 'I'll just go stand in front of the old coot and look *thin*,' she said.

My labors had not gone in vain. *Smithers 25* looked to be the best-attended reunion since 1991 (the last year the Colorado and Arkansas branches of the family had managed to come in force), with upwards of a hundred of us all milling around in one spot. 'What a triumph,' my dad remarked drily, but not loud enough for Mom to hear. He's really a pretty good soldier about these things.

I am sixteen, over at Josie's place. Her father is out of jail for the last time. For some reason the three of us are playing Indian, the world's dumbest card game, where you slap a card face out on your forehead and then bet that it's probably better than what you can see on the other players' heads. Josie's dad is happy and not even drunk. 'I'll see that and raise you *five Yankee dollars*, Will!' He's grinning like anything. The card on his head is a three.

By the time Fonteyne and I got to the reunion, the picnic tables were already beginning to sag under the weight of food. Aunt Dot had brought celery casserole, and jellied Waldorf salad made with diet Jell-O, and something called Georgia Satay, which was lean chicken-breast skewers with peanut-butter sauce, which she said she had learned to cook in Java during the reign of Queen Victoria. 'I'm so sorry about you and Tom,' she said.

'Hanlon? Did you know him?'

She pulled the plastic wrap from her Waldorf salad. 'I met him a few times. You know we never were that close to Eugenia. But when I read the news on the family list-serve, I can't say I was terribly surprised.' My grandmother's generation have become demon e-mailers now that they can spread family gossip literally at the speed of light.

'You think Hanlon was paying for something he did in a past life?' I said politely.

She pinched my cheek. Great-aunts are apparently allowed to do this no matter how old you are. 'Now you're teasing me.' She arranged toothpicks around her Satay. 'He was just that kind of boy things never do work out for.'

I am thirteen, climbing into my cousin Danny's 'Vette. The red upholstered interior is hot and smells faintly of mildew. Danny is taking me on a Slurpee run. He has wanted to join the Air Force for ten years – now boot camp is only three weeks away. I buckle up, then look over. 'No seat belt?'

He grins. 'I like to live dangerously.'

The always-reliable Aunt Patty contributed the best brisket I'd had in years; you could have scooped that meat into an ice-cream cone and licked it down. Patty also brought lemon and poppy-seed pound cake, which she discouraged me from eating on account of she had learned it could make you test positive for pot, so should be avoided by people like me, who might be going for job interviews soon, and also like my cousin Jerome, who was out of prison again and speaking confidently of his chances of bringing his new parole officer around to accepting Jesus into his life.

My cousin Suzy Colbert, the journalist to whom I owed my fifteen minutes of Houston fame, brought along a big Frito pie. My cousin Raider's ex-wife Juanita supplied Smoked Poblano Soup and her famous enchiladas verdes and a meringue palace of a dessert smothered in strawberry sauce, which had a Spanish name I immediately forgot. My Uncle Chase did show, as promised, with his inevitable stash of jalapeño jam and a hundred pounds of fresh corn to throw on the grill.

I was especially pleased to see my cousin Andy, the computer whiz, who wandered around the campsite with a big grin on his face and pale white skin rapidly going red. His Connecticut wife, Sonia, brought water crackers and Melba toast and Brie on a little silver platter. She watched the platter real close. I made eye contact with my cousin Jerome – a good guy in a tight spot, really – and between us we finished off the appalling cheese inside half an hour. '*Man*, that's good,' Jerome said, through a fine mist of Melba crumbs. Sonia blinked and gave an uncertain little smile. 'I lived with a girl and we used to eat this all the time with maybe some red wine,' Jerome said nostalgically. 'Back before I put alcohol behind me.'

'Glad you liked it. I never know . . . I always feel like I'm not going to bring the right thing,' Sonia said.

'There ain't no such thing as wrong food,' Jerome laughed. And then, possibly sensing that this was as good as it was going to get with Andy's wife, he gave her a wink and sauntered off toward the 42 tournament. For her part, Sonia drank several glasses of Adult Punch in quick succession, after which she stopped worrying about her cheese platter and seemed to have a pretty good time.

*

I am eighteen. It's the Fourth of July, and my stoner cousin Alice is lit like a sparkler, in spite of a court date waiting after the long weekend. 'Possession, man.' She giggles. Smoke comes out her mouth and nose like her face is leaking. 'Nine-tenths of the law.'

For as long as I could remember, Uncle Walt had worked the barbecue pit at the family reunion, but this year he had to watch from the sidelines. His memory had finally started to come back, but the shake in his hands wasn't clearing up, and he got tired if he had to stand for any length of time. We put him in a big old patio chair next to the barbecue and let him spend the afternoon correcting my dad's grilling technique. That seemed to keep him happy.

When I swung by the barbecue pit with a box full of hamburger meat, the other person stationed there was Hanlon. He was over by my dad, still wearing his raincoat in spite of the blistering heat, still all black and white, standing with one hand casually resting on the grill. He gave me a little wave as I came over. His palm was crossed with char-lines, like a good grilled steak. 'Hey, DK, what's cooking?' he said with a grin. 'You know it's not over.' He made a gun out of his thumb and forefinger, just like Mamaw had the day I went down the ghost road. He pointed it at the back of my father's head. 'Ka-pow!'

I ignored him. 'Burgers on the hoof,' I said, putting the box of meat down on the table next to my dad. 'Cook 'em quick before the botulism grabs hold.'

My dad peered dubiously into the box of meat. 'A hundred Texas rednecks had gathered at a family reunion *when* –'

'If he knew what you thought of him, man, it would break his heart, wouldn't it?' Hanlon said.

I kept on ignoring him. The dead are only ghosts, after all.

My dad asked Uncle Walt about his youngest boy, who was pitching at Baylor. 'He's doin' purty good,' Uncle Walt allowed. His face had aged ten years since the accident, and his head shook as he spoke. 'They ain't played but a couple of preseason games, but he pitched the one time and did real well. I don't expect he's a serious prospect. They have this one ol' boy the scouts come to see, got him clocked in the high nineties. Bryce is more of a nibbler. But he'll play some ball and have some fun and it's just possible those professors might sneak a little education into him if he lets his guard down.'

I headed back toward the kitchen. 'Weren't hoping to see me here, were you?' Hanlon called.

'You're family,' I said. But I kept my back to him, and I didn't turn around.

When I got back to the lodge I spotted a door marked 'Caballeros' and ducked into the bathroom, where I splashed cold water on my face as if I could wash the smoky stink of Hanlon off of me.

In the spring of '96 I saw a dead man playing at a Carolyn Wonderland show. I'm thinking it was her Tuesday gig at the Last Concert Café, but that might be wrong. I got there between sets, people were just milling around the way they do, and there was this dead guy onstage, playing incredible slide guitar, but so softly I could barely hear it under the clink of bottles and people shooting pool. This was only a couple of weeks after Jeffrey Lee Pierce of The Gun Club had died.

It didn't make sense it would be him – he was an LA guy, and spent the last part of his short life in Europe, anyway. No earthly reason he should be playing a room in Houston, of all places. But the guy onstage had the blond hair, and his hands were thin and sick-looking. He seemed strangely at peace, as if his guitar was talking and he was just listening to what it had to say. I guess I liked the idea that Pierce had finally got some rest. He was every bit as good a writer as Cobain, but he never got famous the way Cobain did. I guess he never will now.

Before he was anybody, he was the head of the Blondie fan club. Not everybody knows that.

I guess if I ever came back – and let's face it, it could happen – that's how I'd want it to be. Not out to hurt anyone. Just listening.

It can be like that, AJ said.

She was in the bathroom mirror, looking out at me. 'Hey,' I said.

Hey yourself.

'I got to wondering, about your boyfriend, what happened to him. Andy looked it up for me. He's still in Huntsville. I actually called the parole board, and I guess he has a hearing coming up in a year and a half. I couldn't find out why he did it, though.' AJ looked at me over the tops of her glasses. 'I mean, he must have had a reason. Not a good reason. No reason is good enough. But I just . . . wondered.'

I washed my hands. The last time I had seen AJ, she was standing in Josie's window, watching me nearly shoot my ex-wife.

I forgive you, AJ said.

'I don't.'

I know.

'Okay.' I splashed my face again. 'Okay.'

Are you ready?

'Not yet.'

Her eyes were full of love. She reached out and put her blood-stained hand against the mirror, like she had the very first time I saw her, in the bathroom of her parents' house. *Be thou faithful unto death*, she said, *and I will give thee a crown of life*. I lifted my hand up, shaking, and met her fingers with mine. Where we touched, the glass felt cold, cold.

Time stopped.

I looked at her face for a long time. Then I pulled my hand off the mirror and got the hell out of that bathroom.

*

I am fifteen, and it's the first time the reunion is being held on Lake Conroe. I haven't talked to AJ in almost a year. She rides in on her boyfriend's motorcycle, bare arms tight around his waist. I mean to say hey, but she's introducing him around and I'm supposed to be running a treasure hunt for the kids. I'm busy up through dinner, and by the time we all settle down to eat, it turns out the two of them have already left.

You never know which time will be the last.

Back in 1994, we had a shitkicker of a storm in Houston, twenty inches of rain in less than forty-eight hours. Eighteen thousand people were flooded out of their homes, and the San Jacinto River, which flows through the middle of town, was at its highest level ever. Thirteen people drowned. To top it all off, when the rain finally stopped and the clouds broke up, the river exploded. Two giant pipelines, carrying one sixth of all the fuel delivered in the United States, are buried three feet under the San Jacinto. Somehow the storm scoured out the riverbed, and then a piece of debris punctured the line. Two hundred thousand barrels of diesel and gasoline burst to the surface and ignited, sending a wall of fire racing down the river at eighty miles an hour, destroying everything it touched. My point being that when shit blows up, you've got to figure there was gas under the fucking river.

I'm talking about AJ's boyfriend here, obviously.

Gas under the river.

The phone call came while I was playing 42, which is a fairly complicated bid-and-trick dominoes game. I was paired up with my smart cousin Andy, and we were playing against my Uncle Chase and Sonia. One of Chase's rules is that he never lets a couple play partners in dominoes or cards – saves on bickering, he says. Chase is ninety-four years old, but an acknowledged master of the game (and fourteen-time Reunion Tournament champion). As for Sonia, while they don't play a lot of 42 in Connecticut, they apparently play a fearsome amount of bridge. The two of them were cleaning our clocks. Sonia, now up by many points and several cups of punch, was nakedly gloating, but Uncle Chase said it was on account of he and his partner were sitting samewise to the nearest bathtub.

'Will?' my mother said, heaving into view around a table full of pinochle players. 'Mrs. Moreno says there's a call for you at the registration desk.'

'Well,' Andy said brightly, 'I guess we better pack it in.'

Sonia clamped one steel hand on his arm and turned to my mother. 'You'll sit in a hand with us, won't you, Susan?' Mom, who was determined to make Sonia enjoy the reunion or die in the attempt, allowed as how she'd love the excuse to get out of the kitchen for a spell. Andy eyed me reproachfully as I left him to his fate.

There was a dead guy hanging around the motel registration desk. Nobody I recognized as kin, just a big old redneck with his head tipped back, squinting up at the stuffed fish mounted on the walls. The plaques claimed they'd all been pulled out of this very stretch of the Little Blanco River, though seeing as how one of them was a fine sailfin marlin, I had my doubts. I could tell the dead guy wasn't buying it either.

I wracked my brains trying to think who could possibly be calling me. My whole family was already here. It might be Lee, I supposed, calling to tell me my apartment had burned down, or sunk into the swamp, but he and Vicky were supposed to be gone for a romantic weekend on South Padre Island. It was a mystery.

'Hello?' I said.

'Hey.'

It was Megan.

So I guess why I'm writing is to say, thanks for nothing.

'Hey,' I said.

'I called your place and you weren't home, so I called Grandma and the machine said y'all were at the reunion and gave the number in case of emergencies.'

'Yeah.' My mother is very thorough with her answering machine messages. The reception from Megan's end was crappy. I could hear a crowd in the background, and maybe a fountain. Mall noises, like at a food court. 'Does Don know you're using his cell phone?'

'He's got all these weekend minutes,' Megan said. 'So . . . have they had the watermelon-seed spitting contest yet?'

'In another hour.'

'That was always my favorite,' she said.

'Me too.'

It didn't seem like that much to ask: *Don't Screw Up.*

'I love you,' I said. Because it didn't matter what she wanted to write to me, that was her business. But I was a grown-up and it was my job to let her know I gave a damn.

'Yeah, I know. Listen, I sent you this letter, and it's going to get there like today or tomorrow, back at your house, but when you get it, I want you to just tear it up, okay?'

The ghost in the lobby stooped forward to examine a three-and-a-half-foot-long pickerel someone had allegedly pulled out of the Little Blanco in 1978. 'Okay,' I said.

'I was really mad when I wrote it and I'd just had a fight with my folks and – anyway, it doesn't matter. Just throw it out, okay?'

'Okay,' I said.

'Promise?'

'Promise,' I said. 'It's good to hear from you. How's California?'

'Good. They have these really big trees.'

'How about the kids?' I asked. 'Are you getting along okay?'

'You forget I'm very cool,' Megan said. 'I land on my feet.'

'Don't stop playing soccer.'

'What?' she said sharply.

'A lot of girls drop out around your age. They start talking about boys all the time, and they drop out of soccer and math classes. And you don't want to do that, because boys, man . . .

Not worth the time. Not at this age.'

'No fear. Guys only look at girls with boobs,' Megan said. Silence.

'Do you think I'm pretty?' she asked in a small voice.

I felt a stab of pure hate for all the boys who *weren't* staring at my daughter's chest. One thing about being a parent, it never stops surprising you. 'Sweetie, you are gorgeous. Swear to God. You light up a room. Even the stupid boys will figure that out soon.'

'That's what I wished for, you know. That day at Six Flags, with the balloons? Boobs.' Pause. 'Didn't get them.'

'It's four to six months shipping on balloon wishes.'

She laughed and I felt like a good parent. 'Really?'

'Yeah, it's not like shooting stars at all, or the tooth fairy. Whole different delivery schedule.' I was smiling at the phone. 'So you're going to keep playing? I really enjoyed watching those games.'

'Yeah, that's what it's all about, your viewing pleasure.' Megan relented a bit. 'I guess I probably will. Look, I gotta go. Just touching base,' Megan said. 'You should see a counselor or something.'

I will when I see your team picture, I didn't say, because it wasn't her job to make deals with me. It wasn't her job to take care of me. 'I should go now,' I said. 'I'm supposed to judge that spit-off.' That was a lie.

'The minutes are free, I think. The weekend ones.'

'I love you,' I said. I tried to make it sound like it was no big deal. Like I had always loved her and always would, and it was something that didn't have to be emphasized, like the sun coming up. 'You know that, right?'

'I know,' she said. Then we hung up.

Confession time: when Megan was ten, I bought her an ABBA's *Greatest Hits* CD. She loved it. I can still remember her vamping in Hermann Park after a trip to the zoo, kicking her legs on the swings and warbling 'Dancin' Queen' at the top of her lungs while I gave her pushes and did the ooo-wah-ooos. Because the truth is, when I was ten, I loved those songs.

I headed back to the family reunion, trying to think what I could send her next.

Maybe Supertramp?

I am six. It's the first Friday of first grade. The air smells like plastic burning and there's a big black cloud spilling from the Philips plant where Uncle Billy works. The cloud keeps growing, and Uncle Billy is up there somewhere, melting into the dirty sky like sugar dissolved in a glass of iced tea. Every family in Deer Park is waiting by the phone.

Unless you are a hardcore domino player, the watermelon-seed spitting contest is generally considered the highlight of the family reunion, but that afternoon I decided to skip it. I waited until the whole clan had been summoned to the hastily converted horseshoe pit and then slipped out behind the main ranch and made my way down the dusty half-mile track to the river.

It was not a bad day, as days go. Heading on to four in the afternoon, hovering around ninety-five or ninety-six degrees, humidity only sixty percent or so. A little sticky, but not the saucepan heat of Houston. Later on, when the sun went down, the night air would be soft and warm and drowsy, but for now the day was still bright. Sunlight fell hard on the pasture, beating the smell of hot straw out of it. Farther along, big trees began to close over the dirt track, live-oak and valley oak and cottonwood, and willows right by the river, thick enough to turn the light dim and green at the corners of my vision, though where I looked everything was still black and white.

There was a path that ran along the river bank. I turned up it, heading for the swimming hole and the tire swing I remembered from when I was a kid. The swing was still there, and so was Uncle Billy, as I sort of guessed he would be. Even in life, he hadn't been a seed-spitting sort of guy.

He was black and white, of course. Dead. He was standing in a shallow stretch of water, as if he had been waiting on me for days. Forever. 'Hey,' I said. I could see his bare feet, white as biscuit dough under the slow river.

'I cry unto thee, and thou dost not hear me,' he said testily. 'I stand up, and thou regardest me not.'

This sounded pretty much like the Uncle Billy I remembered. I pulled off my shoes and socks and sat down on a tree root and paddled my feet in a shady part of the river, scaring the water skaters there.

'Did I not weep for him who was in trouble?' Uncle Billy said. 'Was not my soul grieved for the poor?' He glowered at me for a spell, then peered down and rolled up the cuffs of his Brown & Root jumpsuit. We looked at one another. He finally broke down and smiled.

Cool water ran over my feet. I smiled back.

Uncle Billy held out his hand, and after a moment's hesitation, I took it. He started out into the stream, tugging me after him. His fingers were cold as winter dirt. I followed him for a couple of steps, then stopped and looked around for AJ, to see if her reflection might be floating on the surface of the water. I didn't want to get dunked under the Little Blanco River and drowned, either by a ghost or my own addled self. I wouldn't do that at a family reunion. My mom would never get over it.

No sign of AJ. Maybe Uncle Billy had his own kind of AJ repellent, or maybe she was still back at the reunion, listening to the kids fight, or scaring the piss out of Hanlon. *That* struck me as entirely likely.

I let Billy lead me a couple more steps into the river. The current was still lazy here, but the last step was a steep one. I squeaked, suddenly balls-deep in river water. After a second I relaxed. The cool felt good against the heat of the day. Really good.

Billy reached up to cradle the back of my head. With one sharp pull he yanked me backward under the water and held

225

me there, while I spluttered and struggled to get free. Then he pushed me back upright.

I broke the surface gasping and swearing. 'What the *fuck*!' I started, but the cold hands dunked me back in again. This time I at least managed to get a breath on my way down, and I hardly had to hold it before Billy returned me to the surface. 'I will give thee a crown of life,' he grouched.

I figured it out and stopped struggling. He let me sink back gently as he prepared to baptize me for the third time. 'You know this doesn't do any good for us unbelievers,' I said, but I didn't stop him. If it made him happy, what the hell.

I took a deep breath and let my head go back as I sank underneath the river. I kept my eyes open, looking up through the cool water at the twisting haze of willow branches overhead, and the leaf light. I had the strangest feeling that the current was passing through the bullet hole in my chest, and all kinds of things inside me, smoke and blood and disappointment, were streaming out the exit wound in my shoulderblade, floating up to stain the Little Blanco like oil spilling from a cracked pipe.

The sounds of the world receded, all dim and muffled but for the voice of the waters, which rushed and murmured around me, crying, laughing, complaining. It was as if I could hear the voices of the dead, that otherwise were hidden under the ground, or the river.

When I came up with a whoop and a splash the world had changed. Nothing was black and white any more. Everything was wet and glistening with color, as if the whole planet had just been painted. A cardinal flicked by, all swagger and attitude, his scarlet crest like a candy red Mohawk. Around him, the hanging willow leaves were sticky with afternoon light. The world was dipped in color, dappled in it, tree trunks mottled brown-gray and pale green, crusted with fans of lichen. And the jumbled, wavering colors of the Little Blanco itself! Where I had first sat down, in the shade under the tree-root, the river was dark and mysterious brown . . . deeps of it, like years pooled under the water skaters. Out a little farther from the bank, where the sunlight dripped through the canopy overhead, the water ran amber, like strong iced tea. A few yards downstream was a shallows, caught full in a patch of yellow sunshine. There the stream ran busy and clear as glass, with coins and spangles of light glimmering and glancing off the pebbled bottom.

The color had even managed to leach into Uncle Billy. Not all the way – his clothes were still gray and his skin was white as mushrooms – but his eyes were brown and quick as river water, and I could see a red trace of sunburn around his neck.

I found I was crying. Uncle Billy pretended not to notice. He just gave me a gruff nod and started wading for shore.